The Earl Pretender

by

Caitlin Callery

Copyright Notice
This is a work of fiction. Names, characters, places, and incidents are either the product of the author's imagination or are used fictitiously, and any resemblance to actual persons living or dead, business establishments, events, or locales, is entirely coincidental.

The Earl Pretender

COPYRIGHT © 2023 by Hilary Mackelden

All rights reserved. No part of this book may be used or reproduced in any manner whatsoever without written permission of the author or The Wild Rose Press, Inc. except in the case of brief quotations embodied in critical articles or reviews.
Contact Information: info@thewildrosepress.com

Cover Art by *The Wild Rose Press, Inc.*

The Wild Rose Press, Inc.
PO Box 708
Adams Basin, NY 14410-0708
Visit us at www.thewildrosepress.com

Publishing History
First Edition, 2024
Trade Paperback ISBN 978-1-5092-5520-7
Digital ISBN 978-1-5092-5521-4

Published in the United States of America

Dedication

To my wonderful son, Steven,
the people who care for him,
and to carers everywhere.
You are the world's true heroes.

Chapter One

1817

If Jane Frobisher hadn't been so preoccupied with her family's problems, she would have been more aware of her surroundings. Then, she might have seen the gentleman leaving the Hay Wagon in time to prevent their collision.

As it was, Jane was still angry at the butcher's presumptuousness, and irritated by Ben, her brother, who thought it funny to run too far ahead with not a care that his sister had called him back and was, even now, racing to catch up to him. At the same time, she was frantically trying to fathom where on earth she would find four pounds, ten shillings by Friday without distressing her mother.

She saw the blur of movement as the inn's door opened, and heard the noise of the taproom. The unmistakable smells of yeasty beer, stewed steak, and sawdust were carried on the draught of air through the door, and in the back of her brain she registered the fact that someone was coming out. At the speed she was travelling, though, she could not hope to stop in time. All she could do was turn sideways to avoid crashing into him head on, which caused her shopping basket to swing around and hit his midriff. It flew from her grasp as he gave a loud "Oof!" and knocked into her, solid muscle pushing against her tiny frame. She took one step back, then another, and teetered on the edge of the curbstone, her arms windmilling in a vain attempt to save her balance.

Everything slowed down. The noise of Bloomfold High Street faded into a thick silence. Jane seemed to float, every movement exaggerated, clear and detailed, and completely unstoppable.

Just as she fell back toward the cobbled road, bracing herself to land in one of the myriad puddles of cold, muddy water or, worse, to sit on a steaming horse apple no one had yet collected, her shoulders were grabbed by firm, strong hands and she was pulled upright. The man held onto her, steadying her, his eyes dark with what looked like concern. His lips moved, but she couldn't hear him through the deafening whoosh of blood pulsing past her ears.

For a full twenty seconds, Jane stood there, blinking stupidly, while the stranger held her, and the world tilted on its axis, nothing behaving as it ought. The wool of her pelisse should have prevented her feeling anything but the pressure of his gloved hands cupping her shoulders, yet she was strangely conscious of his warm touch heating her skin and sending a frisson of danger down her arms and into her fingers. Her heart missed a beat, even as her stomach flipped over itself, and her legs turned to jelly. No doubt at the scare from her near fall.

She took a moment to steady herself, then breathed in deeply and turned to the man who had barreled into her. If it turned out to be one of the farm laborers, taking time from his work to fill his skin with beer, he would get the sharp side of Jane's tongue. How dare he come running out like that, without checking the pavement for pedestrians?

He wasn't a laborer. He was not a working man at all, judging from the clothes covering the broad chest level with her eyeline. Which, she thought inanely, would make him a couple of inches over six feet tall. A whole twelve inches more than she was. Power and strength and authority emanated from him, filling the space around her, imposing and intimidating. He wore a dark coat, made from superfine, its buttons gleaming and solid, under an open greatcoat with three capes. A finely embroidered blue waistcoat covered a white linen shirt, and his cravat was simply folded, held in place with a silver stickpin, its broad, flat head sporting a design that reminded Jane of...

She gasped. The design was unusual enough to be instantly recognizable: a bird, its beak open in song, its body hidden inside an open-topped barrel. It wasn't a design Jane would expect to come across often, and yet she had now seen it on two things: the stickpin this man wore, and a ring which belonged to Ben.

Was there a connection between this man and her brother? She couldn't, for the life of her, think what it might be, but it frightened her. Ben could not protect himself, so if this man posed any sort of threat to him, Jane needed to deal with it. Now.

She looked up, hoping to gauge his measure, and found herself staring into a face that was far too handsome for his own, or anyone else's, good. His jaw was firm, almost square, and she would not have been surprised to learn it was hewn from granite. His lips pressed together in a long, straight line that made him seem stern and disapproving, although his countenance was softened somewhat by the dark blue skin on his cheeks where new beard growth formed.

His eyes were dark beneath the brim of his hat, neither their color nor the expression in them easy to discern. She *could* see his high cheekbones, the long, thin, aristocratic nose, and the light brown hair curling below his hat. His cologne smelled like the woods after a summer rain, green and fresh, vibrant.

The caped greatcoat gave him bulk, not that he needed it. He was taller and broader than any man Jane knew. Considering half the men in this village were laborers who lifted huge bales of hay as if they were no heavier than Mama's cross-stitch, that was saying something.

She thought she should be frightened of him, but she wasn't. Anxious, yes, but that was because of his stickpin and the threat it might represent for Ben, and it was not the same thing as fear.

His gaze met hers and her heart hiccupped. Her mouth dried, and her breath caught in her throat, and…

It was happening again! Had she learned nothing from the last time? Although, as she recalled, with Sydney her reaction had not been so immediate, nor so stark. Sydney had had to encourage Jane, and it had been several months before she'd so much as put her hand on his arm. Although, when she had…

No! She would not let history repeat itself. She couldn't go through that again. And anyway, what on earth was she thinking? This wasn't a man to spin dreams about after a harmless flirtation at a village gathering. This was the lout who had rushed from the pub and almost sent her flying. He probably thought she should apologize for having the temerity to be walking where he wished to tread!

He let go of her arms, and she stepped back, spine straight as a ramrod, shoulders squared, chin tilted defiantly. Her fists clenched, pulling her worn gloves taut across her knuckles.

"I do beg your pardon, miss," he said. His voice was rich and deep, like the rumble of distant thunder. Jane shuddered. This moment felt like the calm before a heavy storm. "Are you hurt?" he asked.

"No. I thank you." Her own voice seemed soft and shaky, nothing like the sensible and practical Jane Frobisher who had, not five minutes earlier, negotiated a stay of execution at the butcher's shop.

The butcher! Her chicken!

That tiny bird had cost her dear, not in monetary terms, but in the humiliation of having to accept it gratefully from Mr. Turner's pudgy hands while he eyed her bosom in a way that made her feel he could see right through her clothes to the body beneath. He had leered at her as he told her how much Mama now owed. "Four pounds, ten," he'd said, his tone apologetic, though his eyes were not. "I can't let it get any bigger, my lovely."

"I will remind Mama," Jane had answered, taking a step back, out of his reach.

"We don't have to worry your Mama." He smiled, and it sent goosepimples across her skin. "I'm sure you and I could work out a…repayment scheme." He licked his lips. "And to prove my good faith, I'll only charge you tuppence for the chicken."

Jane wanted to throw the chicken, which should have cost a shilling, into his face. She wanted to tell the repulsive man exactly what she thought of him and then to walk away, head held high, never to darken his doorstep again. But she couldn't. Mama owed him far too much for cuts of meat he'd allowed on account. And they did need to eat.

So, instead of putting Mr. Turner in his place, Jane had swallowed the bitter shame, curtseyed and fled from his shop.

And now she'd dropped the chicken they needed if they were going to have any dinner tonight. All because this arrogant man hadn't looked where he was going.

Her basket lay on its side in the road a few feet away, the chicken still half inside the paper, half on the ground. There were a few pieces of grit on the bird's skin. Nothing she couldn't wash off, she told herself, and took a step toward it.

Before she could reach it, however, the stranger bent and scooped it up. "My humblest apologies," he said. "I will, of course, replace the meat."

As was only right. She meant to thank him and accept his offer. Even though the chicken was still edible, he had knocked it from her hand, and besides, the extra meat would come in handy. Except, when her words came, they were not the ones she was thinking.

"Th-there is no need." she answered. The sound of her own voice was shameful. She sounded breathy, and she was stuttering, for goodness' sake! She cleared her throat, but it made little difference. "I—I must be going. Th-thank you for…"

For what? Preventing her fall? He was the reason she'd lost her balance in the first place, so she hardly needed to thank him for that. For picking up her basket, then? She supposed it had allowed her to keep a little of her dignity, which would have been completely lost had she been forced to scrabble in the mud herself. But Jane didn't think this man would care a fig for her dignity.

Saving her face had been a fortunate consequence of his action, not the reason for it.

Perhaps she should be thankful he had alerted her to a threat to Ben. She glanced at his stickpin once more, gulped, and took a step back.

"I…Good day." She made to go around him, anxious to hurry home and tell Mama what she had seen here. And then, they would probably have to pack.

Inwardly, Jane groaned. The last thing she wanted was to leave Bloomfold and start another new life, once again surrounded by strangers. In her twenty years, Jane had moved home ten times that she remembered. Surely, that was enough for anybody.

"Janey!" Ben's voice made her start. He ran to her.

Oh no! She did not want Ben to come too close to this man. Not until she knew exactly who he was, and how he was connected to her brother.

"I'm coming." Trembling, she took the basket from the man's hand, then made to hurry away.

Ben, however, had other ideas. And whereas he was normally slow and lumbering, today he was quicker than Jane. Before she could move past the man's imposing frame, her brother reached her, a puzzled frown on his open, honest face. He eyed the stranger, then asked, suspiciously, "Who you?"

"Time to go home, Ben." Jane gave the stranger one last glance, then stopped, her anger rising to see him staring at Ben, intently. How dare he? Ben was not some exhibit in a carnival sideshow, to be gawped at by anyone with a penny!

It had happened before, of course; Ben hadn't reached the age of thirty without attracting some curiosity, and even Jane had to admit he was different to most people. Added to his clumsy movements and the childlike way he behaved, Ben's distinctive features meant he was bound to be noticed, but she expected better manners from people of "the Quality," and this man—she refused to call him a gentleman—was most definitely a member of "the Quality." His coat was expensive and well-made, and his boots, though spotted with the mud of a day's riding, were clearly the best money could buy.

His breeches were well made, too, and they fitted him perfectly, molding to his muscular thighs like a second skin. His flat stomach did not spoil the line of his buttoned coat…and Jane knew better than to look at a man's flat stomach! Or his thighs.

Of such things was the road to hell made.

Besides, he was studying Ben like an insect under a scientist's microscope. There was nothing attractive in a man who would do that. She stepped past him and looped her free arm through Ben's.

"Come along," she said, throwing the stranger a look of contempt.

The man shook his head as if to clear it and gave her a tiny bow. "Forgive me," he said. "That was rude of me."

Jane wanted to say, *Yes, it was*, and berate him for his boorishness. She did no such thing, but behaved instead like the lady she'd promised Mama she would be on the day she'd also sworn never again to do anything to shame the family name.

"It's just…" The stranger smiled at Ben. "You remind me of someone I know."

His explanation did not mollify Jane. She was aware there were others who looked like Ben. Not many, since most did not survive infancy, but enough to be noted. They weren't pattern copies of Ben; each one bore the stamp of their own family, but they were similar, with their almond-shaped eyes and button noses. However, that was no reason to stare, and a mealy-mouthed apology did not make it all right.

"Good day, sir." She made sure he heard her anger and disgust in those three words.

Ben, however, understood the man differently, taking his words to mean that he knew Ben himself. He frowned. "I not know you," he said. "How you know me?"

The stranger looked nonplussed. He glanced at Jane, then at Ben. "I didn't mean…"

"I not know him, do I, Janey?" Ben's voice rose with his agitation. Yet another crime to lay at the feet of this oafish man. Jane spared him one more glare before moving to comfort Ben, something she needed to do quickly, before his anxiety became a full-blown tantrum.

"No, Ben," she soothed, "you don't know him. The—gentleman—" she hoped her eyes told him she used the term for Ben's sake and not because the man deserved it—"has made a mistake. Let's go home."

She led him along the street, away from the stranger. With every step, she felt the man watching her, and she fought the urge to look back when she reached the corner and turned off the High Street, onto the lane where their rented cottage stood.

With luck, she would never see the oaf again.

Chapter Two

Robert Carrow watched them leave. There was something about that man, Ben. It was something he couldn't be certain of, and yet…had he seen Father in his features?

It wasn't easy to tell. The young man's eyes were dark like Father's, like Robert's own, come to that, but many people had dark brown eyes. Robert had wanted to look more closely for more certain signs of familial resemblance, but staring at him had been unforgivably rude. No wonder the young woman had bristled.

She was very protective of Ben, which was good, for he was clearly vulnerable and in need of someone to care for him. But who was he? Could he possibly be the brother Robert had spent the last year searching for?

His stepmother would say it was impossible. She would point out that Robert's father himself had said, in one of his more lucid moments, that his oldest son had died. "It broke his heart," she'd said, shortly after Robert had become aware he'd ever had an older brother. "He's put that in the past, where it belongs. Why would you drag it all out again?"

"I didn't. He did." Robert had answered through gritted teeth. He had always disliked Jessica, although he tried to hide it for Father's sake. The man was besotted with this, his third wife, and thought she could do no wrong. It wasn't an opinion Robert could bring himself to share.

He did try. He wanted to believe she loved her husband, that she tried to dissuade her stepson from searching for his brother because of her concern for his father's feelings; the Earl of Barwell had been devastated when he'd spoken of his firstborn son during one of his "episodes." There had been tears at the remembrance of his beloved first wife, and the child she'd borne him, the child who had disappeared without trace as his mother lay dying.

Jessica had begged Robert to forget the whole sorry story. "Your father is not a well man," she'd said. "He doesn't always make sense. I would spare him the pain of your wild goose chase."

All of which sounded reasonable, something a loving wife might say. Unfortunately for her, Robert did not believe Jessica so altruistic. If she wanted Robert to stop his search, it was because it suited her. Sparing her husband's feelings was a lucky side effect.

"He is an old man," she continued. "Old men, especially those with delusions, say foolish things that aren't true."

To which Robert had retorted that old men, especially those with delusions, were like men in their cups: they spoke the hidden truth.

"And tell me," she went on. "What if this Benedict is real? What if he did survive infancy, and you do discover him? Have you thought through the ramifications of that? He would be the firstborn son. You would lose your place as the earl apparent."

"I have never coveted the title. I certainly don't want it if it isn't truly mine."

"You say that, but you surely don't deny it has

greased wheels for you throughout your life. Being the second son is quite a step down. And my poor Barnaby will only be the third son. He will have no status at all."

Robert could not fathom her argument. Barnaby, the son she had borne Father, had never been destined to inherit the title at all, so whether he was the second son or the third made little difference. He had no cause to worry. His pedigree meant, no matter how many were ahead of him in the succession, he would never want. Sometimes, Robert thought, Jessica was a little too preoccupied with position and society.

Neither of which mattered to Robert a whit. If Father's memory was a true one, there was someone out there to whom Robert's place truly belonged, and honor insisted he search for him, no matter what it cost Robert, nor what Jessica may say.

He'd left home the next day, following the flimsiest of clues around the countryside. Dorset. Devon. Somerset. Hampshire. Back to Dorset. And now Sussex. Always one step behind, always too late.

Had his luck turned this time? The woman's defensive attitude just now made him think it might have.

He wondered who she was. She was too young to be the person Robert had expected to find caring for his brother. That person, an old school friend of Ben's mother, would be in her mid-fifties now; the woman today was about twenty. A nurse, perhaps, employed to look after Ben?

Whoever she was, she was the kind of woman a man remembered. She was tiny, the top of her head reaching no higher than midway up his chest, and slender. No, not slender. Skinny. There'd been very little of her, and her pelisse was too big, as if it had been made for a fuller figure. He recalled her arms beneath his hands. He'd grabbed her to stop her falling after he bowled into her, but he'd been shocked to feel sharp shoulder bones, an indication she did not eat enough. Robert had had the insane urge to take her into the inn and order her the biggest meal they offered.

Which was ridiculous. She was not the only person in England who needed more food. Twelve months after the Year without a Summer, half the population were skeletal, their cheeks hollow, shoulders stooped.

But most of the hungry wore rags. They had the look of what Jessica called "riffraff," and they spoke in uncultured, uneducated accents. This woman was not like that. She'd spoken well, indicating a certain level of breeding. Her clothes might be old and worn, but they were of good quality, and she carried herself with an innate pride. Yet her face was gaunt, her eyes too large for it.

They'd been arresting eyes, all the same. Not quite blue, not quite gray, the color of the clouds on a day when it might rain but equally might not. They were ringed by long eyelashes, darker than the blonde hair curling around her bonnet, and her skin had the look of a soft, white rose. A smattering of freckles on her pert nose gave a hint of mischief, and the edges of her lips turned up as if she was perpetually ready to smile.

She hadn't smiled for Robert. Judging by the look of contempt she'd directed at him, she never would. But then, he had nearly knocked her down.

His fault, entirely. He'd stormed from the inn in high dudgeon, with no care for anyone in his path, angry that the landlord and his clientele had intended to be less than helpful, answering Robert's questions with riddles and jiggery-pokery. It was plain they would tell him nothing, even though he put several coins down.

He'd intended to secure a room and a meal, but their attitude changed his mind, and he had decided instead to ride to the next village, where he hoped to find a friendlier innkeeper before returning to Bloomfold to resume this part of his search.

But that had been before he bumped into Ben and the young lady called Janey.

It struck him how fortuitous their meeting had been. If he'd stayed in the taproom a few moments longer, if she hadn't come past at that exact time…Robert might never have found them. Come to that, if she'd not had Ben with her, he *still* wouldn't have found them.

Robert had no guarantee that Ben was his brother, of course. This could be another false trail. Although, how many men born with that condition could be found in one small village, then lived to adulthood? Few lived long at all, yet were there two here, both around thirty years old? What were the odds of that? And Ben could be short for Benedict…

Was Robert catching at a straw?

If he followed Ben to his home, made himself properly known, mayhap he could learn more. If Ben was not his brother, if this was just a coincidence, Robert could beg pardon and go on his way, searching for new clues. But if this was his brother…

Father would be overjoyed to have his son returned to him, although, Robert knew, he would also be anxious about the future of his title and the estates. The Ben Robert had just seen was not capable of administering them. But then, Robert would help him, and there were capable land agents.

If Ben was Benedict, and if he returned to Barwell with Robert, would Janey come too? She clearly cared for Ben, so it stood to reason she'd want to satisfy herself he was comfortable, his every need supplied.

Robert wished he could promise her the same for herself.

He imagined her after a few of the hearty meals his father's cook prepared. Her cheeks would no longer be sunken, but rounded and pink, her eyes bright and healthy. As she filled out, would she become more curvaceous? Or would she remain slight, so delicate a puff of wind could blow her away? He closed his eyes and enjoyed the images his mind painted: Janey, in satin and silk, pearls in her hair and at her throat, smiling up at him in a ballroom; Janey in sprigged muslin as they walked by Barwell's lake; Janey…

Robert blew out a heavy breath and pushed the woolgathering aside. He had no business thinking such things. There were two types of women who crossed a man's path: those who shared his fun and accepted his gifts, knowing it would never lead to anything more, and those who expected marriage. Janey belonged to the latter group, but even if he felt so inclined, Robert couldn't marry her. For one thing, he was the son of an earl. If and when he married, it would be to a lady of suitable family, not to the nurse caring for his possible brother. Besides, until Robert knew for certain what his own future held, he could not offer to share it with anyone else. On the one hand, it wouldn't be fair for a woman to marry him with expectations of a title and wealth, only to discover she was the wife of a younger son, and therefore entitled to neither. On the other hand, until he knew for certain that his brother had survived,

Robert couldn't disclaim the title, and that wouldn't be fair to a wife either.

On top of this, if the childlike Ben did indeed turn out to be Benedict, Viscount Burbage, heir to the earldom of Barwell, then Robert was going to be busy helping prepare for a difficult future. His first priority must be ensuring the estate's interests were safeguarded. All in all, it would be a long time before Robert could even think of marriage for himself.

Which was by-the-by. First, he needed to find this Ben again, and discover what he could of him.

He strode along the High Street, his eyes fixed on the corner where Ben and Janey had disappeared, his mind focused on what he would say when he caught up to them. "Hello, I believe I'm Ben's brother," didn't sound as if it would put her at ease, and Robert suspected if he didn't put Janey at ease, he would get nowhere with Ben. The pang in his chest at the idea she might think badly of him took him by surprise. It shouldn't matter at all what her opinion of him was. All that mattered was…

There was a shout of warning from across the street. Robert looked around and saw a carriage bowling toward him at a fast clip. The horse hooves sounded like thunder on the uneven road, the animals' snorting and the jingle of harness-brasses joining the crack of a whip and the sharp shouts of the driver as he pushed them on.

Robert should have been safe. He was on the pavement, well back from the road. All he should feel was the wind as the carriage raced by. But then the driver seemed to lose control and the horses pulled to the right. They mounted the shallow curb, and the carriage wheels followed.

In a strange slow motion, the vehicle drove straight

at Robert. The gap between the wheels and the walls of the shops narrowed until they scraped the brick with a sickening crunch. There was nowhere to go.

He took a step back, turned and tried to run, though he knew he could not outpace the horses. They were so close he could smell the sweat on their flanks, feel the heat of their breath.

The bakery door opened and Robert dived through it, landing heavily on the woman who had been coming out. Her surprised yell was cut short as he knocked the wind from her. The woman behind the counter shrieked. The carriage wheels screeched and sparked as their hubs again struck the wall outside. It didn't even slow down.

Robert scrambled to his feet. This was the fourth near accident he had had in as many months, and his closest shave yet. Each incident, considered alone, seemed unfortunate, but taken as a whole, he wondered now if there was something more to them. Surely no man could be so randomly accident prone.

Then again, how could they be linked? They had happened in different places, many miles from each other. As far as he knew, nobody wished him harm, and even if they did, they didn't know where he was or where he was going. He hardly knew himself much of the time, letting the clues to his brother's whereabouts lead him. So how could anyone plan an attack on him?

"Are you all right?" The man from across the street rushed into the bakery. He spoke with a soft Sussex burr, his forehead creased in concern as he helped the woman up. Robert bowed and apologized to her.

"Weren't his fault," the man said. "He'd nowhere else to go. He might've been killed."

"Thank you for the warning." Robert took a deep

breath and willed the trembling to stop spreading through him. His heart raced, and the world around him suddenly seemed clearer, much more sharply focused.

"I seen him coming like Ol' Nick hisself was on his heels. And then he just swerved. Idiot! Shouldn't be allowed on the road if he can't control his cattle. Do you know," the man spoke to the shop worker now, "he didn't even slow down?"

The shop worker expressed her horror and asked what the world was coming to, while her customer told Robert that it didn't matter about knocking her down, and really, no harm was done, he may even have saved her life, and she was glad he was uninjured.

The crowd grew. People told each other what they'd seen, and how bad this road was getting these days, it nearly happened to old Mrs. Jenkins a week ago and, mark the words, there'd be someone killed ere long. And where exactly was the constable when you needed him? The indignation grew, until they forgot Robert and his part in the adventure altogether.

So, taking his chances, Robert slipped out of the shop and stared up the road. The carriage was long gone. Even if he ran back to the inn and collected his horse, he doubted he could catch up now. And for what? A drunken coachman was more of a danger to himself than he was to anyone else, Robert's near-miss notwithstanding. The idiot would probably be thrown into a ditch soon, where he would be found in the morning with a broken leg and a princely hangover, insisting he'd done nothing wrong.

Robert pushed the incident away and concentrated instead on the matter that had first brought him to Bloomfold. He hoped he hadn't lost too much time and that he could still find Janey and Ben. Quickening his stride, he turned the corner and hurried along the road they had taken.

The tiny lane twisted and turned, limiting his view of what lay ahead. High hedgerows darkened the road, making it seem narrower, giving way at intervals where fields changed into small copses of trees.

Ten minutes later, he rounded a bend and came upon three cottages. They were very small, all three together not as big as the Dower House at Barwell, and they were built for people who were not as tall as Robert, if the small doors and low roofs were any indication. Those roofs were thatched, the eaves hanging over the windows like the lids of half-closed eyes. They were probably very dark inside, even in the fullest light of day. They looked to be well-maintained, though: the thatch on the roofs was thick and fresh, and the walls in good repair. Flowers grew in the gardens and the fences stood upright and strong.

Did Janey live in one of these cottages? And Ben, of course. It was Ben he sought. He'd merely thought of Janey because…because he'd need her help when he talked to Ben.

Three cottages. Which one, he wondered, might be hers—Ben's?

As he stood, pondering his next move, a small child wandered into the garden from the nearest cottage. She wore a gray dress with a blue pinafore over it, and her soft, blonde hair was gathered into bunches tied with bright red ribbon. In her hands she carried a ball that had seen better days. Misshapen and tatty, Robert doubted it would roll, let alone bounce.

He grinned as she threw the ball. It landed with a

soft thud on the lane. She toddled to it and bent to pick it up, but accidentally kicked it, sending it out of her reach once more. She took a few more steps and bent again. When she kicked it a second time, Robert had to bite his lip to stop himself laughing out loud.

This time, he heard the carriage before he saw it. The thunder of hooves, the jingle of harness and the creak of wheels over rough ground. Then it was rounding the bend, so fast the wheels on one side left the road. The same driver stood, whip in one hand, reins in the other, a maniacal grin on his face.

The driver saw the child and his grin turned to a snarl. He roared and waved his whip, warning her to get out of the way, but the movement only spurred the horses faster. The child stood in the road, watching, transfixed. In the distance, someone screamed.

Instinct took over. Robert dove at the child and shoved her. He saw her land in the cottage garden, her eyes wide with shock and terror. He tried to roll after her, but the skirt of his greatcoat caught in the spokes of a wheel and he was pulled backward, jerked from his feet, and dragged along the ground. The driver shouted at the horses, but they didn't slow.

A terrible pain shot through his shoulder and down his arm. His back bounced against the wheel and his cravat tightened, cutting off his air. He heard shouts, a child yelling, the snorting horses, the sickeningly loud crack of a breaking bone.

Then nothing.

Chapter Three

Jane stood in the doorway, removing her bonnet and watching Lucy play with the ball. The child followed it into the road and Jane pursed her lips. She really must drum it into Lucy that roads were not for playing. Although the prospect of any traffic along this lane was remote, it was better to make all roads forbidden rather than confuse the child.

What happened next was over in an instant yet seemed to last an eternity.

The rhythmic pound of galloping hooves.

The creak of wood.

The "Hah! Hah!" of an impatient driver.

Lucy in the middle of the lane, frozen in place, watching the danger race toward her.

Jane may have screamed. She didn't know. She picked up her skirts and ran forward but knew, even as she tried, she was not going to reach Lucy in time. She pumped her arms and legs, leaning forward as if to arrive sooner. It made no difference.

A blur of movement. Lucy sailed through the air and landed in the garden, shocked, frightened, but not badly hurt.

The coach raced past.

Everything stood still.

Then Lucy yelled, and Jane reached for her, speaking nonsense in a soothing tone. She picked her up and held her close and tight, the child's crying blocking out all other sounds for several seconds while Jane tried to slow her own heartbeat and calm her own breathing.

Ben shouted and rocked from foot to foot, slapping his hands against the sides of his head as he stared at the road. Jane followed his gaze and froze. The stranger with the stickpin lay still, both legs and one arm bent at impossible angles. His coat was torn, his eyes closed. An ugly crisscross of red lines and black grit scored his forehead and slick, dark blood stained the road.

For perhaps half a minute Jane stood, unable to move, unable to think. Then common sense kicked in, and she sprang into immediate and instinctive action. "Ben, stop that noise and go and fetch Doctor Bull," she ordered, sternly.

"He dead?" sobbed Ben.

"No," answered Jane, though truthfully, she had no idea whether the man was dead or not. Ben needed reassurance, so that's what she gave him. "Fetch Doctor Bull," she repeated. Ben lumbered away toward the village, while Jane prayed the doctor would come quickly, be able to help, and wouldn't insist on immediate payment.

"Lucy," she said to her daughter, "fetch Grandmama." She prised the child's starfish fingers from her neck and put her on the ground. "Fetch Grandmama." She watched the little girl toddle into the house before she finally ventured into the road to see to the downed man.

By the time Mama came, Jane had established that he was breathing but the gash on the back of his head was deep, and besides the graze on his forehead, he had a scrape on his cheek and an ugly, bruised swelling around his eye. She didn't have to check to know there were broken bones—nobody's limbs could twist like that and remain intact.

Gently, she stroked back a lock of hair that fell across his damaged face. It was silky and soft, well cared for, proclaiming that this was a man of means. No doubt his family would be expecting him. Would they be angry at Jane? If she hadn't allowed Lucy to run into the road, he would not be hurt now. Was that how his people would see it? Was that how he would see it himself when he regained his senses?

He hadn't seemed unreasonable in the High Street. Grim faced, perhaps, brusque even. But he had apologized for his rudeness, and he had offered to replace her shopping.

Perhaps he had a servant travelling with him. A man like this would surely have a valet, or a groom, or someone. When Ben returned with the doctor, she would send him to the inn to fetch the servant so he could see to his master's care. Until then, she must do her best to make him comfortable and ensure his injuries were not made worse.

Mama brought a blanket and laid it over him as the doctor came along the lane, Ben huffing and puffing in his wake. Two other men followed, their faces creased with concern.

"It's the gentleman from the bakery," said one as he squinted down at the unconscious stranger.

"Twice in one day?" replied the other. "That i'n't no accident."

"Shouldn't have thought so. We'll need to tell the constable."

"The constable," said Doctor Bull, his tone brisk,

"can wait until we've tended to him."

"Is he dead?" asked Ben, breathless after his exertions.

"No, he isn't," answered Jane. She stood and took a step back, out of the doctor's way.

"Sorry to disappoint you, young Benedict," added Doctor Bull.

"Not dis'ppointed," argued Ben, affronted.

Jane grinned at him. "Doctor Bull is making sport of you," she told him. Ben didn't look completely convinced, but he said nothing more.

The doctor diagnosed two broken legs, a broken arm, and some cracked ribs, along with a possible concussion. He ordered the men to load his patient onto a trestle and to carry him, carefully, into the cottage.

"It seems, Mrs. Winter," he bowed to Mama, then turned to Jane, "and Mrs. Frobisher, the pair of you will have a house guest for a time."

"But we are not acquainted with the gentleman," argued Jane. "My reputation…"

"Your reputation is safe, Madam," said the doctor, impatiently. "I realize it is an inconvenience to you, but your Christian duty to a person in need is clear."

Mama put her arm around Jane. "We have not had houseguests since my daughter became a widow," she said. "She has never had to remember a widow can do things an unmarried maid could not."

"To be honest, that is a moot point," said the doctor. "This gentleman is so severely injured it would not matter to me were there a dozen maidens living under your roof with no chaperone between them. Moving him into your cottage is the limit of his endurance for now. He certainly would not survive the journey to the inn.

Forgive my bluntness, but Mrs. Frobisher must forget her sensibilities and take him in." He raised an eyebrow, daring Jane to argue with him further.

Instead, she nodded. "Of course he will stay here. I was not thinking properly. The shock…" The doctor smiled, kindly, and Mama gave her shoulder an encouraging squeeze.

The men carefully carried the injured man into Mama's bedchamber, where Mama set to, collecting what was needed and helping Doctor Bull tend to the man's wounds. Lucy watched from the doorway, eyes wide, two fingers stuck in her mouth.

Jane gave the child a tight smile. "Come along, Missy Lou," she said in a voice that was far brighter than she felt. "This is not the place for you." *Nor me*. She picked up Lucy and carried her downstairs to the parlor.

"Is Mrs. Frobisher not going to help?" asked the doctor as she walked away. Jane's face heated at the thought of being in that chamber as Doctor Bull removed the gentleman's clothing and bound his wounds.

"She must take care of Lucy and Ben," said Mama. "She'll help later."

Doctor Bull harrumphed. Jane hurried away before he could try to commandeer her again.

"The gentleman will doubtless be here with you for some weeks," Doctor Bull said two hours later, when he had tended his patient and come to the parlor for a cup of tea. "I have reset his bones and bound his ribs, and he's young and strong, so he should heal well, but he cannot be moved until those bones have knit together. You will both have to care for him."

Jane sipped her tea and avoided eye contact with the doctor. If he saw how uncomfortable she was, he might wonder why. If he investigated, he would learn there had never been a Mr. Frobisher, or at least not one who had wed Jane. Desperate to protect herself from Society's censure and Lucy from the taint of illegitimacy, Jane had become a widow in name, if not in fact, although she had been saddened when Mama insisted she change her name.

"As a married woman, you would no longer share my surname," Mama had pointed out. "And a married woman you must be, Jane."

So Jane had taken the name from an ancient gravestone and invented a whole life that was far removed from her own.

"Henceforth," said Mama, once their story had been created and rehearsed, "you are not Jane Winter. You must think of yourself, at all times, as Jane Frobisher, for to do otherwise for even an instant is to risk making mistakes that will lead to discovery."

Sydney Greening had a lot to answer for.

If he'd been the least bit honorable, Jane would now be married in truth, and unafraid of anybody's questions. She was honest enough to know she would also be desperately unhappy.

"Our patient has a fat purse," said Doctor Bull, bringing her attention back to the present. "I have taken my fee and will send him a receipt. You would be within your rights to take the cost of his board, as well."

Mama fixed him with a frosty stare. "We will take nothing."

Doctor Bull cleared his throat. "Yes. Well. Plenty of rest, keep him calm and still, and if he develops a fever, cool him down. Call me if he should take a turn for the worse."

Mama saw the doctor out of the house and Jane went to the bedchamber. She needed to get over her discomfort at seeing a man unclothed, the sooner the better, she told herself, checking on their sleeping guest.

He looked much more peaceful now. His face had been cleaned and liniment applied to the cuts. The sickly-sweet smell of the ointment filled the room, threatening to overpower her. A bandage was wrapped around his head, the white of it contrasting sharply with the brown of his hair and the tone of his skin, although the tan she had noticed earlier was now reduced by the pallor of sickness. One eye was swollen, the stretched skin already shiny and black, and the beginnings of new beard growth shadowed his jawline.

His arm was splinted, white linen wrapped tightly around it to prevent movement, and a makeshift cage had been placed over his legs to keep the weight of the blankets off them. His shoulders were bare, their breadth suggesting he was unafraid of physical activity, while a smattering of dark hairs covered his chest above the bandages wrapped tightly around his ribs.

Jane swallowed against her suddenly dry throat. The tip of her tongue dampened her lips. The only other man she had seen without his shirt had been Sydney Greening, and he had looked nothing like this. Long-limbed and slender, with no discernible muscles on his skinny arms, Sydney had looked like the boy she now knew him to have been. This stranger was all man.

The direction of her thoughts shocked her. Had she learned nothing? Gazing—among other things—on Sydney's body had led to her ruin and almost destroyed her family. They had lost their home and been hounded from their neighborhood, the jeering and sneering ringing in their ears. Poor Ben had been insulted and threatened, his very existence deemed a punishment on the family by some of their more superstitious neighbors. In fact, the only good thing to have come from it was Lucy. Jane would not, could not, regret her daughter.

Which did not mean she was anxious to repeat the mistake that had led to the child's existence.

Jane swallowed hard and closed her eyes, determined not to look at the man anymore. It did her no good. She could still picture him lying there, his form beautiful, even in its brokenness.

She was lost! She truly was the devilish, wanton temptress Sydney had accused her of being. She dreaded to think what Mama would say, were she to discern the direction of Jane's thoughts at this moment.

"You should not be here." Mama's soft whisper made Jane jump and she whirled, breath caught in her throat, heart racing.

"He requires care," she answered, amazed that she sounded so unaffected.

"I will do it," said Mama.

"I am a widow too."

Mama's look remained steady. "Not when we are private, you are not."

"It is too much for you to do alone." Surely Mama couldn't argue with that. She was, after all, only a flesh-and-blood woman, and she had her limitations.

Mama sighed. "You may help with some of the more seemly tasks once he is properly attired."

That was as far as Mama would bend, Jane knew. She took one last look at the sleeping man, committing his beautiful form to memory, and then she left the room.

Chapter Four

The first thing Robert became aware of was the pounding at his temples. It felt and sounded like someone had taken a large hammer and was using his head as an anvil. Light seeped in through his eyelids, but he made no attempt to open them, knowing instinctively it would be painful to do so. His body was stiff and his legs pained him, as did his arm. He tried to move and found he could not. He frowned, then groaned as this set off the bruise-pain around his eye.

"Lie still." The voice was gentle. Soft fingers pushed the hair from his forehead before a cold damp cloth dabbed at him. It soothed the pain and seemed to lessen the pounding between his ears.

He took a deep breath in and flinched at the sharp pain in his chest.

"Gently," said the voice.

Images tumbled over each other in his head. A carriage, a bakery, a child, horses, a white-hot burning in his legs, the ground rushing toward him…

"Am I dead?" he asked. His voice was a rasp. The words hurt his parched throat. If he was dead, clearly he was not in Heaven.

The voice chuckled. It was a pretty sound, the ringing of a silver bell. "No, sir," she said. "You are not dead. Although for three days we thought you might soon be so."

Three days? Robert snapped open his eyes and tried to sit up, then collapsed back into his pillows, crying out at the double pain of the light attacking his head and the sharp, piercing needles in his chest.

A firm hand touched his shoulder. "Rest. Stay still."

"Three days," he said, then promptly fell asleep again.

The next time he woke the light had dimmed. His head still pounded and one side of his face was sore, but opening his eyes did not increase his pain as it had done earlier. He took stock of his condition as best he could. His chest stung like the devil, every breath a sharp knife digging into him, and the muscles in his back protested, urging him to stretch, though he knew he should not. His mouth felt as if he had been chewing sand, and his throat hurt. "Water," he said. Or at least, he tried to say it. No sound came out.

Robert turned his head and saw a man sitting beside his bed, staring intently at him. The man looked familiar, though for a moment Robert couldn't place him. He had a round face with a wide forehead, tiny, almond-shaped eyes and a button nose over a wide mouth, with thick lips and a tongue too big to be contained.

Ben, he remembered. His brother?

He couldn't think properly. And if he didn't quench his thirst, he might well die. "Water," he said again. This time, the word came on a growl.

Ben stood. But instead of fetching a jug of water so Robert could drink, he yelled, "Janey!" and ran from the room. Robert winced and groaned as the pounding in his head worsened, and he saw green and red dots dancing in the air.

"You're awake." It was the angelic voice. He had

thought he'd dreamt it last night, but he was definitely awake now, and it was real. He turned toward the sound and blinked, clearing his vision.

Janey. The woman from the High Street. She wore a plain white apron over a coarse brown dress, the lace fichu tucked into her bodice making it modest to the point of primness. Pity, he thought, then chastised himself for his inappropriate reaction to her.

Although, he reasoned, any man could be forgiven for wanting to see more of her. She was beautiful. Without her pelisse to hide them, he became aware of her tantalizingly full breasts, her slender arms, and the long, graceful line of her neck, exposed by the tight bun she'd pulled her light blonde hair up into, scraping it away from her face in a style that favored practicality over fashion. Her throat was bare, and Robert had the fleeting thought that she should wear pearls. They would enhance her cream-pale skin perfectly. Pearls, and nothing else. He pictured her standing before him, glorious in nakedness, a rope of pearls around her neck, rolling softly across the skin of those luscious breasts, caressing the darker skin around her nipple, bringing it to life, making it peak, reaching out for him to touch…

His breath caught and his heart pounded, increasing the pain in his chest. He tried to swallow, but his throat was dry as Ezekiel's bones. Guiltily, he glanced at her. Her eyes were filled with wariness. Of him?

As well she should be, when the only thoughts he had were crude and salacious. The blow to his head must have sent his wits packing and pushed his manners and decorum out with them. This was not some loose-moraled doxy. This was a respectable woman, a nurse, already caring for a man who might well be Robert's brother, and now, it seemed, caring for Robert, too. He thanked God she could not read his mind as he wrestled it to respectability.

Robert wanted to tell her that all was well, that he would not harm her and she had no need to fear him. But when he opened his mouth to speak, just one word came out, and that was strangled and strained.

"Water."

Janey moved to the table beside his bed and poured water from a jug into a tumbler, then helped him to drink. "Sip at it," she said, when he would have gulped it down. "You'll be sick otherwise."

It tasted cool and fresh on his tongue and soothed the fire in his throat, though it did nothing for the pounding of his heart at her nearness. Her skin was soft against his face, though not silky soft like the ladies he'd met in the drawing rooms of Mayfair. Janey's hands were firm, hands that were used for work, though not the red, rough, calloused hands of a servant. Her wrists were delicate, so small and fine he thought they must surely break under the weight of anything she carried, and there was a gap between her skin and the wool of her sleeve, as if her gown had been made for a larger woman. Which it likely had. A nurse wouldn't have money for new dresses. She would, no doubt, wear hand-me-downs from the local Ladies Bountiful, or she would buy them at the secondhand shops where ladies' maids sold their mistresses' cast-offs to supplement their incomes. She smelled, faintly, of lavender.

He looked up at her as he lay back against his pillows. In the dim light, her eyes had darkened to the color of pewter, though he could clearly see the smattering of freckles dotted over her pale cheeks. He knew the ladies of the ton would be horrified at what they saw as her disfigurement, but Robert could not agree. All he saw was her beauty, natural and unaffected and…

Lord, above! This had to stop. He was not a randy schoolboy who lusted after every woman who crossed his path! Vaguely, he remembered a friend who'd been in the army, and who had described the soldiers after a battle at some Spanish town or other. They'd run amok, raping and pillaging and rioting.

"It's a manifestation of joy at having survived," his friend had said. "A need to meet the most basic needs to affirm they are alive. Happens to every man who faces death and walks away."

Was that what had happened to Robert here, now? He winced, then tried to swallow the groan the movement elicited. Smiling sympathetically, she offered him more water.

He closed his eyes and forced his emotions under control. He was a gentleman, and, by God, he would behave like one. He cleared his throat and concentrated his attention on something else. "What happened to me?" he asked, his voice croaky.

She frowned. "You don't remember?"

Robert shook his head, then wished he hadn't when the hammer pounded harder at his temple. "I remember the carriage, the accident," he assured her. "I meant, what happened to *me*? What are my injuries?"

Janey ballooned her cheeks and breathed out, hard, making Robert nervous. It did not seem a good sign.

"Let me see." She counted on her fingers as she listed his ailments. "You have two broken legs, although Doctor Bull said one was a clean break and easy to mend, and the other could have been worse. A broken arm, and there was a dislocation of your elbow, although he was able to put that back in place. He said it probably hurt like the devil, and he apologizes but it had to be done. You have cracked ribs, but none of them pierced anything so, while painful, they are not life threatening, and they will heal with rest. You had a gash on your scalp which needed stitches, and you are covered in cuts, scrapes, and bruises." She smiled. "And you have my eternal gratitude." He frowned, pulling on the swollen skin around his eye. She smiled, sheepishly, at him. "I wish you hadn't been hurt, of course," she continued, "but to me, your injuries are badges of the honor and courage you displayed when you saved my daughter's life. Something I can never repay."

The child was Janey's daughter? Disappointment swept through him, followed by resignation. She was a beautiful woman. It stood to reason some man would already have snapped her up and married her.

"Is your husband about?" he asked. He didn't truly want to meet the man, yet felt compelled to do so. It was as if he needed to meet him, to discover whether he was worthy of her. Which, of course, he would not be. Nobody could have been.

Janey blushed. "I am a widow."

Even as he offered his condolences, elation bubbled up within Robert. *She's not taken.*

"I made a chicken broth," she said. "The meat has been eaten, but the broth is still tasty and filling." She blushed again, giving him a lopsided smile which highlighted her discomfort. "If there is anyone who needs to know where you are, I can write to them for you, if you like." Her color rose even more. "That is, I will write it for you, for your injuries make writing unfeasible." She swallowed, nervous. "I'm sure your wife would like to know you are safe."

"I have no wife."

Her mouth opened in a tiny O, and there was a pause. He wondered what was going through her head. Was she glad that he wasn't married?

"Your mother, then?" she asked, at last. "Surely, someone needs to know your whereabouts?"

Robert thought of the people at home. Father would worry if he knew Robert had been hurt, but only if he was lucid. The older man's failing health was enough to concern himself with. He did not need to worry over Robert's ills. As for his stepmother, Robert doubted she would care very much. Oh, she was always polite to him, but he'd never flattered himself that his welfare truly mattered to her.

"There is no one I need to notify," he said.

She nodded, then left to fetch him something to eat.

The broth she brought back was warm, if a little thin, and Robert assumed he'd been given this because he was an invalid. After delivering it, Janey hurried away, muttering about having things to do.

Almost immediately after she'd gone, a little girl sidled into the room, two fingers in her mouth, eyes wide as she watched him. Robert knew little about children; the only one he was acquainted with was his half-brother, Barnaby, and Jessica did not encourage him to know the boy well.

"Hello," he said softly to this child. With her free hand, she twirled a lock of her hair. "What's your name?"

"Lucy," she said around her fingers.

"That's a pretty name."

She took a step farther into the room. "I eated all my broth," she said, proudly. "Ben not finish his."

Robert frowned. The broth was not only for invalids? It turned to ash in his mouth as he realized this must be the main meal for the whole family. A memory came of the basket in the road, its meagre contents spilled. The chicken had been scrawny, barely enough meat on it to satisfy one person, let alone a family. Now he suspected it had fed them all for the three days he'd lain here, and the bones had been boiled to get one more supper from them.

He thought of the meals at Barwell. The table groaned under the weight of hearty soups and plates full of meat and vegetables, potatoes and bread, sauces, gravy, and stuffing. After those there would be jellies and jam, pastries and cakes, syllabubs and fools, to say nothing of fruit and wine and tea. So much food, too much for them to eat before the remains were carted away, probably given to pigs by servants who then sat down to a feast of their own.

Here, he'd seen no evidence of a servant at all. Janey had been the one who tended him, whilst she also cared for a small child and a mentally disabled man. Yet her accent was cultured, with no trace of a country burr or the rounded speech of the lower orders. This was a woman who should have a maid, at the very least.

There could be only one reason why she did not have one. The same reason she would make a thin chicken that had lain in the road feed her family for three days.

That was something Robert could address, although he suspected he would need to be clever about it. The Janey he was coming to know wouldn't take charity, nor would she accept a gift from him. He took another mouthful of broth and smiled at Lucy, half listening to her babble while he worked out what to do.

When Janey came back for his bowl, he addressed the issue carefully. "I am putting you to a great deal of trouble," he said.

"No, sir," she replied. "You are no trouble at all."

Robert did not believe that. He looked around the room, hoping for inspiration. There was a femininity about the chamber, with its pretty lace curtains and embroidered cushions on the chair seat.

"I have evicted you from your own bedchamber."

Janey grinned. "No, you haven't. This is usually my mother's room, but she is more than happy to share with me and Lucy."

"She shouldn't have to."

"What else do you suggest, sir?" Her smile faded and her shoulders stiffened. "You cannot be moved, and I'm afraid the west wing is currently out of commission." She took a deep breath in through her nose and visibly relaxed her shoulders. "I apologize. Sarcasm is never becoming, and I did not intend to be a shrew."

"You were not. And I deserved the sarcasm." He rolled his left shoulder, trying to ease the ache caused by the weight of his splinted arm. "I wished to say something and was clumsy about it. Would you hear me out? Please?"

Primly, she sat on the chair, hands in her lap. Robert took a few seconds to collect his thoughts. How he broached this subject now would decide the entirety of his stay here.

"I will be here for some time." She nodded. "That's quite a burden on your family." She opened her mouth and he held up his uninjured hand. "I am aware of the extra work and expense caused by one more person in a household. I would pay my shot."

"No." The word was firmly spoken. "We will not take charity."

"I did not offer it. I offer a fair transaction. You are housing and feeding me, nursing me and helping me to heal. You deserve remuneration."

She stood. "If that is all, sir, I will bid you good evening."

Desperately, Robert cast about for a way to convince her. She walked toward the door. His opportunity was slipping away.

"You don't want charity, but you expect me to accept yours," he said. "I have my pride too, and if I cannot pay my way, I will have no choice but to remove myself from your care."

Janey turned and stared at him. "You cannot be moved."

He raised an eyebrow. For several seconds, they glared at each other. Then she nodded, one curt movement of her head. "Very well. If it means so much to you, you may pay for your..." she cast around for the right words, "room and board."

"Thank you. If you would be so kind as to pass my coat? My purse is in the pocket." On a heavy sigh she did as he asked, and he counted out ten guineas for her.

"That's too much!" Her eyes widened in horror.

"You can always return what you do not spend," he said. He did not promise to accept any returned money. Janey looked as if she would argue further, then changed her mind and took the coins.

Tomorrow, he would see about employing a

manservant to help him, and perhaps a maid to share her burdens. For now, he would accept the victory he had secured.

Chapter Five

Jane sat at the kitchen table and stared at the pile of coins in front of her. She didn't think she'd ever seen so much money at one time.

"What am I to do, Mama?" she asked in an awed whisper. Part of her wanted Mama to insist she return it and call his bluff, although she hated to think he might be true to his word and leave. Only because moving him would be detrimental to his healing, she told herself. She cared not a fig for the presence of the man himself. True, he was charming and good natured, kind to Lucy, and he seemed honorable and decent…

Which was exactly what she'd thought of Sydney, and look how that had ended.

She should return the money, watch him move to the inn, and cheer when he had gone.

And yet…they needed the money. For one thing, Mr. Turner wanted four pounds, ten shillings by tomorrow for the meat he had supplied. She hadn't told Mama how he had proposed Jane pay his bill, nor would she. But oh! this money would be welcome when she went to him. She relished the look of disappointment he would wear.

Mama poured herself a cup of small beer, sat across the table, and eyed the money for a long moment. "He is right that looking after him means added expense. He seems to me to be a man who is used to the finer things.

He'll want decent cuts of meat, and coal in the grate." She sipped her drink and grimaced. "And tea. A gentleman will want tea. Coffee, too, if we can get it."

"You told Doctor Bull you wouldn't take any money for caring for him," Jane reminded her.

"No, I said I wouldn't take his money without his permission, which is what the doctor encouraged me to do. But if the gentleman offers to pay his way, we should not refuse."

A great weight lifted from Jane's shoulders. If Mama thought this was acceptable, that was good enough for her. Now she could pay what they owed, buy decent cuts of meat, and stock the larder. More, their guest would not need to leave. He could stay until he was properly healed, and Jane could care for him. Because she enjoyed being useful. That was all.

"By the way," she said, putting the coins into her reticule, relishing the soft chink as they settled, "he told me his name."

There had been nothing on the injured man to identify him. His clothes were well made and expensive, but anonymous, and he hadn't booked a room at the inn, so hadn't identified himself there. The only thing about him that might lead to clues about his identity was the stickpin from his cravat. That had fallen out when the carriage knocked him down and had lain in the road beside his broken body. Jane had scooped it up and put it in her pocket and, afterward, slipped it safely into his bag, hidden by his spare shirts and neckcloths.

"Oh, yes?" asked Mama. "Who is he?"

"He is Mr. Carrow," answered Jane.

Mama gasped and her face paled. "Carrow?" She gulped. "Where is he from?"

"I didn't ask. He did say there is no one to inform of his present circumstances. Do you not find that sad?"

Mama nodded, but she was clearly distracted.

"What is the matter, Mama? Do you know him?"

"No. No, I don't." She stood and walked to the far end of the kitchen, where she busied herself preparing vegetables, presumably for tomorrow, since today's meals were already sorted. She kept her back to Jane. Her defensiveness was disconcerting. Mama was never defensive, or evasive, so why should she react this way to Mr. Carrow's name?

"I knew a Carrow once," she said, after a moment, as if she'd heard Jane's questioning thoughts. "He married my friend."

"Perhaps they are related. I could ask him…"

"No!" The violence in the word startled Jane. Mama took a deep breath, then said, more calmly, "The poor man has been at death's door. He is healing. The last thing he will wish to do is answer idle questions on his lineage." She huffed a humorless laugh. "Good grief, girl! He might even think you were throwing your cap at him."

"Mama, I—"

"My acquaintance was many years ago. My friend is long dead. Besides, you said he had no family, so what good would it do to ask him?"

****

It was with smug satisfaction that Jane entered the butcher's shop on Friday. The bell over the door tinkled, announcing her arrival, and Mr. Turner came out of his back room, rubbing his hands down the front of his apron, adding to the bloodstains there. His stomach bulged forward like that of a pregnant woman and his jowls pulled down his cheeks, giving him a hangdog expression. His bare forearms were thick and covered in dark hair, and his hands were like hams.

He leered at Jane and she struggled not to show her revulsion. They still needed to buy meat from this man, and it served no purpose to insult him as well as to disappoint him. Jane had no illusions that he would be disappointed; if he'd wanted to be paid in money, he would never have allowed the debt to grow so big. She knew he thought of Mama as a lady, and tradesmen did not dun ladies as a rule, but even so, two years' worth of unpaid-for meat was a lot for a butcher to overlook.

"Mrs. Frobisher." He licked his lips. "What can I do for you?"

"It's Friday," she said.

His grin grew broader. "Come to pay what you owe, have you?" He looked her up and down, the way he might inspect a cow or a sheep. Disgust roiled in her stomach and left a bitter taste at the back of her throat. She couldn't bring herself to speak. Instead, she reached into her reticule, drew out five of the golden guinea pieces and offered them to him.

Mr. Turner's smile fell away. His eyes darkened with displeasure. "What's this?"

Jane bit back the sarcastic response she was tempted to make and said, as sweetly as she could, "It's five guineas. I owed you four pounds, ten shillings, plus tuppence for the chicken we had the other day. I'd also like a shilling's worth of steak, please. I make that four pounds, eleven shillings and tuppence altogether, giving me 13 shillings, ten pence change." She held out the coins for him. He made no move to take them.

"Five guineas?" His voice dripped ice. "Where did

you get five guineas?"

Jane bristled. "I took them from my savings."

His cheeks reddened and his jaw clenched. Jane said nothing. "If you had this," he continued, "why didn't you settle the bill before? You've had almost two years' worth of meat from me, and you've had it all on the never-never."

She wanted to retort that he'd had no business extending them credit for that long, but she bit her tongue. Until the money changed hands, she was still in his debt, and it wouldn't do to anger him, especially since he was clearly upset that she'd found the funds anyway.

"You've got that toff staying at your cottage, haven't you?" he asked. He turned and began chopping steak. "He give it to you?" The words were flung at her over his shoulder.

Jane lifted her chin and fixed him with her haughtiest stare. "Do you ask all of your customers where their money comes from?"

He wrapped some of the meat in brown paper for her. "You shouldn't take money from gentlemen."

Jane stared him straight in the eye. "I don't recall saying that I had."

"'Course you did. You couldn't afford it otherwise." Heat rushed into Jane's cheeks, making her skin burn and prickle. "Thing is," he continued, his head tilted to one side as he thought, "what did you have to do in return?"

"I beg your pardon?" Jane's eyes widened in shock.

"Hit the spot, did I?" He tied the paper with a small piece of string, wiped his hands on his apron again, and thrust the package at Jane. He snatched the guineas from her and bit down on one before he counted her change and threw it at her.

"Doesn't matter who you lift your skirts for," he spat. "Just because he's got money, doesn't make you any less of a harlot."

Jane's cheeks burned and her vision blurred behind her unshed tears. In her head she heard that word ring out across the square in the small town where she'd grown up.

Harlot. Women who'd once passed the time of day now held their skirts close as she walked by, so they might not touch her and be contaminated.

Harlot. Men who had offered respectful greetings now leered openly at her.

Harlot. Sydney looked at her down the length of his patrician nose, turned his back, and walked away, arm in arm with his advantageous match.

She blinked, clearing the tears, and lifted her chin. "Good day, sir," she said, proud at her steady curtsey, which betrayed none of her crumbling courage and withering spirit. Last time, she had taken the insults because she was guilty. This time, she'd done nothing but her Christian duty to a stranger in need.

And if you looked with interest on his sleeping form, touched the skin around his wounds with a little more longing than a nurse should have, who was to know? Surely, thoughts did not carry the same weight as actions, no matter what the Bible might say.

Perhaps she was the harlot everyone said she was. Surely, only a harlot would entertain such thoughts, such wanton longing for a man to whom she was not married? Yes, Mr. Carrow was handsome, and he had a fine form, but Jane had no business watching him, taking in every detail, then woolgathering about him whenever she was alone!

She pulled open the shop door with more force than necessary. The bell jangled and seemed to give voice to her anger and shame. She tugged the door closed and stood on the street, composing herself.

There was no reason for her to feel shame, she told herself as her heartbeat slowed and her face cooled. She had done nothing wrong. What was the old saying? A cat may look at a king. There was no crime in looking, and Mr. Turner had no right to make her feel there was.

Mr. Turner was a bully. His actions were intolerable, and Jane would not grace his shop with her custom again. That meant going to the butcher in Robertsbridge, but the three-mile walk was a small price to pay for the satisfaction of never dealing with that odious man again.

Meanwhile, she had enough steak for two or even three substantial meals. On that thought, she straightened her shoulders, pasted a smile on her face, and walked away briskly, enjoying the decisive clicking of her heels against the stone.

****

Over the next week, life at the cottage changed dramatically. First, Mr. Carrow insisted he must have a man to help him. Instead of sending to Hastings or Brighton for a valet, he hired a local man, Jem, saying he didn't need a fop who could tie fancy cravats, but a man strong enough to lift him when nature called, or to turn him so he didn't develop bed sores. And when he didn't need Jem's attention, he was sure Jane and her mother could find things to occupy him. As he had paid Jem handsomely, Mama saw no harm in working the man, and Jane had to admit it was good to see him doing all the jobs she couldn't manage. He was patient with Ben, too, who followed him around like a puppy, eagerly telling Jem anything and everything that came into his mind. Jem let Ben help where he could, and it was wonderful to watch her brother's confidence grow.

A few days after Jem came, Mary arrived. Having a bedridden guest created a great deal of extra work, Mr. Carrow had reasoned, and it wasn't right for ladies like Mrs. Frobisher and Mrs. Winter to do it all, when he had the coin to pay a girl. Jane would have argued but she saw how tired Mama seemed, with her drawn face, sallow skin, and the dark circles under her eyes. If Mary's help gave Mama some respite, so be it. All too soon he would be gone and, without his money, so would Mary and Jem. For Mama's sake, Jane would enjoy the interlude while it lasted.

Lucy was fascinated by Mr. Carrow. Other than Ben, she had never really known a man, and Jane was thankful her first encounter was with someone who was gentle and kind, and ready to tell her nonsensical stories that made her giggle. He didn't take offense at some of her more forthright comments, either.

"You not lay in bed in the day," she told him. "Lazy slug-a-bed."

Jane turned, wide-eyed with horror, ready to scold her, but Mr. Carrow laughed.

"I am, aren't I?" he agreed. "You must tell me that every day."

He caught Jane's eye and winked. Her cheeks heated and her heart pounded. She lowered her gaze, then looked back up to see him watching her, his eyes sparkling with humor. She turned away, but she couldn't keep the smile from her face as she did so.

After two weeks, Doctor Bull removed the splint from Mr. Carrow's arm and replaced it with a sling. He instructed Jem to help Mr. Carrow walk about the room, to strengthen his legs and improve the healing. Jem cut two long, sturdy branches and made crutches, which Mr. Carrow quickly mastered. When she was in the kitchen, Jane heard the steady clump, clump, clump of him practicing walking in the room above her head for hours at a time. Part of her was pleased that he tried so hard, for it boded well for a full recovery. Another part of her, the selfish, unattractive part, lamented the speed of his healing, for the quicker he healed, the sooner he would leave, and that was not something she looked forward to at all.

Only because his leaving meant losing Mary and Jem, and the money for good quality meat, she told herself. There was no other reason for wishing he would stay longer. It wasn't because of the long, comfortable, satisfying talks she had with him of an evening, when Lucy and Ben were in bed and she had the time to debate art and politics, books, and other such things. It certainly wasn't because of his strong jaw and his well-defined cheekbones, the mischief in his dark brown eyes, or the flop of an errant curl over his forehead.

No. If not for the ease of living his generosity had afforded them, Jane would not miss Mr. Carrow for a single moment. And so she would keep telling herself, until she finally believed it.

Chapter Six

When Robert was able to come down to the parlor, it felt like one of the greatest events of his life. Several weeks of staring at the same four walls had tested his sanity to its limit. He'd taken to counting the number of cracks in the paint on the ceiling and imagined joining the age spots on the mirror to make different pictures and patterns, simply to pass the time.

He hadn't been completely alone, of course. As well as Jem, who came in each day to wash and shave him and make him look respectable, Robert had regular visits from Ben, who had clearly been commanded to keep him company. Judging by the small talk he made, Ben had been given topics of conversation with which to maintain Robert's interest and he had committed these topics to memory, making certain to use them every time. This gave his visits a predictability that was at once soul destroying and yet comforting.

Robert tried to vary the conversation by asking questions which should have required answers leading to tangents. They never worked; Ben just blinked and moved on to his next prepared speech, like an actor doggedly delivering his lines. After several days, Robert gave up and went along with whatever Ben said.

He longed to ask the man about his heritage, but knew it would be a waste of time. Even if Ben was Benedict, he would be unlikely to know anything.

Asking him would just confuse him and destroy his trust in his family. Robert didn't want that on his conscience.

The one person who could give him the truth, Mrs. Winter, rarely came near, and so couldn't be asked.

Robert did broach the subject with Janey, but she frowned as if she thought he was mad. "Ben is my older brother," she'd said in a tone that implied Robert was foolish for thinking otherwise.

He pointed out that Ben bore no resemblance to either Janey or her mother, then asked about the man's real family.

"We *are* his real family," she answered, confused and more than a little offended.

"I had the impression he may have been adopted by your mother. I simply wondered if you ever met his real parents."

Janey gave him a long, unblinking stare, as if she tried to see past his facade, deep down into his soul. "Ben is my older brother," she repeated, at last, using a tone she might take with an obtuse student. "His father was my mother's first husband. He died when Ben was a baby, and my mother then married my father. Does that clear your confusion?"

"If I have offended you, I apologize."

"I am not offended." Her brusqueness gave the lie to the statement.

With every day that passed, Robert became more convinced that Ben was the man he had searched for, but he needed to know for certain before he returned to his father with the news. The earl was frail and confused enough as it was, without building up hope only to destroy it again. Robert needed proof. He thought Janey could provide it, but before she would do so, she would have to trust him. Clearly, where Ben was concerned, she did not.

Perhaps she would be more forthcoming if he told her the whole story. So, now that he was downstairs, he asked her to sit and listen to his tale. She narrowed her eyes, suspiciously, but she sat in a chair beside the fireplace, hands folded in her lap and a look of patient resignation on her face. She would, he saw, indulge him, but she was unlikely to change her mind without a compelling reason.

"Where to begin," muttered Robert. He looked around the parlor for inspiration. The room was tiny, no more than fifteen feet by ten, and cluttered with chairs, a table, bookshelves and a small chest in one corner. Most of one wall was taken up by the fireplace, to one side of which was a small pile of logs and a bucket of kindling. On the other side of the hearth was a stand on which were balanced a shovel, a hearth brush, and a poker. A rag rug stretched in front of the hearth. Robert could imagine spending winter evenings in this place, a book on his lap from which he would read aloud while Janey sat across from him, sewing, Lucy playing at her feet.

He shook his head, dispelling the absurd images.

"I find the beginning is a good place, usually," Janey answered his muttered question in a carefully emotionless voice.

He gave her a sidelong look, then took a deep breath. "My father had a wife before my mother," he said. "By all accounts, it was a great love match. But when their first child was born, everything turned to ash."

****

Horror mounted as Jane listened to Robert's tale. His father had loved his first wife to distraction, he said, but when their son was born weak and ill, he was devastated. That, Jane could understand. Any parent who'd planned a life for the child they thought they were having would be devastated at first, upon learning all was not how they had dreamed.

But there was a world of difference between grieving the child you had expected to have, and turning your back on the one God gave to you, which was what Robert's father had done. Overcome with his own heartbreak, he could not even be in the same room as the child for more than a few moments before he claimed he was sick and raced away, his rejection complete.

Jane pictured Ben in that unfortunate baby's place, and anger bristled in every nerve. How could anyone not love a child, simply because he wasn't perfect?

"My mother was widowed before Ben was born," she said, and disgust deepened her voice. "She would have struggled to bring up any child. Yet I can, hand on heart, say she would no more have discarded Ben than she would have tried to fly to the moon. You are saying that, to your father, a child's worth is diminished if it is less than whole."

"I am saying nothing of the sort." Robert stood in front of the fireplace and ran a hand over his jaw. "My father readily admits he behaved badly after Benedict was born. He said things he did not mean, which led his wife—and everyone else—to believe he wished the child gone, but it was grief talking." He swallowed and looked away. "Unfortunately, his wife took him at his word and felt she needed to protect her son."

Jane sniffed. "It can't have been the wondrous love match you claim, if she could believe that of him." She had only thought she loved Sydney, but she had refused to hear any ill of him for weeks, even after he had rejected her and spread rumors about her wantonness and betrothed himself to another woman. Yet this baby's mother had believed the love of her life capable of infanticide?

"I am told that sometimes, when a woman has just given birth, she does not always think in the most rational manner," said Robert. "When my stepmother was confined with my little brother, she had several…less-than-perfect moments. The midwife told my father it was common after childbirth. Apparently, it usually passes quickly." He looked sad. "In the case of Benedict's mother, it didn't pass quickly enough to prevent thirty years of heartbreak."

Jane stared into the hearth. She could not argue with him. After she had delivered Lucy, there had been times when she said or did things that were at odds with her character. On occasion she had actually wondered if she was losing her faculties. At the time, she had attributed it to all that had happened to her. She'd been seduced and betrayed, shunned by her neighbors and shamed as a harlot. Worse, the vicious tongues had attacked Mama and Ben, too. People had blamed Mama for Jane's immorality, and it had been a very short step from there to accusing her of being responsible for Ben's disabilities as well. It hadn't taken long in a small, largely uneducated community for people to conclude the problems of the son were a judgment on the mother.

Faced with such vitriol, Mama had moved the family away, to make a fresh start. In the middle of all this, Jane had given birth. Was it any wonder her mind had not been its normal efficient self?

But even in her darkest moment, she could not

imagine sending Lucy away. And even if such an action had been forced on her, she couldn't think she would have waited thirty years to put things right. "If this was known," she said, "why did no one look for your brother sooner? Why did your father not search for him?"

Robert sighed. There was a wealth of pain in the sound. "From what I can gather, for a long time, he thought the child had died. His wife died shortly afterward, and the secret of the baby's whereabouts went with her. The pain of her loss was so great, he never spoke of her." He snickered. "Until recently, I wasn't even aware he had had a wife before my mother."

"What changed?" What had alerted Robert to the secret in his father's past, and sent him out on his quest to find his lost brother? For that matter, why did he wish to do so? There could be no filial affection, since the brothers had never met, so there was surely no longing for a reunion. She supposed he could be searching because his honor compelled him. Or he could have other, darker motives. Robert had been raised to be the heir, but if there was another claimant…would he want to secure his own position at the expense of the true heir?

Jane did not wish to think so ill of a man she had grown to like over the past weeks. But then, Jane had not wished to think ill of Sydney, either. She was the last person who could be trusted to read a man's character and gauge his actions.

"Over the past couple of years," Robert answered her question, though he seemed reluctant, "my father has…become frail. There are times when…" He folded his arms, pulling his coat taut across his shoulders, emphasizing their breadth. "At times he is not altogether lucid. His memories are jumbled, and sometimes, he seems to have slipped into the past. He speaks as if it were now."

"Oh." It was all Jane could say at such a revelation. There was nothing else to say. One could not offer comfort to those who watched a loved one slip into such a madness, because there was no comfort to be had. No hope. "When we lived in Dorset," she told him, "we knew a lady with such an affliction. It was very hard for her family."

"I can imagine."

"It must be…worrying for you. Your father's responsibilities…"

"I have employed agents. Men I trust to oversee his estates and holdings. They are in safe hands."

"But…your brother?"

Robert nodded. "At first I thought my father was just confused, but an old retainer told me of the first wife, and of the rumors that the baby had not died, after all. Father became obsessed with those rumors, with learning the truth. They filled his mind. So much so, he wouldn't be easy until I promised him I would search for my brother."

"To actually do so was good of you." He frowned and she explained. "Many would have said they had searched whilst only paying lip service to it."

Robert looked appalled. "My word is my bond. I would never give it and then go back on it." He grimaced. "My father was so distressed, so desperate to find… I promised him I would look for Benedict, and I would not return unless I found him, or definitive proof of his demise. And I meant it."

Her heart swelled with admiration for this man, so honorable and true to his word that he had put his own life into abeyance while he searched for a brother who might not even exist anymore.

"Even so," she said. "After so many years... How did you even know where to begin?"

He huffed, a humorless chuckle. "It wasn't easy. But the estate records are meticulously kept. The muniment room holds papers going back to the time of the Restoration. In the first instance, I simply read every entry from around the time of the birth, hoping something would stand out and lead me where I needed to go."

****

Robert stared into the cold fireplace. It hadn't been long before he found the name of the midwife in the accounts book. She had been paid well for her work, more than most midwives could expect, which had made him suspicious, although finding her after thirty years was no easy task. She had long since retired and moved away from the village to be with her daughter.

When he found her at last, she was not eager to talk to him. It took him several days, much reassurance that his motives were good, and not a little money before she opened up.

"Baby wasn't right," she said, her arms folded tight across her chest, as if protecting herself from what she had to say. "I could tell that right off. There's telltale signs with a baby like that, see? I'd seen them before, and I knew straight away." She stared into the fire in the cottage's hearth, her lined face grim. "Her ladyship was heartbroken, o' course, who wouldn't be? But she loved that little scrap from the first moment. Wasn't anything she wouldn't have done for that child." She sighed. "She had so much love inside her, did her ladyship. Fair shone with it." She smiled serenely into the fire then, as if she could see the events of the past in its flames, before turning back to Robert.

"She heard the doctor say as the baby wasn't right. Said as how it probably wouldn't live long." She nodded, sagely. "He had the right of it there, I'll give him that. Most of them don't survive. But it's not a given. I've seen a couple that have gone past infancy."

"You told the countess this?"

"She was in a terrible state. That doctor's bedside manner left a lot to be desired. Young mother, she needs hope. Childbirth is hard, it takes it out of her, leaves her wrung out. Last thing she needs is some man telling her it was all for nothing." She huffed. "But then, what can a man truly understand about it? They don't just ask for midwives because we're cheaper than doctors, you know. Women prefer women when they're laying-in."

"You gave her hope, then?" asked Robert, keen to steer the conversation back to the specifics of Benedict's birth.

"That fool doctor. Never minded his tongue. He stood there, in the corridor outside her bedchamber with the door ajar, and told her husband exactly what he thought, never once considering—probably never caring—that the new mother could hear every word. Said as how they should send it away to an asylum, or better, get rid of it altogether. Not taint the family line. He said "it," mind. It. Not him."

"What did her husband say?"

"Nothing I heard. There was a silence, and then he walked away and the doctor followed him, still talking at him. That poor lady, she didn't know which way to turn. I've never seen anyone so distraught. Took me the best part of an hour to calm her. But then she came up with a plan to save the child. A lady through and through, she was. Mind you, we already knew that. Everyone in the village knew her for a kind-hearted, caring woman. Why, there was one time…"

"A plan?" Robert encouraged her to return to the subject of the baby.

"Aye. She wrote a letter, to an old schoolfriend, asking the woman to take care of the child and keep him secret until she could come for him. She called the steward and got him to release sixty guineas to her. Fifty went in the letter to pay for the child's care, and ten to me for delivering it, and him.

"Her schoolfriend was happy to help. I went home and carried on like nothing had happened for a while." She shook her head and rubbed her hands up and down her arms as if to ward off a chill, though the room was warm. "My lady died. And questions were asked about the babe. The doctor called on me, asked if I knew what happened to him. 'Course, I said no, but I wondered if he believed me. Always felt like his eyes were on me, watching me. Made me nervous. So I put it about that my daughter needed me to help her and I left and come here."

The memory faded and Robert's attention returned to Janey's parlor, where he stood, hand resting on the mantelshelf, one foot resting on the stone hearth.

"I set out to look for the schoolfriend the next day," he said.

****

Jane was incredulous. "It sounds like the plot of a fantastical novel." It was all she could think of to say. She was tempted to dismiss it as a fiction, but then, why?

What possible motive could this man have for making up such a strange tale?

She looked up at him, trying to gauge the measure of the man. Their eyes met and he gave her a wry half smile, shrugged his shoulders as if to say he understood her skepticism, then winced and rubbed the upper part of his wounded arm with his good hand. His fingers were long, the nails neatly rounded and clean, but the hands were strong and masculine, the hands of someone who was used to working, not someone who sat at home languishing and being waited on. There was a smattering of hair on the back of them, which thickened and darkened slightly before disappearing under his shirt cuff.

Jane remembered the strength of those hands as they'd held her arms that day in the High Street. Even through the thickness of her clothes, and his gloves, she had felt the warmth of him flowing through her. Now she wondered how those hands would feel gloveless, his skin against hers. A shiver tickled her spine and the hairs at the nape of her neck stood to attention as she imagined his fingers upon her breast, his callouses abrading her nipples. The thought made them stand to attention, chafing against the lawn of her shift and setting her heart racing. She knew instinctively that his touch would be different to Sydney's. Sydney's hands had been smooth, unsullied by anything resembling work, and his skin had been cold, but his touch had been harsh, insistent, squeezing her until she cried in pain. Jane thought Robert would never do such a thing…

Heat flooded her cheeks. Why was she contemplating what this man would or would not do to her? Had she learned nothing? He might be as lecherous as Sydney, and as treacherous. For all his denial, he might be promised to another. He might even be married!

A quick glance showed no ring on his left hand, nor any indentation or change of skin color to suggest he had ever worn one. There was a plain gold ring on the little finger of his right hand, but that seemed to be the only jewelry he wore, save for the stickpin…

The stickpin! The memory of it pushed all else aside. Nausea swirled in her stomach and her mouth dried, the taste of her own thoughts bitter. The design on that stickpin was identical to the design on Ben's ring, nestled in Mama's jewel box.

After meeting Mr. Carrow in the High Street and seeing his pin, Jane had checked Ben's ring, hoping she had remembered it incorrectly and that the designs were actually different. They had been exactly the same. A bird, its beak open in song, its body hidden inside an open-topped barrel.

Ben's ring had come to him from his father, Mama had said. It was the only thing Ben had of the man, and it was a family heirloom. Even when things were at their hardest and it was uncertain how the family would afford to eat, even when Mama sold the pearls she'd inherited from Grandmama to pay their rent, she had refused to part with that ring. It was Ben's inheritance, she had insisted.

If the ring was a family heirloom, did the same apply to the stickpin? Could Ben be…?

No! If Ben were Mr. Carrow's brother, then Mama had lied. Jane's entire life, all she had ever been told about her family, would be a fabrication.

Although, Mama had had a school friend who married a man named Carrow…

"Janey?" Robert spoke her name softly, his face filled with concern. Jane stared at him, took in his dark brown eyes as he studied her. At first glance those eyes seemed solidly dark, almost ebony like Ben's, but now she saw tiny gold and green flecks in them, softening them. A curl flopped resolutely over his forehead, giving him an air of—something that drew her in, made her want to know him better…

Which was exactly what had caused this family so much trouble in the past. Jane could not, would not, go through that humiliation and vilification again. She would not subject Mama and Ben, and now Lucy, to speculative stares and gossiping tongues.

She stood and clasped her hands in front of her, every inch the prim and proper widow. "I will retire for the night," she said, her voice flat, giving away none of her turmoil. "Shall I fetch Jem to you?"

He watched her for a long moment, then shook his head. "I can get upstairs unaided," he said. "Coming down is the hard part." He kept his eyes fixed on her. She felt his gaze right through to her soul, and she shivered, though the room was warm.

"Goodnight, Mr. Carrow," she said, and she left the room with alacrity, although it probably did her no good. She had a feeling she would dream about that deep, dark stare all night long.

Chapter Seven

Another week passed. The weather brightened as spring became summer, although it was still cold. The spring flowers in Mama's garden died back, making way for the colors summer would bring. With Mary helping in the house, Mama had time to tend the garden properly, tidying and training plants, growing flowers and some vegetables. Lucy spent time with her, paying rapt attention as Grandmama pointed out the different plants and allowed her to help with the easier tasks.

Jem helped Robert downstairs every day. After that, the manservant would chop wood or mend the hedge, or do the myriad other jobs that needed more strength than Jane or Mama possessed.

Ben followed Jem around like a poodle, so close on his heels he ran the risk of tripping over him. Jem had infinite patience with him. Many people would—had—grown weary of Ben. Some were cruel to him. But Jem spoke to him in friendly terms, enlisted his help and swore he couldn't have completed the work without it. Ben's proud grin split his face and he seemed to grow several inches.

Robert was a dreadful patient, far too eager to move about and prove he was no invalid. When Doctor Bull said he might leave his bed and sit in a chair, Robert came downstairs. When he was told he could come downstairs and sit in the parlor, he practiced walking around the furniture. Now he tried to walk back and forth without leaning on anything. His legs were stiff, and he walked with a rolling gait, not quite limping but not wholly healed. He moved across the room, first one way, then the other, stumbling over his own feet and cursing as he grabbed onto furniture to prevent a fall.

Jane watched from the doorway, unable to help herself as the muscles in his broad back flexed and shifted with his efforts. He no longer needed the sling, although his left arm was still markedly thinner than his right.

He took another step. Jane's eyes travelled down from his wide, strong shoulders to his narrow waist and hips and on to his legs and buttocks, which were firm and well-shaped, his muscles well defined beneath his snug-fitting trousers. She licked her lips and a strange feeling, like the buzzing of a million bees, filled her stomach.

She closed her eyes and willed herself to behave. When she opened them again, he had turned and now watched her intently. Nonplussed, she asked in a waspish voice, "Should you be doing that?"

"The more I do, the more I can do." His deep voice seemed to make the air vibrate. He smiled, and a tiny dimple showed in his cheek.

"If you do too much, you might undo the good of your previous efforts." To her ears, Jane's voice sounded breathy, as if she had run before speaking.

"You are correct, of course, and I am ready to rest." He gestured to a chair, inviting her to join him. She was about to refuse when she realized he would not sit until she did. Over the past weeks, he had, of necessity, stayed seated while she or Mama stood, but now his strength was returning and he would be a gentleman.

Jane saw something else as well: he had reached his limit for today. His face was pale, and there were beads of sweat on his upper lip. His eyes, ringed by dark circles, held pain. She guessed it took a great effort to remain standing.

Startled by this epiphany, Jane hurried to the chair. She sat, then he did. His movements were careful, slow, as if he tried to hide the pain in each movement.

At the very last moment, he knocked the occasional table beside him. It teetered and threatened to topple. Robert grasped it, preventing its fall, but grunting as his muscles jarred.

Although he saved the table, he wasn't quick enough to save his book, which fell to the floor. Jane moved to retrieve it at the same moment he reached for it, and their fingers brushed. The sudden jolt of electricity made her jump, and she pulled back her hand as if she'd been burned. He pulled back just as quickly. Had he felt it too?

She looked up. His eyes were darker than ever, his gaze seeming to bore through her.

This was a dreadful idea. A mistake she couldn't afford to make. She should break eye contact, stand, back away. Now.

Her legs refused to straighten; her eyes refused to look away. Her heart raced until the beats melded into one long, continuous note, loud and insistent, drowning out the tiny voice of caution.

His hand touched hers again, this time a soft caress, light as a flower's petal against her skin. Jane shivered. He moved closer. She could see each fleck in his eyes, every individual lash around them. His warm skin held the fragrance of woods in summer. It mixed with the scent of laundry soap on his shirt and that of the starch in his cravat, and an indescribable, undefinable something that was unique to him.

Jane didn't know if she moved toward him or he moved toward her, but the gap between them disappeared. His arms enfolded her, warm against her back, and she felt his breath, soft against her cheek. He lowered his gaze, studied her mouth, then slowly, slowly, came closer until, finally, his lips brushed hers, soft, barely there. She tasted the coffee he'd drunk at breakfast, and the sharp tang of his tooth powder.

She closed her eyes and willed him to kiss her again.

He obliged. This time his kiss was harder, firmer against her lips. The beginnings of his new beard scratched her. His hand moved up and cradled her neck. She wound her arms around him and her fingers played with the silky ends of his hair. She heard a small noise and realized it came from her. Her nipples hardened and there was a dull, warm ache between her legs.

His tongue pressed against the seam of her lips and she opened, letting him in. His tongue danced with hers. Instinctively, she moved her own tongue, and felt him smile against her mouth. His fingers splayed in her hair, loosening pins, which pinged as they hit the floor. Her hair uncoiled, falling over her shoulders. She held him closer, tighter. A soft growl rumbled in his chest. She wanted this. She wanted more. She wanted…

In the garden, Lucy squealed, bringing Jane back to reality. She was in the parlor where anyone might come in, and she was kissing a man she barely knew.

Harlot.

She pulled away, quickly and took a step back. Then another. Their eyes held. She couldn't have looked away from him had she tried. He made no attempt to come after her. He said nothing. Jane didn't know if she wanted him to or not.

Sydney would have. Sydney had used soft words, called it destiny, because how else could they have shared such a wonderful kiss?

Except Sydney's kisses hadn't been wonderful. Jane had thought they were when he'd been the only man she had ever kissed, but compared to what she'd just shared with Robert, Sydney's were nothing. Robert's kiss was warm and strong and filled as much with emotion as with desire. He left her wanting—craving—more. She couldn't stop it, couldn't control it. And it terrified her.

"I should…" She gestured over her shoulder.

"Yes." His voice was gruff.

She held his gaze for maybe three seconds more. Then she raced from the room, pulling the door firmly shut behind her.

Alone in the corridor, she took what seemed her first proper breath in…forever. What had she done? She had kissed Robert Carrow. *Mr.* Carrow, she corrected herself. It would be best to keep things formal between them from now on.

She touched her fingertips to her lips and shivered. That could never happen again. It would *not* happen again. She would make certain of it. She had far too much to lose this time.

****

Robert sank into his chair. The careless movement jarred his ribs and made him grunt. His shoulder ached, as did his legs where he'd pushed them hard, strengthening his muscles in the hope of healing faster. He thought it was working, since he could stand for longer and do more before the pain came, and his limp was less pronounced.

What he could not exercise away, though, was his anger. He clenched his fists, welcoming the pull on the muscles in his healing arm. His jaw tightened and he wanted to hit something, although if justice was served, the only thing being hit would be him.

He had kissed Janey. Taken advantage of her vulnerability and trust, acted less than honorably. He scoffed. Less than honorably? There was no honor in him at all.

For weeks he had desired her. He watched her move about while he was incapacitated, enjoyed the gentle sway of her hips, the way her bosom lifted when she reached for something on a high shelf. He reveled in the sight of her dress molding to her firm, round bottom when she picked up something from the floor. Everything about her drew him in: the lightly tanned skin above the neckline of her dress, the slender gracefulness of her throat, the dainty curve of her waist.

At the same time, he came to know her better. She read to him, and listened while he read to her. They talked. He told her things he had not confided to anyone outside his family. He'd begun to consider her a friend.

And now, with one stolen kiss, he'd spoiled it all.

Damn! Janey was a respectable widow with a reputation and a family to care for, not some tavern wench out for a good time and a few pennies. She deserved to be treated with circumspection, yet he…he ought to be horsewhipped.

His book dropped to the floor. She'd made to pick it up. That was all she intended, a brief kindness to a man who found movement awkward. It was Robert who had turned it into more, Robert who had touched her hand.

Had she felt the same jolt at that brief, accidental touch? The look of surprise on her face said it was possible. Or was it wishful thinking that saw in her the same sizzle that raced through him, putting every last nerve on edge?

She'd held him, her arms around his neck, her fingers toying with his hair. He smiled at the memory. She had been hesitant, unsure of herself, and there was a naïveté in her that was surprising, considering she'd been married and had a child. Her sweet innocence made him want her all the more, not just with that part of him that had grown so hard it was painful, but with every fiber of his being.

Which was terrible. It didn't matter that she'd kissed him back, or that she'd given that soft mewl of pleasure when his tongue stroked the length of hers. Janey Frobisher was out of bounds. A gentleman—and Robert was a gentleman, despite current appearances—did not play fast and loose with a woman like her, especially when he had nothing to offer her.

A year ago, Robert Carrow could have courted her properly. He'd been the oldest son of an earl, set to inherit the title one day and, with it, large tracts of profitable land, business interests, and a healthy bank balance. He could have offered Janey the life he'd like her to have, one of comfort and ease.

Now, he was no longer certain what he was. He might be a second son, entitled to nothing, destined to make his own way in the world. Or he may still be the heir. Until Benedict was traced, and his identity verified, Robert could not know which he was.

Both would have consequences for a wife. And yes, it was early to think of Janey as his wife, but he had kissed her, felt things for her, dreamed of her. The thought of spending forever with her did not fill him with dread.

Could he make her happy? She was a country widow, of less than modest means. She was not a Society lady, doing the rounds of At Homes and gossiping over tea and cakes. If he *was* the future earl, his wife would have to fit in with that world, and Janey might be overwhelmed and uncomfortable there. It would make her unhappy, more so if she believed, at the time of their marriage, that she was becoming the wife of an ordinary man, with no title, no fortune, and no expectations.

On the other hand, if he told her he might be the heir, would she be dissatisfied if he proved to be no more than a second son? Perhaps she would feel cheated, tricked into marriage with false promises.

He'd concealed his lineage from her. It wasn't that he didn't wish her to know, specifically. He hadn't told anyone about his family connections since leaving home to scour the countryside for a young man who may not even exist anymore. Keeping a low profile made for more honest encounters with many people. He'd been plain Mr. Carrow at the inn in Bloomfold, and the opportunity to tell Janey the truth had never arisen. First, he'd been too ill, then too careful. Now, it was too late.

And really, what did it matter? Unless her brother Ben turned out to be his brother Benedict—and didn't that throw open a whole Pandora's box of complications?—their time together would be brief, and his lineage a moot point.

Plus, there were other considerations…

He dropped his good hand over his bad arm, massaging away the dull ache. The broken bones had knitted and the muscles were strengthening, but Robert could not ignore that someone had tried to kill him.

The first few incidents had seemed like accidents. Negligence on the part of a servant, clumsiness in himself. But after the carriage…

The first attempt to run him down in the High Street might have been unplanned. The horses were out of control, the coachman reckless. But less than half an hour later, the same carriage had come for him again, on a little-used lane. The same coachman had whipped the same team, urging them to hit Robert, to trample him and anyone else who stood in the way.

Anger tightened his throat and burned his eyes. Lucy could have been killed. She was a bright child, full of laughter and mischief, with a curious mind fueled by a thousand questions. Somebody had been willing to snuff out all that, just to kill him.

Robert wanted to tear the villains limb from limb, to break their bones and see how they liked it. He wanted them to rue the day they'd put Lucy Frobisher in danger.

He might get the chance. There had been enough incidents, now, that he didn't believe this was the end of it. Whoever it was, the incident in the lane proved they wanted him dead. Therefore, he must believe they would try again. And this time, he would be ready for them.

Chapter Eight

Although Jane vowed to keep her distance from Robert, it was not a promise she could hope to keep. The house was simply too small to avoid him without drawing attention to herself, and if Mama learned how Jane's wantonness had resurfaced, she would be furious.

Mama had been supportive of Jane last time. She had blamed Sydney, deciding he'd taken advantage of Jane's innocence. Which, to an extent, he had. He'd turned her head with compliments, delivered in an oh-so-sincere voice. He talked about the future, his plans, the sons he hoped for. He asked how she would decorate his house. Although, to be fair, he hadn't actually said she would be the wife who would live there.

He implied it, though, Mama decided, before describing him in words Jane had never expected to hear from her mother's mouth. "I wish him well of his pasty-faced wife," she'd said. "May she be barren and extravagant and leave the idiot without heir or fortune."

"That was unkind," Jane replied.

"I know," said Mama. For a moment she looked contrite, then she gave a wicked grin. "But it felt good to say it."

Mama may have insisted the fault lay with Sydney, but Jane could not lie to herself. Yes, he had been glib and persuasive, but Jane had responded, encouraging him.

And now it was happening again.

For three days, Jane kept herself busy in her efforts to avoid Robert—*Mr. Carrow*. She must call him Mr. Carrow! She helped Mama with the garden and took Lucy for long walks along the lane. Then it rained and she had no choice but to stay inside and, in a house this small, there was no more avoiding him.

"We are adults," she reminded herself as she stood outside the parlor door. "We can be in the same room." But still she stood, making no effort to enter. "You're being ridiculous. Why, it's likely he's forgotten all about it."

After all, Sydney had called her kisses mediocre and uninspired. 'Hardly the stuff poets wax lyrical over,' he'd sneered. Even now, the memory of his casual cruelty made tears well and a lump form in her throat. She swallowed against it, pinned on a bright smile and stepped into the parlor.

Robert—*Mr. Carrow!*—was practicing walking. It seemed to Jane he was a little faster today, his movements more fluid, the limp less discernible. He turned as she entered, his lips curved in a smile that crinkled the skin around his eyes and showed off the dimple on his cheek. It transformed him from merely good-looking to the most handsome man she had ever seen. She wanted to hold him, have him hold her, repeat the kiss…

Oh, this just would not do!

Robert clearly thought so, too. For an instant, his smile wavered. Uncertainty and discomfort showed before it returned, though now it did not reach his eyes.

"Mrs. Frobisher," he said, and he bowed. "How are you this morning?"

Jane's curtsy was stiff and awkward. She glanced at him, then looked away, taking in every detail of the fireplace, the figurines on the mantelshelf, the fireside tools on the hearth. Anything, it seemed, could hold her attention if it meant avoiding Robert Carrow's gaze.

"You look well," she said, at last.

"As do you."

"Thank you."

The awkward moment stretched. The room was silent, save for the soft ticking of the clock on the mantelshelf. Outside, a branch knocked softly against the windowpane. The wind whistled mournfully in the chimney and stirred the thin layer of ash in the grate. Robert scraped his boot on the edge of the hearthstone. Jane flinched at the loudness of it.

"My apologies," he said.

Jane looked at him. He was half turned from her, staring into the hearth, and she was astonished to realize he was as uncomfortable as her. She wasn't sure if that was good or bad.

"You walk better today," she said, more to be rid of the silence than in hope of conversation.

He smiled again, and his eyes softened. "Thank you. Your doctor says I should make a complete recovery, with no aftereffects."

"I am glad." She nibbled her bottom lip. He looked down as if examining his healing limbs. Jane took a deep breath and smiled as brightly as she could. "Shall I ring for tea?"

She made to walk past him to the bell pull. He did not stand aside. Instead, he reached out, his fingers wrapping around her upper arm. It was not a tight hold, but it stopped her in her tracks. The heat of him seared her skin through her sleeve and rooted her to the spot.

She looked up at him, a little alarmed, confused, hopeful.

"Janey, I…"

His gaze held hers. Jane could not have looked away if she tried. She leaned toward him, and thought he leaned toward her. The dark blue of new beard growth showed below his skin, and the flecks in his eyes sparkled like the fireworks she had once seen over Torquay Harbor. The springtime woodsiness of his cologne wrapped around her, mixing with the beeswax Mary used on the furniture and the soft scent of the flowers Mama had arranged in a vase. She could almost taste his lips, firm and full and warm against hers. The rain drummed steadily, matching the rhythm of her heart.

His breath was warm against her face as they moved nearer. He licked his lips. Need jolted through her, and her lips parted in readiness for his kiss. Her fingers itched to smooth their way across his chest, to feel the play of the muscles below his warm skin, to revel in the strength in his shoulders, the silky softness of his hair. Her nipples hardened and her breasts grew heavy as her breathing shallowed.

He swallowed and glanced at her lips, then back to her eyes, signaling his intentions. She lifted her face slightly…

"Mama! Mama!" Lucy's voice reverberated through the room as she pushed open the door and bounded in. Jane sprang back from Robert as if he had burned her. His hand moved from her arm, and he turned to the hearth.

Jane grinned at Lucy, though it felt more like a grimace. "Yes, my love?" She sounded breathless, which was hardly surprising since she couldn't seem to fill her lungs. Every nerve in her body was on edge, every muscle tight, ready for…something that could never happen.

What had she been thinking? Jane was no dollymop, giving herself to a man with no thought of what happened next. Even Sydney had led her to believe he would offer for her before she'd let him seduce her. Robert—*Mr. Carrow!* had not implied any such thing. Yet, had Lucy not come in, Jane knew she would have given him whatever he wished to take.

Lucy tugged Jane's hand and pleaded to be taken into the village. "Grandmama gave me a penny," she said, holding up the coin. "She found it in the garden, and she says the fairies buried it. She said I can use it to buy sweets."

"Grandmama gave you a penny?" asked Jane, her voice too bright, her attention deliberately diverted from Robert. She felt him behind her, watching her. "A whole penny?"

The child beamed. "May I have sweets? The rain has stopped, and Grandmama says it will be fine now. Please, Mama?"

"Well, if Grandmama says that, it must be so." Jane took Lucy's hand and they left the room, as Lucy told a long and convoluted story about fairies who lived in the garden and buried hordes of pennies especially for little girls and their grandmothers to find.

****

Robert had to get out of this house. The temptation was too great, and he was likely to besmirch his family name if he stayed. Not just his family name, either. Janey was far too enticing for her own good. Or for his. The sooner he was able to ride, the better. Frustrated, he ran a hand over his head and felt his hair stand up. He sighed heavily. Now, as well as the evidence of his arousal pulling his breeches out of shape, and the tight look he knew was on his face, his hair probably looked like a cockerel's comb! He was a damned mess.

He needed to regain his strength. Now. With that in mind, he moved away from the hearth toward the window, trying not to limp or walk stiffly. Pain began near where the bones had broken and radiated outward, growing, sharpening, until it was all he could do not to cry out in agony. His steps slowed but he pushed on, determined.

Doctor Bull had been concerned about how much Robert was doing. He thought he should cut the exercise because he was pushing himself too far, too soon. Robert disagreed. To him, the doctor made little sense. How could one do too much exercise? The human body was designed to move, and movement strengthened it. It stood to reason, therefore, that more exercise would strengthen a body more.

It wasn't as if he was running or jumping or trying to throw his horse over high fences. He was just pacing back and forth across a small room. How much damage could that do?

He turned, biting back the groan as his legs protested, and walked back to the hearth for the sixth time, or was it the seventh? He had promised himself ten circuits before sitting down, and he would do them. Sharp needles stabbed at his limbs and raced up into the small of his back. He wanted to stop and arch his spine, knowing instinctively that would make him feel better. But when the relief faded, he would probably feel worse than before. He resisted the temptation to sit, and moved back to the window.

Once there, he allowed himself a small rest while he gazed out at the garden. Wildflowers bloomed, their colors sharper following the rain, and the grass gleamed as if it had been washed. Mrs. Winter must love this patch of ground to make it so pretty.

Mrs. Winter. The only person who could answer his questions about Ben. For it was Ben, not Janey, that Robert should concentrate his efforts upon. He needed to discover more about the man, to either confirm or assuage his suspicions that he was, in fact, his brother.

Janey said Ben was *her* brother and Robert thought she sincerely believed that. But Janey was several years younger than Ben and would not have known otherwise. Only Mrs. Winter could say for certain. But Mrs. Winter never seemed to be nearby to answer the questions Robert wished to ask of her.

Was she avoiding him? When he had first arrived, she tended him alongside her daughter. Then, when he began to re-gather his wits, she made herself scarce. She rarely came into the parlor while he was there, and when she did, her visit was brief. She never took her meals with them, having, she said, eaten with Lucy. She retired early, so never spent her evenings with them, and her days were spent in the garden, where Robert had yet to venture.

It was time to confront her.

Through the window, he saw her on the garden path, a small trug balanced on her arm, shears in her hand. Ben was at her side. They were making the most of the break between showers, something Robert could also do. He limped from the room and out into the garden.

The day was chilled, the sun weak for July, and the air smelled of rain. It wasn't a heavy scent, nothing like the wetness of last year when summer had never arrived at all and the heavy, frigid downpours ruined the crops. By comparison, today was positively balmy.

His feet crunched on the narrow path.

Ben beamed at him. "I helping my Mama," he said.

"So I see," Robert replied with a smile. Ben drew himself up to his full height of five foot three and puffed out his chest proudly as he explained exactly what he was doing.

Mrs. Winter gave Robert a perfunctory curtsy. He bowed in return. The gardening shears hung loosely from her fingers. "You are recovering well, I see," she said, coolly polite.

"I am, I thank you. I thought to take a turn in the garden and enjoy the air." He winced at the inanity of his words, but now he was here, he didn't know quite what to say or do next.

Before he could decide, Ben yelled, excitedly, "I got that. Mama look! Like my ring." He reached out, his earth-covered fingers caressing Robert's stickpin. Smudges of brown soil transferred from Ben's skin to Robert's once-white neckcloth.

"Benedict Winter!" gasped Mrs. Winter, horrified.

"But Mama, look," argued Ben. "Like my ring. Bird in bucket!"

Mrs. Winter paled. The shears slipped from her limp hand and landed on the grass with a soft thud. Ben stroked the bird on the stickpin.

Robert fixed Mrs. Winter with a glower. "I believe, Madam, you and I need to talk."

Chapter Nine

Jane followed Lucy along the lane. The excited little girl bounced from puddle to tree to clump of flowers. She crouched on her haunches to study a grasshopper, talking softly to it. When it jumped away, she cried out in dismay, then ran to the next attraction. Jane watched her, but her thoughts were all about Robert.

He had almost kissed her. Again. She could still feel his warm breath as he drew closer, still smell the coffee he'd drunk at breakfast. If Lucy hadn't burst in on them, he would have leaned forward those last few inches and…

Jane had wanted him to. She had wanted to feel his lips on hers again, warm and firm and full of passion, his arms around her, pulling her closer until she was pressed against his chest, the hard strength of him making her feel protected and safe.

No, not safe. That was the last thing Jane felt when he was near. She knew she was not safe from him, from his effect on her. And she definitely was not safe from herself.

At first, she'd castigated herself because it was happening again, exactly as it had with Sydney. But then she realized that wasn't true. Robert was nothing like Sydney. Sydney had been a boy masquerading as a man. She hadn't known that then, but now, seeing Robert's maturity in the way he behaved, the things he said, the sure way he held her, she could see how lacking Sydney had been. He had never set her on fire with the merest touch like Robert could. He'd never made her feel anything like she felt simply by being in Robert's presence. Just the thought of Robert made her shiver deliciously, and a warm glow moved through her, starting in her belly and radiating to every part of her. The idea that he might touch her dried her mouth and made her heart race, and she knew that if he did, it would be as different to Sydney's fumbling, pinching, and nipping as silk was from pigskin.

There were more differences between the two men. She actually liked being with Robert, something, she acknowledged now, that she had never been able to say about Sydney. With Robert, she enjoyed long talks in the evenings, when he treated her as an intellectual equal. He was kind and patient with Ben, too, never sneering at him as Sydney had done so often. And Lucy adored him.

Then again, there was the stickpin and the story of his lost brother. Did he truly think that brother was Ben? Certainly, there were similarities: both men were thirty, both were called Benedict and both were different from other people. But Ben was Jane's brother, and there was no way he could be the earl's lost son, no matter what Robert suspected.

She felt for Robert, and for his family. They'd lost a child, and they wanted to know what had happened to him. Jane could not imagine how she would be if Lucy disappeared. She would probably go mad with the worry, be unable to sleep, wondering constantly where she was and what was happening to her. Doubtless, she would clutch at any straw, chase any possibility, see Lucy in anyone of a similar age and appearance. But Jane wanting it to be Lucy wouldn't make it so, and the same was true of Robert in his search for Benedict.

The design on Robert's stickpin came to mind. It was a design she hadn't seen before, other than on Ben's ring, and that was enough to put doubts and worries into her head.

On the other hand, it could mean nothing. For all Jane knew, there could be a thousand pieces of jewelry with that design etched into them, all cheaply available in London's shops. Although the pieces had not been cheap. Made of real silver, their quality weighed heavy.

If only she knew where the things had come from and why they belonged to Robert and Ben. There could be any number of reasons for both of them to have items with the same unusual design.

"None of which is any of your concern, Jane Frobisher," she muttered. Annoyed with her own preoccupation, she made a conscious effort to banish the subject from her mind and called Lucy to her side as they turned in to the High Street.

The village was crowded today. Jane took Lucy's hand to walk along the pavement to the general shop where the child could buy sweets with her penny. Because there were so many people, Jane took no heed of the first few women who twitched their skirts aside, avoiding touching her. And when she greeted Mrs. Lucas and that lady did not answer, Jane assumed she hadn't seen or heard her in the hubbub. But when Mrs. Evans and the Misses Michaels also snubbed her, she slowed her pace and took more notice of her surroundings.

People stared at her. Some spoke behind their hands. Others glanced at her, then nodded to their companions, sharing looks of disgust. One or two included Lucy in their glares. Thankfully, Lucy, eager to reach the shop, didn't notice.

Jane felt drained, as if all the blood had left her body, taking with it her spirit and her hope. What had the people of Bloomfold discovered? Did they know she was not truly a widow? That Lucy was born on the "wrong side of the blanket" as the midwife had put it?

How could they know? Sydney's family were not known here; their sphere of influence was a hundred miles away. They had no reason to come after her, nor to destroy her all over again. It was in their interests as well as Jane's that the widowed "Mrs. Frobisher" and her daughter be left in peace.

So how had her neighbors in Bloomfold discovered the truth?

"Come on, Mama!" Lucy tugged her hand and Jane took a step forward. She was jumping to conclusions. These people may know nothing about her past, or about Lucy's birth. There could be another reason entirely for their actions, although Jane was at a loss to know what it could be. After her one indiscretion, she had kept her behavior above reproach and her reputation spotless. She owed that much to Mama and Ben, and Lucy.

Knowing she was innocent of any wrongdoing, her anxiety gave way to anger. How dare these people gossip about her, pointing fingers and looking down their noses? If they believed she had done something wrong, they should have the decency to tell her, and give her the chance to defend herself.

"Harpies and tabbies," she muttered. Unworthy of her attention, she thought, and she straightened her shoulders, raised her chin and walked with Lucy to the shop.

In the general shop, Mr. Palmer watched Lucy choose her sweets. He seemed uncomfortable, unable to maintain eye contact with Jane. Jane's temper flared. The women in the street were bad enough, but she could weather their censure. They had nothing better to do than destroy their neighbors over little, mostly nonexistent sins. But Mr. Palmer ran a busy shop. He should have no time for such nonsense. And if he wanted their money, he should treat his customers with respect. Were it not for Lucy, so eager to spend her penny, Jane would have walked out and taken her business elsewhere.

"Is there something amiss, Mr. Palmer?" she asked, crisply.

The man reddened. "Well, I, that is, where did the child get the penny?"

Jane was nonplussed. She didn't know what she expected him to say, but that was not it.

"My grandmama gave it to me," Lucy told him, her smile bright and wide. "It was in the garden all covered in mud." She held out the penny, which still had small grains of soil stuck to the contours of the etched design. Lucy leaned closer to Mr. Palmer and whispered, conspiratorially, "The fairies buried it there, and we found it."

Was it Jane's imagination, or did Mr. Palmer look relieved? Why should it matter to him where the child's penny had come from?

"If it's fairy treasure, we'll have to make sure you get the very best for it, won't we?" he said. Lucy grinned, nodded, and started to choose her favorites.

"I'm sorry," he whispered to Jane. "I should have known you came by it honestly."

Jane stared at him, astounded. "How else would we

have come by it?"

Mr. Palmer's face went from crimson to beetroot. "Quite. I can only apologize. Old Matt Turner's quick with his gossip, and he don't always make sure he's got his facts."

The room tilted. The air suddenly seemed too heavy to breathe. Jane's legs were like string, threatening not to support her weight. She clutched at the counter to steady herself.

"Mr. Turner gossiped? About me?" The words squeezed from her in a strained whisper. "What…?" She gulped. "What did he say?"

Mr. Palmer shifted, uncomfortably. "He said you gave him five guineas to pay your bill."

Jane swallowed. "What if I did?"

"He…you know what he's like, Mrs. Frobisher. Allus poking his beak into other birds' nests."

"He wondered where I might have come by it." She pursed her lips. Mr. Turner was going to feel the sharp side of her tongue. How dare he make insinuations about her?

"Not exactly." Mr. Palmer looked around as if searching for eavesdroppers, then lowered his voice. "Said he knew where it come from. You don't want to listen to his nonsense."

She tried to calm her racing heart. "Clearly, some people do. I've received the cut direct several times today. I wondered why."

Mr. Palmer's blush deepened. He ran his hands through his thinning hair and looked down at his feet.

"Tell me what he said," she continued, "for I will not settle until I know."

Five minutes later, she ran from the shop into the

alley alongside it and was sick. Mr. Palmer followed, Lucy's hand in his. Lucy watched Jane, her concern plain.

"Mama not well?" she asked.

"No, Precious," said Mr. Palmer. "Mama needs you to take her home so your grandmama can care for her. Can you do that, like a big girl?"

Solemnly, Lucy took Jane's hand. "Come along, Mama. I look after you."

Jane straightened, found her handkerchief in her reticule, and dabbed at her lips. Ignoring the bitter taste in her mouth and the churning shudder in her stomach, she gave Lucy a weak smile.

"Go on home, my dear," whispered Mr. Palmer. "I'll see what I can do to put Turner's gossip in the dust heap where it belongs."

Jane nodded, but she knew whatever he said would not be enough. The damage was done.

"What's the matter, Mama?" asked Lucy. She clutched Jane's hand tightly.

Jane smiled, but she knew it was weak. "Nothing is the matter, Sweetness," she said in as cheery a voice as she could muster. "Mama's just tired. Shall we go home?"

Home. Where she would have to tell her mother that lies and gossip had ruined Jane's reputation in Bloomfold and made it impossible to stay. Once again, Mama and Ben, and Lucy too, this time, must suffer the upheaval of moving far away, and the uncertainty of beginning again from nothing, because of Jane and a man. What was worse was, once again, Jane could not claim complete innocence.

She hadn't lain with Robert like she had with

Sydney. But she had let him kiss her. She'd kissed him back. At what point did a woman's behavior go beyond the pale?

Mama would be furious, though not at Jane. Even last time, when Jane had been increasing and unmarried, Mama had not been angry with her. Disappointed, yes. There'd been regret for what might have been. But not anger. That was reserved for Sydney, and the tittle-tattlers who were only too keen to tell a half-true story. It was her defense of Jane that had made targets of Mama and Ben. The gossips had gone on to question Ben's parentage, pointing out that Mama had said she was a widow, but no one had ever seen the proof.

"Like mother, like daughter," they whispered. "Always were a havey-cavey lot." And the cruelest jibe of all: "That boy's a visitation from God. Punishment for his mother's sin."

That time, there had been no friendly Mr. Palmer to try to tell the truth. Not that it would have done much good then, nor would it do so now. People liked to think the worst of their neighbors, and the truth, though it be spread by a dozen Mr. Palmers, inconveniently spoiled the narrative. Besides, Mr. Turner was so outspoken and opinionated others always listened to what he said.

He'd been angry when she paid the bill. Angry she'd found the money to do so instead of agreeing to the alternative payment he'd hoped for. Thwarted, he'd said hateful things.

Doesn't matter who you lift your skirts for. Just because he's got money doesn't make you any less of a harlot.

Now the butcher had taken his revenge, passing on tales of Jane's immorality as if it were the truth. Jane dashed her tears from her cheek with the back of her hand and heard Mr. Palmer's kindly voice in her head.

"He's also saying you tried to pay your meat bill in kind," he'd said. "Said he turned you down and insisted on coin, so you befriended that toff." Mr. Palmer smiled, sadly. "Didn't believe that for a moment. I know Matt Turner far too well." He added quickly, "And you aren't that kind of a lady."

Jane was under no illusions. It wasn't that Mr. Palmer didn't believe she'd made the offer. The thing he found hard to accept was that Mr. Turner would refuse her.

A sob escaped her as she hurried along the lane. She didn't want to tell Mama but, knowing she had to, sooner was best. Then they could begin to face the problem, find the solution, and rebuild their lives.

Lucy patted her hand. "Don't fret, Mama," she said, echoing words Jane had said to the child many times. "It could be worse."

Jane resisted the urge to say no, it could not. Which was just as well, because a few minutes later, she was proved wrong.

She arrived home and went straight to the parlor to tell Mama what had happened as quickly and concisely as she could. Vowing not to cry, determined to tell her tale dispassionately, she opened the parlor door. And heard Robert and Mama talking.

"I believe I deserve answers, Madam," said Robert. "Exactly who is Benedict Winter?"

Mama seemed to deflate. Her voice filled with defeat. Jane took a step forward to defend her, then stopped when Mama said, "If you are the son of Joshua Carrow, Earl of Barwell, then Ben is your older brother."

Chapter Ten

Jane stood in the parlor doorway. Her shoulders stiffened, and a dull ache started in the back of her neck, travelling up through her skull. Her eyes felt impossibly, painfully wide, and her mouth was dry, a bitter taste on her tongue. Her stomach churned and she thought she might be sick again.

Robert did not seem shocked by Mama's words. He nodded, as if she had confirmed something he already knew.

"Mama?" Jane whispered. She clutched the door frame, needing it to hold her upright because her legs were suddenly boneless. The room spun, out of focus, and there was a buzzing in her ears, as if a thousand angry wasps had taken residence in her brain. A wave of heat washed over her, and her breath seemed to catch, rasping over something sharp in her chest. Lucy clung tightly to her leg and, in a daze, she reached out and patted the child.

She was vaguely aware of Robert leading her to the sofa, where he sat beside her, holding her hand. His touch was firm and warm, and calmed her somewhat. The scent of his cologne and of the starch in his cravat were oddly comforting.

Mama stared into the unlit fireplace. Mary came with the tea tray and took Lucy out. Jane took a sip of tea. The world finally stopped whirling.

As soon as she was herself again, Robert moved away. The space around her seemed to chill, and Jane shuddered. He stood, hands clasped behind his back. "I believe I deserve an explanation," he told Mama, his voice low, almost a growl. The air vibrated like the plucked string of a harp.

Mama poured the tea, then sat, hands in her lap. "I knew Ben's mother at school," she said, softly. "We were friends, though our lives were different. We were both orphans, but Mary's parents had provided for her, and her guardians gave her a Season, which is when she met the earl, your father. I, on the other hand, had a small inheritance, enough to maintain a frugal lifestyle but not enough to join her in London.

"I never met your father, though Mary and I corresponded regularly." She held out her fingers and studied her nails as if they were the most fascinating thing in the room. Jane found her own attention drawn to them. Short, tidy, with just a hint of grime from the soil under them and around them.

"Go on." Robert's face was grim, his jaw clenched. His eyes glittered and there was an energy about him that reminded Jane of a cat about to pounce on a bird. Mama glanced at him, then stared down at her hands again.

"I knew she was increasing, and I wished them well. It should have been the happiest time of their lives, but when the baby came…" Her breath caught on her emotions, and she paused for a moment to compose herself. "I was told your father took it badly. And when the doctor said the child should be taken away…Mary feared for her baby."

A lump formed in the back of Jane's throat, making it painful to swallow. Her eyes burned and a fresh tear slid down her cheek. She wanted to reach out and take Mama in her arms and tell her all would be fine, though she knew it would not be. She wanted to rant and rail at Robert and push him from the house, never to distress Mama again, but she could not.

This was all her fault! If she had not gone into the village the day he arrived…if she'd been more careful and not collided with him…if she hadn't let Ben come with her to the shops…

If ifs and ands were pots and pans, there'd be no need of tinkers. The line her father had recited so many times throughout her childhood came to mind. The remembrance made her want to giggle. Recognizing that urge for the hysteria it was, she held her breath until it passed, and concentrated on what Mama said.

"She sent him to me with five hundred pounds. Asked me to care for him until it was safe to bring him home. She didn't trust the doctor. She thought he would take it upon himself to…" A sob escaped Mama and she put two fingers to her mouth as if to hold the next one inside. "She died a week later. I didn't know that then, of course. By the time I discovered it, several months had gone by and I understood your father believed Ben had…" She breathed out noisily, all her emotion carried on the sigh. "The least I could do for my friend was to abide by her dying wish. And by then, I…I loved him.

"I moved home and told everyone I was a widow, and that he was my son." She turned to Jane and smiled, sadly. "Then I met your father, and you came, and the years went by." She shrugged her shoulders. "I did my best for the child of a friend. Is that really so wicked?"

"It depends upon your perspective," said Robert. He moved to the window and stared out over the garden. The rain had started again, and drops of water slid down the windowpane. "You stole my brother, raised him in poverty…"

"I raised him with love."

"You denied him his birthright!"

"I saved his life! That doctor was going to…"

"He wasn't yours to keep."

"I did what I thought was best for him…"

"Enough!" Jane stood, every muscle rigid, every nerve on edge. They stared at her as if they had both forgotten she was there. "You are brangling like children in the nursery," she said. "Ben is not a toy to be fought over. You should be ashamed of yourselves."

Mama stared into the hearth, her lips pressed into a thin line, jaw tight. Robert closed his eyes, took a deep breath and opened them again.

"Mrs. Frobisher is correct. I apologize."

Mama glanced at him, then at Jane, who raised an eyebrow, daring her to argue. "As do I," she said. "It seems we are both protective of Ben."

"He does have that effect on people," agreed Robert.

"His mother didn't believe that of everybody."

Jane glared at Mama while Robert pursed his lips. "My father would not…"

"I meant the doctor," Mama interrupted him. "He was the one Mary heard threaten the child's wellbeing."

For a moment there was silence as the two combatants stared at each other. Jane sat down again, on the edge of her chair, her hands clasped in her lap, her spine rigid. Robert returned to his seat and rested his forearms on his knees, his hands hanging loose between his legs. His head was bowed, and he looked heavily burdened.

Mama watched Robert. Her expression said she wanted to ask him something, but she bit her bottom lip and said nothing.

Jane felt a sharp stabbing pain in her chest. Her heart was breaking, but she didn't know who for—Mama, whose secrets were about to cost her so much, Robert, deprived of his older brother for so long, herself, for the sudden loss of the family she'd thought she had, or Ben, who wouldn't easily understand why his life had changed forever.

Robert spoke first. His voice was softer now as he addressed Mama. "You lived with your husband in Dorset?" Mama looked surprised and he smiled, ruefully. "I have spent months looking for you. You did not leave an easy trail to follow."

"I did not intend to." Mama's words were flat. "Although after so long, I did think…"

"My father has been… The fate of his firstborn son has weighed heavily upon him. He needed to know for certain what had become of him." He gave a wry smile. "I found the midwife the countess entrusted him to, and she confessed her part, but even so, you were difficult to find. Five different addresses in five different parts of the country, and in each one hardly anyone remembered you, let alone where you had gone next."

"We have always kept ourselves private. Our neighbors were never privy to all our comings and goings." Mama huffed. "And when we left a place, it was usually because I had perceived a threat, so I was hardly likely to give a forwarding address."

Jane listened to them calmly discussing this turbulent past she had lived through and yet known nothing about. Her own thoughts tumbled chaotically.

Her brother, Ben, was not her brother, he was Robert's brother. But how could he be anything but her brother? Her head pounded and a vise gripped her neck and squeezed.

"When you lived in Dorset the second time, you stayed for many years," said Robert.

"I was born there." Jane's voice sounded as if it had been dragged over sharp rocks until it tore.

"My husband was from Dorset," added Mama.

"Ben was happy there? Settled?"

Mama nodded. "Yes."

"Then why did you leave? You were established, and as you say, after such a long time, your fear of discovery must have dissipated. Why uproot yourself and begin again in Sussex?"

Panic roiled within Jane. She glanced at Mama, willing her to say nothing. Surely, these candid confessions of the past involved Ben's history, not Jane's. Robert did not need to know.

"Circumstances change," said Mama with a tiny shrug of her shoulders. "It was time to move on." Jane breathed out, relieved. Mama raised her chin, defiant, although the trembling of her hands indicated she was not as brave as she tried to seem. "Now that you know all, Mr. Carrow, I should like to ask you about the future as it pertains to Ben. What do you intend to do?" She swallowed. She clutched her hands tightly to stop the quiver in them.

"Naturally," said Robert, "my father will want to meet Ben."

It hit Jane then that there might be serious consequences to this strange history. Robert's—and Ben's—father was an earl, probably a powerful man. He would doubtless be angry that he'd been robbed of thirty years with his son. When he arrived here and saw how Ben had lived…

She looked around the parlor. It was a cozy room, warm and welcoming, neither austere nor too cluttered. Today, with the clouds low outside, it seemed dark, but on a sunny day sunshine lit every corner and covered everything in a glowing gold. But through the eyes of a man used to living in—what did an earl live in? A manor? A castle? Whatever it was, it was sure to be grander than this house, and he would undoubtedly look with contempt on the conditions in which his son had been brought up.

Worse than his disdain for their lifestyle, another question arose in Jane's mind. What if the earl wanted to punish Mama for hiding Ben from him? Had Mama broken the law? Could she go to prison?

Jane didn't realize she'd said the last two sentences aloud until Robert answered. "I have no idea if any laws were broken, and it's a moot point, for I'm certain my father will have no desire to make life difficult for your mother. She acted in good faith, on instructions given by the child's parent. But my father has missed his son, mourned his loss, and he will wish to become acquainted with him now."

"I should be disappointed in him if he did not," said Mama. Her voice was flat, as if she was trying to keep her emotions under control and therefore could not allow the tiniest inflection lest it open the floodgates. "Have you written to him? When can we expect his lordship to arrive?"

A new wave of horror rolled over Jane. The timing could not be worse. Even if the earl did not disdain their living arrangements and sneer at their poverty, he would be angry to discover the kind of woman Ben called sister. When he heard what Mr. Turner had said of Jane—and how could he not?—he would likely drag Ben away with all haste, refusing them permission to see or contact him ever again. That would break Mama's heart. And when the village tabbies learned the truth…

Lost in her misery, Jane almost missed Robert's next words. Certainly, it took a moment for their meaning to hit her. She looked up at him, her heart pounding furiously with both hope and dread.

"I beg your pardon?" she asked. "Could you repeat that?"

Robert turned his gaze to her. His lips, which had been thin and grim, turned up slightly at the ends. Not enough to make the dimple on his cheek appear, but enough to let Jane know his ire was not directed at her. His dark eyes softened and there was about him a sadness that made her want to reach out, to hold him close and lift his spirits. Her own, too. She wanted to feel the warmth of him near her, to let him banish the chill foreboding that tensed her every nerve, to be wrapped in the comfort of his scent and feel the cool silkiness of his hair against her fingertips while the rasp of his shadowed beard chafed her skin…

What was the matter with her? Why was she so determined to ruin herself and her family? The gossips already believed her a harlot. She did not need to prove them right.

"I said my father will not travel to Bloomfold. He is not a well man and does not venture from home. I will take Ben to Barwell."

Jane's spirit soared. The earl would not come here.

He would neither hear the gossips' tales, nor give them new ones. Then she frowned as her spirit dropped again. "Ben won't know anybody there," she said. "He doesn't like the unfamiliar. He'll need people he knows."

"Oh, Jane," scolded Mama. "Have you been gathering wool these last five minutes? We agreed it is not in Ben's interests to make him leave everything and everyone he has ever known in one fell swoop. I will accompany them and stay at Barwell until all is settled and the future is decided."

"Your mother said you would not object to her leaving. You and Lucy will have each other for company while she is gone, and she will be home again before you can properly miss her."

"No!" The word burst from Jane before she could stop it. Both Robert and Mama stared at her, shocked. "That is, I mean to say…" She cast around for a good reason that she must come too. She could not stay here alone while the villagers spoke of her with contempt and picked holes in her reputation. She closed her eyes to hide her guilt over the fact that her excuse was less than truthful, and she spoke slowly, keeping her voice steady. "All my life, Ben has been my brother. I would see for myself where his home will now be. I am certain he will be well cared for there, but…I would see for myself."

She opened her eyes and stared at Robert, willing him to agree. Their gazes met and held, and she could not have looked away if the world had ended.

After a few seconds, Robert nodded once. "You are more than welcome," he said.

Chapter Eleven

Over the next two days Jane was kept busy. She helped Mama pack what they needed to take with them. She explained, several times, to both Ben and Lucy, where they were going and why, then reassured the bewildered and frightened Ben that, yes, she would still be his sister and love him, yes, he could still refer to Mama as Mama, and no, they weren't sending him away because he had been naughty.

"You will still have us," she told him, patiently, crossing her fingers behind her back and hoping it was not a lie. "But now, there are other people who love you, too." Then she watched him walk away, frowning as he pondered this information. Jane shook her head, knowing he would be back within the hour to ask all over again.

Mary and Jem were happy to accompany them, and Mama found a woman who would look after the cottage while they were gone. Of course, that meant the entire village knew of their plans before the first day was over, although Mama was careful not to give the gossips any hint as to why they were leaving. Jane tried not to dwell upon what people would say about their upcoming journey: she was certain it wouldn't be complimentary.

It was only at night as she lay in bed, the house in darkness, the only sounds the creak and crack of cooling floorboards and the rattle of rain on the windows, that

Jane had time for the thoughts swirling chaotically through her brain. There was so much to make sense of: Ben's incredible history, Mama's subterfuge, Jane's own problems in the village, which she had not yet shared with Mama, who had enough to contend with for now without Jane adding to her cares.

And then there was Robert.

Jane smiled as her mind conjured his face. In her imagination he smiled back at her, his eyes full of warmth and promise. She studied every detail of him the way she would study a great painting, taking note of every part of him and committing it to memory so she would still be able to see him after he was long gone from her life.

She was thankful he'd agreed to let her go to Barwell with them. It would give her a little more time before she must say her final goodbye to him. Some might say she was prolonging the agony, but Jane didn't see it that way. To her, there were a good many years of loneliness in her future and she wanted to delay it for as long as she could.

Oh, she knew she wouldn't be completely alone. There would still be Mama, of course, and Lucy, and perhaps when they reached their next home—wherever that may be—she might make friends whose company would bring her enjoyment. But there would never be a special person, a man who loved her enough to offer marriage. She wasn't the kind of woman a man married. Sydney had proved that when she had gone to him, pregnant and expecting him to keep his promises.

"I cannot marry you," he'd said, and his lip had curled in a sneer. "I am a gentleman, of good family. When I marry, it will be to a lady."

"I am a lady!" she answered, shock and anger making her voice high and her cheeks burn.

He laughed, and the cold cruelty of it made her shiver. "You, my dear, are no lady," he said. "You're not a guttersnipe, that's true. But what is your family? Your father was a seaman…"

"A ship's captain." She stiffened, offended by his offhand dismissal of her father's rank.

"A ship's captain, but not of good birth. 'Tis a pity he and your mother educated you above your station, but that doesn't alter the fact that you are of mean birth, with no dowry, and with passable but not striking good looks. In short, you are not a suitable bride for a man of consequence."

Jane's bottom lip quivered. "You said you loved me," she whispered.

Sydney laughed again. "A man in the throes of desire is not always in full control of his tongue."

Jane slapped him. The crack of her hand against his cheek rang in her ears, and his skin reddened angrily. Malevolence glittered in his eyes.

"Because I have fond memories of you, I will let that go this time," he said, his voice low and menacing. "But if you ever assault me or any of your betters again, I'll see you transported."

The memory of that moment, the hatefulness in Sydney's eyes, the coldness in his tone, made Jane shudder even now. She pulled her blankets closer. No, she thought. She would never marry. Nor would she ever be foolish enough to give herself to a man again, no matter what he promised. That included Robert.

Robert, who was honorable enough to search for his lost brother, even though he knew it would reduce his own consequence. Robert, who had not simply taken Ben away, as he'd had every right to do, but who had taken into consideration not only Ben's feelings, but Mama's, the woman who had, from his perspective, wronged his father. Robert, whose strong arms had held Jane so gently, making her feel warm and safe, while his kisses created havoc within her, making her wish for things she knew she could never, *must* never, have again. Robert, who…she put her hands over her ears as if she could blot out the sound of her own thoughts, and resolved never to think of him again. Nothing good could come of it, and the sooner she accepted that, the better off she would be. She turned over in her bed, closed her eyes, and stifled a scream as her imagination conjured him again.

On the third day after Mama's confession, two carriages arrived and men loaded the luggage. The neighbors stood in their gardens, watching. Mrs. Sutton, who lived next door and had always been forthright, asked bluntly where they were going.

"We are visiting relations," answered Mama. "I am not certain when we will return."

"You never said you had relations," Mrs. Sutton accused.

"The subject never came up. No!" Mama called out, and she hurried away to supervise the men. "Don't put that there. I'll take that one with me in the carriage. I may need it on the journey." Mrs. Sutton watched, her lips pursed in frustration.

"In normal circumstances, I would ride," said Robert, when the last case was secured. "I'm not sure my legs will stand it, though, so I hope you won't mind if I sit inside with you and your family?"

Jane's stomach swooped at the prospect of spending

several days in a vehicle with him, and the only reason a blush didn't burn her cheeks and reveal her desire for his company was that it was countered by her pallor at the thought of being so close to him for so long, without respite or escape.

"Of course we don't mind," she said. Inside she screamed her refusal and wished she could travel in the second coach with Mary, Jem, and the luggage.

The carriage was more spacious than she expected, although Jane thought it could have been the size of the much-publicized ballroom in the Prince Regent's Pavilion at Brighton and she would still have felt encroached upon, suffocated by Robert's nearness, taking up the space and air around her. His scent filled the vehicle, making her more aware of him with every breath. He sat beside Ben with his back to the driver and stretched his long legs out, his feet resting dangerously near the hem of Jane's skirts. If she moved more than an inch, her soft woolen dress would rub against the black leather of his boots. Desire shot through her at the thought, causing a warm ache between her legs that made her want to shift in her seat. There was a sudden dryness in her mouth and an uneasy quickening of her pulse. Quickly, she picked up Lucy and set the child on her lap, hoping no one else had noticed her reactions to him.

They drove through Bloomfold and Ben waved at someone. "Everyone see us off," he said, happy to be the center of attention. Lucy slipped from Jane's lap and stood beside him, and the two of them waved enthusiastically at the villagers. Jane did not look out to see if anyone waved back. She didn't need to see the knowing smirks and scandalized horror on the faces of her erstwhile neighbors.

Robert did not look out, either. His gaze was steady, watching her. In the shaded carriage, his dark eyes were impossible to read, but she could feel them, feel their powerful pull, willing her to stare back. But if she did, he would know her every secret, every thought, every emotion. There would be no hiding from him.

Jane swallowed, lowered her eyes, and studied her worn gloves instead.

****

They made good time, reaching Sidcup before darkness fell on the first evening. Robert gave a smile of satisfaction that, so far, the journey had gone well. He had expected it to be a time of purgatory, because the only other people he had travelled in a coach with were members of his family. His stepmother, Jessica, complained every mile of the way about the state of the roads, the lack of facilities at the taverns, and anything else that occurred to her, while his half-brother, Barnaby, slowed them down with his constant need to stop and be sick. Robert and his father usually rode, which helped them escape the worst of it, although they could only go at the pace set by the carriage. When father's illness had made him too weak to ride and he'd been forced into the carriage, he'd watched Robert with an envy that made Robert feel guilty.

Robert had, therefore, viewed this journey with dread. However, this first day had been surprisingly pleasant. The roads were rough, of course, and the bouncing, rocking, tilting, and swerving of the coach was uncomfortable, while prolonged sitting stiffened his legs and made them ache so that when they did stop, it took time for him to climb out and walk steadily into the inn. At their first stop, Mrs. Winter had whispered to Jane, who came and put her arm through his. To the world, they looked like an ordinary couple, and only they knew how much strength she gave him, allowing him to walk properly and saving him the embarrassment of hobbling so everyone would know he was weak and in pain.

Mrs. Winter kept up a pleasant commentary, explaining to Ben and Lucy where they were. Sometimes, she gave a history of a place. Sometimes she told a story of something that had supposedly happened there. Robert didn't know if the stories were old legends or if Mrs. Winter had made them up, but they were fascinating and helped make the journey better. He found himself eagerly awaiting the next town, simply to hear what she might say.

The motion didn't affect Lucy in the slightest, and they never had to stop for her to be sick or take fresh air. In fact, the only regret Robert had of today's journey was his lack of interaction with Janey.

As they'd passed through Bloomfold, he saw how resolutely she refused to look out the window, staring across the carriage instead. He doubted she stared at him; he didn't think she stared at anything in particular. She'd seemed lost in thought, weighed down by misery.

She had lived in Bloomfold for some years; she must have friends there. Yet she seemed reluctant to acknowledge them, holding herself erect, shoulders stiff with pride. Did she regret leaving this place, these people? Did she fear breaking down at the goodbye?

Her time away was supposed to be short, just long enough to settle Ben and see all was well with him, but Robert was under no illusions. Mrs. Winter had cared for Ben for thirty years. She was not about to give him up and walk away without a backward glance. She would want to stay close. And if Mrs. Winter moved to Barwell, so, of course, would her daughter.

Robert wasn't certain how he felt about that. On the one hand, joy surged through him at the thought that she would be nearby. He could see her whenever she visited Ben. He wouldn't have to resign himself to never meeting her again, never being able to hear her voice or smell her perfume, or see her eyes sparkle with mischief as she teased Ben and Lucy.

On the other hand, a clean break with her might be better. He still didn't know how things would go for him; he was not familiar enough with the law to know whether Ben's disabilities affected the rules of succession, nor did he know the likelihood of Ben siring an heir. Until he did know, all Robert could offer Janey—any woman—was a life of uncertainty, which meant he could not court her. And to have her living nearby, to see her, talk with her, yet maintain his distance emotionally: that would be torture.

If she had had some town bronze, they might have come to an arrangement. Widows in London were worldly-wise and discreet, happy to embark on an affair, knowing it could never lead to anything else. It was simple and straightforward, and mutually satisfying. But Janey Frobisher was not a widow in London. She was from the country, innocent and with a refreshing purity of spirit. She would no more embark on an affair than she would stand naked on Bond Street at noon.

Even knowing that, even aching all over with a lust he could never act upon, Robert knew he would sooner sit across from her in this carriage than be anywhere else on earth.

They put up for the night at the Black Horse in

Sidcup. The tiny hamlet was little more than one street of houses, which was why Robert had chosen it: he didn't want to encounter anyone who knew him, who might spread the news about his travelling companions before his father had had the chance to meet Ben. The earl deserved that much. Besides, Robert thought Janey would prefer to go unnoticed. She wouldn't want the speculation that would follow if people saw them together. Even though there was no impropriety with her mother and Ben making perfectly good chaperones, tongues would wag, and who knew what tales they would concoct by the third or fourth retelling?

Robert secured them rooms and a private parlor where they ate a simple stew with crusty bread. Lucy, tired and out of sorts from the journey, soon grew fractious and Janey took her away. As soon as she'd gone, Robert wished her back. Ben chatted nonstop, reliving the day, recounting things he had seen on the journey. Mrs. Winter encouraged him, reminding him of details, adding to her stories. Robert didn't join in. He gazed, unseeing, at the door Janey had gone through and wondered what she was now doing. Was she hugging Lucy to her, rocking from side to side as she murmured soothing words until the child's sobs subsided and she drifted into sleep? Did she sit beside Lucy's bed, watching her sleep, the child's soft snores bringing an atmosphere of peace? Did Janey read by candlelight while she watched over her daughter? Or had she prepared for bed herself?

An image of Janey in her nightgown came to him. A chaste garment, it would cover her from her neck to her toes, the white cotton buttoned to her throat, exposing nothing. Still, in his mind he saw the gown outline her body, the curvy shapes of her breasts and her hips. If the light shone from the right angle, would he see her legs silhouetted, displayed as if she had covered them with nothing? Would he see the large dark circles of her nipples pressing against the cotton? The patch of hair at the juncture of her thighs? Would bare toes peep from beneath her hem, tempting him to pick up her foot and rest it in his lap, massage it deeply until she groaned with pleasure?

The thought of her foot in his lap, his fingers kneading at her sole while her toes flexed and stretched and brushed against him was almost more than he could bear. His thighs stiffened and the fall of his trousers became tight, a delicious, wanting ache pulling at him. He thanked God he was still seated at the table, his lower half hidden from view.

Later, when Mrs. Winter and Ben retired, he took a turn in the garden, hoping the cool night air would relax him. It was what his mother would have called a pretty night. The sky was a deep dark black, the kind of black it could only be in the country, where its beauty wasn't marred by streetlights. Stars winked at him, some faint, too shy to fully show themselves, others bold and bright. The moon hung low, just over half of it on show, which was enough to see his way along the gray path lined with silver grass. Dark bushes and trees ringed the garden, their leaves shushing on a faint breeze as if warning him to stay quiet, to not spoil the peace of the place.

Peace. Ha! Robert would find no peace on this journey. That had become clear during the long hours in the cramped confines of the coach. Sitting across from Janey had been sweet torture, her soft lavender scent calling to him more than any of the seductively heavy perfumes worn by the ladies he usually encountered. Her face had been carefully composed to show no emotion—or at least, she clearly thought it had. Robert saw her discomfort in the way she kept her eyes averted from his, the paleness of her cheeks, the tight way she held her hands in her lap.

He had done that to her. He'd made her uncomfortable, although he didn't really know why. Could it be the memory of their kisses? That seemed likely. After all, *he* hadn't been able to push them from *his* mind. Even now he could feel her soft, warm lips against his, the heat of her cheeks, and the cool thickness of her hair, the frantic beat of her pulse beneath his fingertips. He remembered the way she let his tongue play with hers. He could still taste the fresh mint of her tooth powder, mingled with the bread and cheese she'd eaten at nuncheon. He fancied, too, that he could hear her voice, softly murmuring quiet words…

Robert tensed as he realized the sound was not part of his imaginings. He really could hear Janey talking softly. He frowned, wondering why she was out here, and who she might be speaking with. Who could she know in this out-of-the-way place?

Carefully, quietly, he moved over the moon-coated grass, staying as close as possible to the bushes, hiding among them. He heard a groan. Was she in despair? In pain? Or was that a moan of pleasure? The thought made his jaw clench and set his teeth on edge. Annoyed with her for being out here, meeting someone, with himself for caring, he turned the corner to where the rest of the garden curved around the side of the inn, then stopped dead. There, sitting on a wooden bench, was Janey, her arms around Lucy, who was tightly wrapped in a blanket.

Janey murmured softly at her daughter while Lucy moaned her tired displeasure.

Emotion flowed through him, crushing and swirling like a river after heavy rain. He couldn't even describe all he felt: relief that she was not in a lover's arms, shame that he'd thought she might be, irritation that the idea of her with another man had upset him so, and above all that, a tenderness, a true liking for this woman that went beyond any feelings of physical desire. It scared him witless.

Lucy's moans grew quieter, then stopped altogether. Janey ceased murmuring, although she continued rocking. He could see her adjust, changing the way she moved as the sleeping child grew heavier. Soon she would stand and take her daughter back to their room. To do that, she must pass the point where he stood hidden in the shadows.

He fought the urge to step forward and take the sleeping child from her. Janey believed herself alone here. How would she feel to know Robert had been watching her? Would she think he was spying on her? Consider him a voyeur? Or would his own need be mirrored in her eyes?

He couldn't take the chance. Silently, he moved around the corner and out of her sight, then ran quickly across the grass and into the inn. He reached his chamber and locked the door, then leaned back, his head against the rough wood. His pulse beat loud and fast, and his breaths were shallow. Because he had hurried here, he assured himself. Nothing more. What more could there be?

He swallowed, but his mouth was dry and there was a strange feeling inside him, as if everything had moved out of place. His thighs were hard, and his bollocks ached.

"This is ridiculous," he whispered. "Get a grip on yourself."

He walked painfully to the bed and threw himself onto it, willing his body under control and telling himself over and over, "She is not for you."

Hopefully, if he said it enough times, he might convince himself it was true.

Chapter Twelve

On the second night of their journey, they stayed at a small inn just outside St. Albans. It was fully dark by the time they arrived, and Jane was exhausted. Two days of confining an energetic three-year-old inside a carriage, together with constantly reassuring Ben that all would be well when she had no idea whether that was the truth, had left her with a tense headache. She spoke quietly to the innkeeper's wife, who brought her a welcome tisane. Jane could not afford to be sick, not now, when her family needed her.

The tension within her was not lessened by the long hours sitting across from Robert. She tried to call him Mr. Carrow, even in her private thoughts, but it didn't happen. They had kissed, and now he would always be Robert to her. As long as she never called him that out loud, all would be fine.

This evening Mary took care of Lucy, who was too out of sorts to dine properly. After a wash that she wished could be a bath, and a change of clothes, Jane went downstairs to the private parlor where she found Robert and Ben waiting.

It was a comfortable room, big enough for a party of four, though more would have been crowded. A table took up much of the space, its top covered with a white cloth embroidered with pretty flowers. The same pattern was embroidered onto the place mats, the chair backs, and the fire screen which stood to one side of the hearth, while friendly flames danced around half-burned logs. Two armchairs were placed on either side of the hearth, each flanked by an occasional table, and two more armchairs were nearby. The walls held pictures of hunting parties, and a Cambridge yard glass took pride of place on the chimney breast. A rag rug on the floor picked up the colors of the embroidered flowers, as did the curtains framing the windows. The glow of the fire mixed with the light shining from the lamps and gave the room a warm and welcoming atmosphere.

The only thing the parlor lacked was Jane's mother. It was unlike Mama to be the last one down; she would normally want to stay near Ben, not to mention her worry at the possibility of leaving Jane and Robert unchaperoned.

"Mama not coming," said Ben, as if he had read her thoughts. "Mama got the headache." He grinned and puffed out his chest. "I 'portant. I…" He frowned, concentrating on his words… "I chap roam for you."

Jane nodded, trying to keep her surprise from showing. Ben looked so proud of the role which Mama had obviously given to him. "That sounds excellent," she said.

"Dinner will be here shortly," said Robert. "Would you like an aperitif?" He poured Jane a small glass of Madeira and gave Ben a long drink that looked like lemonade.

They enjoyed a hearty dinner of roast beef with Yorkshire pudding, potatoes, parsnips, and vegetables. The good food, warm room, and mellow wine made for a convivial evening with easy and pleasant conversation.

Afterward, Ben sat in one of the chairs by the fire

and was soon snoring. Jane and Robert looked at him, then at each other and shared a grin.

"I'm afraid we've fatigued our chaperone," said Robert.

"It's been a long day for him."

"And for you?" His eyes filled with concern. "Travelling is arduous even when you're accustomed to it."

"I have travelled before," she reminded him. "Although, I confess, it was good to stop this evening. I needed to move about after so many hours in the coach."

As if to prove her point, she felt a sudden need to move, so she walked to the window and looked out. In the dark, she could see little: the silhouettes of the outbuildings, light seeping through the cracks around the stable door. A faint glow on the horizon indicated a large town where streetlamps shone and people were awake long into the night. She saw no stars and, from this angle, the moon was hidden from her, too.

"We are halfway there," he said, his voice low, not much more than a whisper. His boot heel clicked against the floor as he came to her. She felt the heat of him at her back, his soft breaths caressing her hair, sending delicious shivers along her spine. His cologne sweetened the air, mixing with the scent of the burning logs in the hearth and the fragrance of the wine they'd drunk with dinner.

For several moments, they stood still. Jane didn't want to move, she didn't want to end this connection between them and break the spell. For, surely, a spell it was, to have her so in thrall, wishing this time could last forever, that there was nobody left on earth but her and Robert. She closed her eyes and imagined him putting his hands on her shoulders, his warm fingers branding her skin, his touch sending tingles and crackles through her, like the static that made her hair stand on end after too vigorous a brushing. Her heart seemed to flip in her chest and her nipples stiffened, chafing against the linen of her shift until she shuddered.

It took her a moment to realize she wasn't imagining it. His hands really were resting on her shoulders, and her body really was reacting to him. He leaned closer. She felt his breath against her neck, her ear, her cheek. She turned her head. His hand left her shoulder, his finger stroking her jawline, so warm against her skin, so gentle, so…wonderful.

A million butterflies took wing within her, making her want to dance and jump and leap, though her legs were like jelly and, for an instant, she feared they would not support her and she would crumple at his feet.

He steered her around to face him and pulled her closer. She felt the hardness of his chest, his arms warm and firm around her, protecting her. His eyes, almost black with need and want, stared into hers, holding her trapped within their gaze.

He moved so slowly she barely realized that he drew closer. His lips brushed hers softly, and he pulled away again. She moaned at the loss of him, then grinned as he kissed her again, harder this time, more possessively. His lips were warm and full, his breath mingling with hers, tasting of roast beef and brandy.

Jane's arms wrapped around his neck and her fingertips played with the ends of his hair while his tongue danced alongside hers, simulating the moves of love. His hand caressed her back, her shoulder, then stroked her side, coming to rest under her breast, his palm cupping her. His fingers moved over her nipple, rubbing her through her clothes. She longed for him to undo the buttons on her bodice, to peel away the layers of her clothing, to free her to his touch, skin on skin.

Her hips swayed of their own volition, pushing her core nearer to his, desperate to cure her of this beautiful pain and end this exquisite torment. Behind his trousers, she could feel he was hard and ready, and she wanted to unbutton him, to take that part of him into her hand…

In his chair by the fire, Ben snorted. The sudden noise acted upon Jane like a bucket of cold water, shocking her back to reality. She pulled back from Robert as if his touch had stung her.

Robert looked as discomfited as she was. He rested his thumbs into the tops of the pockets in his waistcoat and turned to stare out of the window into the darkness, lifting his chin as if in haughty denial of what had happened between them. Jane couldn't stop the pang of pain and disappointment at the thought he might regret it. A muscle twitched in his cheek and she knew, instinctively, that he was about to apologize.

She didn't want him to apologize. She was not sorry for the kiss they had shared, and she didn't want him to be sorry, either. An apology now would ruin one of the most wonderful moments of her life. So, to prevent him saying anything she would regret, she clasped her hands together at her waist, straightened her shoulders, and spoke herself. "Well," she said, briskly. "I should go and see to Lucy. Mary will want her bed."

That was the wrong thing to say, she realized as soon as she had spoken. The image of a bed came to her, its mattress deep and soft, blankets rumpled, and Robert Carrow lying on it, his nakedness partly covered by a sheet, carelessly draped over him, snow-white against the lived-in tan of his skin. His chest, she knew from weeks of nursing him, was broad, muscles firm, shoulders and arms well defined. The dark hair she had seen during his convalescence would surely spread down from his throat to cover the whole of his torso, and…

Jane pursed her lips. She had no business imagining this man naked, or anything like. She certainly had no right to think of him in a bed. Thoughts like that led to ruin and misery, as she already knew. She had weathered the storms of scandal once and worked hard to rebuild her life and her reputation. She was not going to do it again. She was not certain she *could* do it again. So, mumbling a quick goodnight, she hurried from the parlor and ran upstairs to her chamber, where she dismissed Mary, checked on the sleeping Lucy, undressed hastily, and climbed into her bed, pulling the covers up to her neck to ward off the night chill.

It could not happen again. Jane would not allow it to happen again. One ruination was more than enough for any woman. For the remainder of their journey, she must keep her distance from Robert—*Mr. Carrow*! Since it appeared she could not trust herself, she must ensure they were never alone together. And, she added with a wry smile, she would also ensure future chaperones were a little more diligent.

On that thought, she turned over, beat her pillow into submission, and tried to sleep.

****

Robert broke his fast in the public bar, not wishing to chance coming upon Janey—*Mrs. Frobisher*!—in the parlor. What he had done last night was unconscionable. He'd as good as pawed at her like an out-of-control schoolboy with a willing milkmaid, eager beyond belief to slake his lust.

He ought to be horsewhipped. He knew better than to act like that with a gently bred female—and she was gently bred, no matter the straitened circumstances in which he had found her and her family. Even as a widow, a woman of her station could only go so far in relaxing Society's rules, and besides, Janey—*Mrs. Frobisher*—was not that kind of widow. She had none of the world-weary cynicism of the fading ladies of London. There was an air of gentility and naïveté about her that bordered on the virginal. If not for Lucy, Robert would have doubted she had any experience at all. Which made his actions even worse.

His behavior last night had given her a disgust of him, he realized. For one brief moment he'd thought she felt as he felt. Her fingers playing in his hair sent a jolt of electricity through him that shot down his spine, straight to his most sensitive part. He'd been so hard he could barely stand. And her kiss! She'd responded to him, meeting every thrust of his tongue with an inexpert one of her own, and her lips had been warm and soft against his. He'd heard her little mewls of pleasure and his heart soared with pride that he had coaxed those noises from her. His hand had moved, without conscious effort from himself, to cup her wonderfully full breast, his fingers playing with the taut little nub of her nipple...

And then it was over. The shock and horror he'd seen on her face when she realized what they were doing, where he'd been leading her, had almost floored him.

He should have apologized then. Apologized, and made it sound sincere, though that was always going to be an impossible task when the last thing he felt was regret. He was not sorry for the kiss—for any of their kisses—and he couldn't convincingly say that he was. Not when he knew, given the slightest encouragement, he would do it again in a heartbeat.

Lord, but he was in a mess! He rested his elbow on the table and balanced his head on his hand. Two more days. Two more days and they would be in Barwell where he could give Janey—*Mrs. Frobisher!*—for pity's sake, why did his mind insist on making it worse? He could give *Mrs. Frobisher* over to the care of his father's housekeeper and ensure all temptation was removed from him during her stay, allowing her to be comfortable and safe.

Between then and now, though, he should keep his distance from her as much as he could. He toyed with the idea of hiring a horse and riding, but he knew his legs were not yet strong enough. The last thing he needed was to injure himself again and force her to minister to him, because he knew that was precisely what she would do.

He would ride in the carriage, because he had no other choice. But he would keep his distance as far as he was able in such a cramped space, and he would ensure there were no accidental touches, no brushes of his leg against hers, no lingering study of her when her gaze was averted, no euphoria when she looked at him and their eyes met.

Tonight, they would stop near Towcester. He would secure a private parlor, eat dinner with them, then make himself scarce. It was the least he could do. By his actions going forward, he would ensure she knew she no longer needed to worry about him.

And if Robert needed to find a cold stream or two to douse himself along the way, then so be it.

Chapter Thirteen

They finally reached Barwell on the fourth day. Jane looked out of the carriage window, eager to see this place that her brother might soon call home. It was a small settlement, nestling on the side of a low hill, the gentle slope leading from a river at the bottom, up to what was clearly the village center where there was a shop, a church, and an inn. Jane smiled to herself. It didn't matter where in England you went, or how small the community, there was always a church and an inn.

Around the village there were ploughed fields as well as pasture with sheep and pigs. The boundaries between the fields were made of ancient hedgerows, broken now and then by a tree. It looked very much like Sussex, and yet very different.

The carriage travelled through the village and continued for a further two miles before they turned off the road, through a gateway between two stone pillars, onto a well-maintained drive bordered by fenced-in parkland where sheep grazed alongside deer and a few horses. Oak and elm trees dotted the park, along with rowan and yew and a few rhododendron bushes. Along the verges of the driveway, out of reach of the grazing animals, an abundance of flowers grew wild in the grass, splashing color like spilled paints from an artist's palette. Their petals fluttered in the gentle breeze, as if greeting the new arrivals and cheering them on their way. Jane hoped the human inhabitants would be as welcoming.

"Around the next bend you will be able to see Carrow House," said Robert. Ben and Lucy moved to the window to see.

Jane looked over at Robert. It was the first time she had deliberately glanced at him since the evening in the parlor at St. Albans, although the temptation to do so had been, at times, overwhelming.

She knew he had avoided her since then, too, which told her, in clear and certain terms, he thought her a wanton who had thrown herself at him. Shame and mortification filled her at the thought of that, and she wondered how long they must stay here before they could leave.

Deep inside, though, she realized leaving might not be a possibility. If Ben truly was the earl's son, he would need to stay and make this his home. Mama would never leave him, and Jane could not leave Mama. For a start, she had nowhere else to go and no way to make a living, especially with Lucy in tow. She would just have to avoid Robert whenever she could and accept his censure of her when they did meet.

"What it like here?" called Ben over his shoulder. He had lowered the window, and he and Lucy leaned out eagerly. The wind ruffled their hair, revealing the bald spot already appearing on Ben's pate, and pulling Lucy's hair from her ribbons. Jane sighed at her daughter's dishevelment, but she was more concerned that the child did not lean so far forward that she fell. She held the little girl's waist. At first, Lucy struggled and squirmed, trying to get free, but she soon resigned herself to the fact that Jane wouldn't let her go, and turned her attention back to the view.

They rounded a bend and both Ben and Lucy exclaimed their delighted surprise. Jane peered over Lucy's head, and gasped. The house ahead of her was huge. There had to be ten windows on each floor at the front of the house. It was also old, built in the Elizabethan style with three forward facing wings forming the arms of an E. The dark stone walls were draped in ivy, which made the many-paned windows seem smaller. On both ends of the spine of the E, there were towers, and crenulations surrounded the whole roof. In front of the house was a circular driveway surrounding a water fountain, a large round pool with a plinth at its center on which stood three tiers of ever smaller bowls. Water bubbled from the top and spilled playfully down, splashing from one bowl to the next until it hit the pool at the base. Lucy stared at it as if it was the most wondrous thing she had ever seen.

The carriage drove around the fountain and stopped outside the front door. As the vehicle stopped moving, Ben sat back in his seat, arms folded and a stubborn pout replacing the excitement and wonder that had been on his face. "I not like it here," he pronounced. "Want to go home."

"Benedict," said Mama in a tone that brooked no argument, "you cannot say you don't like something until you have tried it." It was a lesson she had instilled into them from their infancy, though it usually pertained to foods they didn't wish to eat.

Ben crossed his legs on the seat under himself in that peculiar, rubber-limbed way of his. His shoulders rose and fell as he tightened the fold of his arms and hunkered down for the fight.

"Ben…" said Mama. Ben ignored her. Robert held

up a hand to her and raised an eyebrow as if asking permission. Mama nodded.

"You don't want to come in?" he asked Ben, gently.

"No!"

"What a pity. Still, I suppose the cakes I asked Cook to make for you won't go to waste, because I'm certain Lucy will eat them." Robert winked at Mama. "Come, ladies, we shall go inside, even if Ben does not."

He stood as the carriage door opened and the coachman let down the steps.

"Cakes?" asked Ben, suddenly unsure.

"I sent a message last night to ask for them. But don't fret, you don't have to come in and eat them." Robert climbed out and offered his hand to Mama.

"You have cake, too?" Ben asked Jane.

"I expect so."

"I have cake," announced Lucy, clapping her hands in glee before launching herself from the carriage and into Robert's arms.

He laughed as he caught her. "A very ladylike exit, you little minx," he said, and he gave Lucy an affectionate hug before he set her down.

Jane felt a pang that he would never take her into his arms again, not even in such an innocent way as he'd hugged Lucy. Which was ridiculous, because in his arms was the last place she wanted to be. Her respectability would never survive it, and her respectability was all she had.

She took his proffered hand demurely, in the same way Mama had done. The jolt at his touch was expected now, and she was largely able to hide her reaction to it. She could not, would not, allow anyone to see the effect this man had on her. Least of all, him.

Ben scrambled out behind her. She glanced up at Robert, who tried to suppress his grin.

"I have cake," said Ben. "Then I go home."

The front door opened. A footman stepped out, but before he could move to the carriage an older man hurried past him. In his late fifties, he was tall and thin, and he looked enough like Robert that Jane had no doubt who he was. He was still a handsome man, although his face had a drawn look and sallow pallor, as if he had not enjoyed the best of health.

"Father," said Robert, and he gave the earl a small bow before he turned to Mama and Jane. "Mrs. Winter, Mrs. Frobisher, may I make known to you Lord Barwell, my father. Father, this is Mrs. Winter and her daughter, Mrs. Frobisher." He picked up Lucy, who had shyly hidden behind his leg, and swung her into his arms again. "And this little imp is Miss Lucy Frobisher." He gave the child a reassuring smile, but she still clung to him, her starfish fingers splayed at the back of his neck and a wide-eyed look of wariness on her face.

"And this," continued Robert, moving to where Ben stood, looking terrified, "is…"

"My son," said the earl, absolute awe in his expression. "Benedict," he breathed, and he stared at Ben as if trying to commit every inch of him to memory.

For several moments, nobody moved. Nobody spoke. Even Lucy was still, as if she understood the importance of this meeting. The breeze died.

Then the earl took a step forward and pulled Ben into an embrace. Startled, Ben looked to Mama, but she just smiled and nodded. At her blessing, Ben relaxed a little.

"My son," the earl said again, and his voice held

wonderment and joy. Then he laughed. "You look like your mother," he told Ben, "although you have my coloring in your eyes." He embraced Ben again. Ben still seemed uncomfortable at the contact, but he didn't pull back.

"Where are my manners?" asked the earl when he stepped back from Ben. He wiped his finger along the damp skin under his eyes before bowing to Mama, then to Jane. "I have asked for tea in the blue salon. It will be served shortly."

"And cakes?" asked Lucy from her position of safety in Robert's arms. Jane watched him hold her as if he had been doing it all his life, and a pang of longing shot through her heart. She willed it away. There was no reason to spoil the moment with things that could never be.

"Of course there'll be cakes," said the earl with a chuckle. "You cannot have a celebration without cakes." He looked at Robert and his eyes glistened. "Thank you," he said, quietly. Jane's heart twinged again when Robert nodded, his own eyes suspiciously bright.

"Let's go and get the cakes," cried Lucy, and the two men laughed, breaking the moment.

As they moved to go into the house, the earl stumbled. Without warning, his breathing changed, as if he had run a long distance, and his shoulders stooped, making him seem much older than he had done just a few moments before. Robert took his arm to steady him, and watched him, his expression one of concern.

"Are you all right?" he asked, his voice little more than a murmur. Jane doubted anybody but she had heard it over Lucy's excited chatter. It was, however, enough to embarrass the earl.

"I'm fine," he replied, testily. "Don't be so picksome, boy."

Robert's anxiety was not assuaged. "It would probably suit the ladies to rest before tea," he suggested. Jane considered voicing agreement with him, not because she felt especially fatigued but because the earl looked as if he could do with some time to come to himself again. Before she could say anything, though, the earl laughed in disbelief.

"You think that little girl is going to want to rest before she has her cake?"

Robert sighed. "Very well," he said, and surreptitiously helped his father over the threshold and into the house.

The square entrance hall was paneled from floor to ceiling with dark wood. Here and there pictures hung, and small tables held flower arrangements. Most of the pictures were old ones in the Dutch style and their dark colors and quiet subjects, while they suited the hall, did not add to its light. The floorboards were highly polished, as were the banisters on the stairs, which were made from ancient wood and almost black with age and the touch of generations of hands. For all its darkness, though, the hall was not oppressive, and the thought of Ben living here did not fill Jane with dread.

At the end of the hall, they moved into a large room. Here, the walls were lined with cream-colored silk, printed with dainty bluebirds. French windows led to a terrace and a vast garden beyond, and there was far more light than in the hall. Pale blue curtains were tied back on either side of the windows, their color picked up by the armchairs, the couches, and the chaises longues that were placed about the room in a way that encouraged conversation. The fireplace was marble, its mantelshelf holding several porcelain figurines, and, in front of the unlit chimney, a firescreen was covered with the same bluebird pattern as the walls. The polished wood floor was mostly covered by a thick rug in shades of blue, cream, and gold.

A maid stood beside a trolley on which were teacups and a teapot, a jug of milk, and a bowl overflowing with cubes of sugar. Beside the tea was a three-tiered Crown Derby cake stand, its gilt handle gleaming above an array of delicate-looking morsels. Lucy's eyes grew round and as big as saucers. Ben stared at the cakes and licked his lips.

"Thank you, Betty," the earl said, and the maid curtsied and left the room. He turned to Mama and gestured at the tea trolley. "My wife is not at home just now," he said. "Could I prevail upon you to do the honors, Mrs. Winter?"

"Of course, my lord." Mama sat in the chair nearest to the trolley. Jane sat near to her, allowing the gentlemen to take their seats. The earl studied Ben as if afraid to take his eyes from him, lest he disappear again. Ben, happily munching on a cake, did not seem to notice, but Mama did, and she looked uncomfortable.

"My lord," she said, "I must make my apology for not writing to you after Mary—Lady Barwell—died." She hesitated, clearly seeking the words she needed to say. Jane swallowed. Was Mama frightened that this man would wreak some terrible revenge upon her for the lost years with his son? Fear for her parent churned in Jane's stomach and made the cake she had eaten lie heavily. The next moment, though, the fear was replaced with almost overwhelming relief when the earl waved his hand, dismissing Mama's concerns.

"You helped your friend and, in so doing, took wonderful care of my son. I can ask for no more." He smiled. "Mary chose well."

Mama blinked several times until the emotions no longer filled her eyes. A look of understanding passed between her and the earl. Feeling she was intruding on a private moment, Jane looked away and found herself being studied by Robert. Their eyes met and he smiled. Jane could not help but smile back before lowering her eyes, hoping the heat in her cheeks did not mean she was blushing furiously.

Lucy broke the moment. She leaned against Jane's legs and patted her hands on Jane's knees. "I have another cake?" she asked, then thought for a second before smiling sweetly and adding, "Please?"

Twenty minutes later the tea was drunk, the cake was eaten, and even Lucy's appetite was satisfied. The atmosphere in the salon was convivial and the gathering laughed heartily like old friends at anecdotes and memories of Ben as a boy. Every now and then a veil of sadness passed over the earl's face, but he quickly pushed it away and asked questions, encouraging Mama to tell him more about his son's childhood. Meanwhile, Robert teased Ben with the ease of several months' acquaintance, and Ben, for the most part, took it in good stead. Lucy forgot her shyness and danced around the room, determined to gather the attention for herself. Jane started to scold her, but the earl would have none of it.

"This house needs to be filled with children's laughter," he said. "My youngest son, Barnaby, who is only a little older than you," he touched his finger playfully to the tip of Lucy's nose, "is altogether too quiet and serious. Mayhap some of your joie de vivre will transfer to him."

Lucy frowned. "What's schwad eve?"

Robert lifted her onto his lap and tickled her tummy, making her giggle. "It means you're a mischief," he told her. Jane grinned, enjoying the sight of him so at ease with her daughter. Yet another image to commit to memory so she could take it out and enjoy gazing on it in the times to come, when he was gone from her life.

The door opened and a tall, slender, and expensively elegant woman glided into the room. The laughter stopped abruptly and, it seemed to Jane, the temperature cooled. Which was absurd, she knew, but she could not help the spirit of uneasiness that came over her.

The woman was beautiful, in the cold, unfeeling way that a white porcelain vase was beautiful. Her features were exquisite, her mouth a tiny pink bow, her nose pert, her eyes the translucent blue of an icicle when the sun shone through it. There was no animation in them, no hint of what she thought or felt. Not a single line marred her perfect cream skin, although Jane guessed the woman must be in her late thirties. Ebony curls were artfully arranged either side of her face. She made Jane feel dowdy and disheveled simply by being near to her.

She wore a day dress in a deep blue, the plainness of it accentuating her exquisite beauty, and a delicate gold locket nestled at her throat, the only jewelry she wore other than her plain gold wedding band. She stood in the doorway and looked around at them all, but there seemed no curiosity, and no welcome.

The earl and Robert stood to greet her, and Ben scrambled to his feet to join them, the manners Mama had instilled in him breaking out. Lucy clung to Robert's leg, her fingers leaving cake crumbs on his trousers as she stared warily at the newcomer.

"My dear," said the earl. There was no more warmth in his voice than there had been when he'd addressed the servant girl. The newcomer looked at him and smiled. It was a small smile, barely lifting the corners of her mouth, and it never reached her eyes.

"Allow me to present my wife, the Countess Barwell," continued the earl, then proceeded to give the names of his guests. When he came to Ben, the countess inclined her head in acknowledgement, then studied her stepson in a way that reminded Jane of the village schoolteacher when he had studied leaves and flowers in botany classes: interested but in no way engaged. Jane shivered.

The countess turned her gaze to Robert. There was no welcome there, either. "You are home," she said to him in a voice that was soft and low. Jane thought it must have taken hours of practice before she bit her lip, immediately ashamed of such an uncharitable thought.

"Jessica," answered Robert. He extricated himself from Lucy's grasp and bowed to his stepmother. "You look as lovely as ever." The words had the feeling of cold duty. The countess inclined her head, before turning to Mama and Jane.

"Has my husband shown you to our guest rooms?" she asked, and Jane thought there was a slight emphasis on the word "guest," as if she was giving notice that their stay would be temporary. As if Jane and Mama were not already aware of that. "You will want to supervise the unpacking of your chests," she continued in her soft, cold tone, "and to rest yourselves before dinner. We keep country hours, so dinner will be at six." She turned to Robert. "Since we have ladies staying, I assume you will move to the dower house?" Jane was uncertain whether what she felt at his banishment was shock or disappointment.

The earl stiffened and Robert's jaw clenched.

"Robert has a perfectly good set of rooms here," said the earl. "He doesn't need to take himself off."

"I insist," said the countess. "For propriety's sake."

"I will not have my son banished from his own home." The earl's voice was quiet but determined.

The countess smiled and glided across the room to her husband. She took his hand in hers and gazed at him. Her look might almost be called adoring, but there was something about it that somehow seemed…calculating. "The impropriety of him being here with these ladies…" she began. "I am sure they would be more comfortable if he were not here."

"There is no impropriety." Mama smiled to soften her words but there was steel in her eyes. "My daughter and I are both widows, and Mr. Carrow stayed several weeks with us, without scandal, while he recovered from his injuries. And if anyone should be removed, it is us, for we are the interlopers."

"We go?" asked Ben, his disappointment plain.

"No," said Robert, firmly.

"Injuries?" The earl frowned. "What injuries? What happened?"

The countess patted his arm, the way one would reassure a child. Robert's mouth flattened and Jane could see why. She, too, was annoyed on the earl's behalf.

"You were unwell, my lord," said the countess. "I did not tell you because you didn't need the additional worry."

"I should know these things. They should not be kept from me."

"I understood it to be no more than a minor accident. Not worth distressing you."

"But if it took several weeks for him to heal…"

"The healing was clearly successful." The countess eyed Robert over her shoulder.

"I am well, Father," Robert said, picking up on her unspoken command. "There was a…carriage accident, but all is well now."

The earl's eyes narrowed. "I want to hear all about it."

"Please don't agitate yourself, dear," said the countess. "We don't need you to suffer one of your attacks. I am sure Robert will tell you all about it later." She turned to her guests. "Allow me to show you to your rooms."

It was only after they had climbed the stairs and Jane was left alone in her bedchamber that she wondered about what had been said. She knew Robert had not sent any letters while he recuperated in their cottage. So how had the countess known about his accident?

Chapter Fourteen

After dinner, Jessica led the ladies into the drawing room for tea, while the gentlemen stayed in the dining room. Ben watched Robert and their father, clearly unsure what would happen next, but pleased and proud to be left with the men.

"Brandy, Ben?" asked Father. Ben's eyes lit and he nodded, eagerly. Father poured him a half measure before filling rummers for Robert and himself. Ben took a sip, then pulled a face of disgust.

"I not like it," he announced, then frowned. "I still a gentleman?"

"Of course," Father reassured him. "Gentlemen are permitted to drink brandy. They don't have to do so if they don't like it."

Ben smiled, relieved.

Robert sipped his own brandy. The familiar burn hit his throat and worked its way down through his chest, but it was followed by a strange aftertaste. It wasn't strong, simply unusual. He might have suspected the spirit was corked, but Father drank his and seemed not to notice, and he certainly would have if the brandy was off. Perhaps the taste had been tainted by the strong cheese Robert had eaten at dinner. He sipped again. The aftertaste was not as marked this time.

"Now we are without the ladies," said Father, sitting back in his chair and crossing his legs at the knees, "tell me about this carriage accident you were involved in."

Robert pushed a smile into place and hoped he looked reassuring. "Nothing to tell."

At the same time, Ben said, "I thinked he was dead." The earl looked from one of his sons to the other.

"Nothing to tell but you looked dead?"

Robert sighed, knowing he had no choice now but to tell his father the whole story. Perhaps it was a good idea to do so at that, for Father might be able to shed some light on what had been happening, and who might want to hurt members of this family. At the very least, the earl should be warned, lest he also be attacked. So, in the most matter-of-fact way he could, Robert told the story of the coachman who had tried to run him down, not once but twice. Ben listened, occasionally picking up crumbs of cheese from the tabletop and putting them into his mouth, nodding at some details, frowning at others.

Father's eyes narrowed. "You were targeted."

"I thought so," agreed Robert. "Although I am at a loss to say by whom, or why."

"Who knew you would be in Bloomfold?"

"Only those who directed me there. But I cannot see that I caused them offense." Indeed, he thought those people were likely to remember him with fondness, considering the generosity with which he had paid for the scantest pieces of information.

"Confound it!" Father hit his fist on the table, making plates rattle and startling Ben. "I've just found one of my sons. I won't lose another." He studied Robert for several moments. "Were these the only incidents of their kind?" Robert hesitated and Father glared at him, sternly. "Don't cosset me, boy. I worry more over half-truths than if I know the whole."

"There were one or two other incidents," admitted Robert. "Things that shook me, but which I would not connect to each other." He then told his father, and the wide-eyed Ben, of all that had happened over the last few months: a poacher's stray shot that took his hat in Dorset, a huge trunk that fell from the upstairs window of an inn near Lyme Regis, missing him by inches, and a quick thinking ostler who saved him when a winch broke and sent a heavy sack of meal at his head at Petworth.

"Then, just outside Winchester, I stayed at a small inn that caught fire."

"Fire?" breathed Ben, his attention riveted on Robert. "Fire dangerous."

Robert nodded. "Yes, it is. But it happens, especially in a two-hundred-year-old house with a wooden frame, wattle walls, and a thatched roof." He smiled and lightened his tone, playing down the incident. "I'm surprised more places don't go up in flames."

The earl stared at him. "What happened?"

"Who can say? A spark from a fireplace? A dropped candle? It was the middle of the night. I was awoken by the clanging of bells and shouts of 'Fire.' Small wisps of smoke were already seeping under my door and the wood of it was hot to touch, so I knew there was fire in the corridor."

"How you get out?" whispered Ben.

"Not through the door," guessed Father, and Robert nodded.

"I tried to, but it was stuck fast. I pulled and hammered on it but it wouldn't budge. So, I climbed through the window." That had not been as easy as it sounded. When Robert had reached the inn that night, most of the bedchambers were taken and he'd been offered a small room under the eaves. It was cold and dark, with the tiniest of windows, but he'd been tired and aching from too many hours in the saddle, dispirited by another failed clue, and happy to take anything with a bed.

It had been a long drop from that window to the cobbled stones of the yard and Robert had faced a stark choice: certain death in the fire, or the chance of a broken neck. Saying a quick prayer, he'd squeezed his body through the window, scraping and bruising his skin on the wood frame, then lowered himself toward the ground. Even stretched out, there was still too big a gap between his feet and the cobbles.

A shout went up and he glanced down to see men holding taut a blanket for him to jump into. Thanks to them, the only injuries he'd sustained were minor.

"Either you are the unluckiest man in England," said Father when Robert finished recounting his adventures, "or somebody has taken great exception to you."

"No," argued Ben. "Robert nice man. Everyone like him."

"Not everyone," answered the earl and Robert was forced to agree. Taken one by one, the events were an unfortunate series of accidents, but when considered as a whole, they were sinister, to say the least.

Ben giggled. "Janey like Robert," he said, then covered his mouth with his hand as if to hold his glee inside.

"Oh?" The earl raised an eyebrow.

Heat spread through Robert's cheeks, and he took a long draft of brandy. "Mrs. Frobisher is a caring woman who likes everybody," he said.

Ben shook his head. "Not everybody. Not Mr.

Turner."

"Who?" asked Father, nonplussed.

"The butcher," said Ben, and his tone implied no more explanation was necessary.

Father talked to Ben, asking him about his life in Bloomfold. Robert stared into his brandy, its dark amber shining in the candlelight, its sour-sweet aroma filling him with a warm and pleasant feeling.

Janey like Robert.

The conversation in the room faded as Janey's face shimmered before him, her smile shy, her eyes full of concern and care, but with fun and laughter too. Eyes that changed, depending on her mood—a light blue when she was anxious, a deeper, brighter blue when Lucy's antics made her laugh. They sparked with ice-fire when she came to the defense of her family, and hazed like the gray mist rolling in from the sea when desire overtook her.

For she had felt desire for him. Of that Robert was certain. Her whole face had softened with it, and her body melted against his, while her mouth had been warm and tantalizing, her tongue sliding back and forth against his, the taste of her filling him, as heady as any spirits he had ever imbibed. He remembered her lavender scent and the little mewls of pleasure she'd made as he wrapped his arms around her slender body.

Several weeks of good food had taken the sharp edges from her frame and filled out her curves. There were roses in her cheeks and her hair held the luster of fine silk, cool and soft beneath his fingers. He'd wanted to wrap it around his hands, draw her closer, feel her press her soft breasts to him, cushion his hardened body against hers…

"Are you planning to answer?" His father's irritated

voice acted like cold water on his skin, making Robert start. The earl studied him, one eyebrow raised.

"I'm sorry," said Robert. "I was—lost in my own thoughts for a moment." *And if you think I will share them, you are very much mistaken.* "What was the question?"

"Question?" The earl's eyebrows lowered, all but hiding his eyes. "You've been wool gathering, boy. It's no wonder your tutor gets so cross with you."

"My—tutor?"

"Threatened to leave if you don't buck up. You're becoming unmanageable. Soon, the only people I'll be able to hire will be sergeants from the army. They'll whip you into shape."

Robert's heart sank. Father had been lucid since their arrival until now, and Robert had dared to hope the worst of his illness had passed. The earl was physically frail, but there'd been nothing wrong with his mind. Until now.

"I'm sorry, sir." It was the best Robert could do. He knew Jessica pandered to him, acting as if they truly were reliving the time where his mind had taken him rather than trying to coax him back to the here and now, but Robert wasn't altogether certain that was the best course of action. However, since he wasn't sure that arguing with Father was the right thing to do either, the ambiguous apology would serve.

Ben leaned forward and pinned Robert with a stern stare. "Papa ask, what first one?"

"Pardon?" Robert studied Ben, searching for a clue to help him make sense of what he'd said.

Father rolled his eyes. "Your first incident," he said, as if the previous moment's confusion had never happened. Robert was grateful it had passed so quickly. There were times when Father was lost in the past for hours. There had even been one time when he was *non compos mentis* for nearly a week. Perhaps he was getting better after all.

"Where were you when the first incident happened, and what was it?" The earl took another healthy gulp of his brandy, then filled his rummer again. "If we can find the first incident, mayhap we can work out who was upset with you at that time. Which, in turn, will lead us to the villain, and the end of the attacks."

That made sense. "I was…" Robert stopped. He had been about to say he was in Dorset, where the poacher's shot narrowly missed taking his head from his shoulders, but even as he remembered that incident, he realized it was not the first. There had been at least one accident before that. "Here."

"In Barwell?"

"At Carrow House. I tripped on the stairs and might have broken my neck. Luckily, I grabbed at the balustrade and stopped my fall, suffering no more than a strained shoulder."

Robert had been hurrying downstairs, intent on his plans for the day, when he'd trodden on Barnaby's wooden horse, which had been left on the step. Even then, he might have come off with nothing worse than a stumble and a few choice words aimed at his brother's nanny for allowing the child to play there, but the stair rod had also come loose and the carpet had moved, literally taking the ground from beneath him. It had shaken him; his shoulder had hurt like the devil, and he had limped for an hour or so until the twist in his ankle righted itself.

He grinned. "I doubt, however, that Barnaby deliberately intended to assassinate me. Boys his age tend not to be cold-hearted murderers." Although, when he'd told the nurse to be more careful she was adamant that Barnaby had not left the toy there, and she had no idea how it had made its way from the nursery.

"It isn't funny, Robert," said Father. "You might have been killed."

"I wasn't."

"Damn it, Robert!"

Ben gasped. "That naughty word."

Father took a deep breath. "Yes. Yes, it is, and I apologize for it. Your brother is sometimes enough to make a saint swear." He turned back to Robert. "Please be careful," he said, an anxious appeal in his eyes. "You are very much needed here. Ben will rely on your help when he takes the title."

Robert gave his father a sidelong look. He did not like the way this conversation was going. Father may not be robust, but he was not at death's door, either.

"I'm not being maudlin," said the earl, waving his hand as if to ward off Robert's objections. "My health is deteriorating, and I suspect time is not my friend. You are needed."

They shared a look. There was no denying his father was not the man he'd been, no matter how Robert might wish it otherwise. Which meant that Robert would be needed, whether the earldom was in Father's hands or Ben's.

"I'll be here," he said.

"Now," said the earl, and he levered himself out of his chair. "Shall we join the ladies?"

Chapter Fifteen

While the gentlemen enjoyed their brandy, the ladies sat in the drawing room and drank tea. The room was large and comfortable, its white walls embossed with gilt curlicues, which also decorated the black metal fire guard. Gold embroidery covered the white cushions on the cream sofa and matching armchairs. Occasional tables were placed around the room and a pianoforte stood near one wall under a picture of the present countess.

Wedgwood Willow bowls were in abundance, and the carpet, which covered the middle of the polished wood floor, picked up the blue of these bowls, mixing it with gold and cream. Altogether, the room had an expensive, delicate atmosphere.

The countess continued to be polite but distant, and Jane felt that she was merely being tolerated. Every time she said something, the countess looked at her as if listening carefully, then she nodded, her expression unchanging as she said, "How interesting," until Jane wanted to scream at her to be truthful and admit she was bored.

Mama sat, busying herself by darning one of Ben's stockings, though Jane was at a loss to know where she'd got it from, because she hadn't been to her room to fetch it.

The countess poured the tea, then studied Mama for

some moments. "There is no need to do that for dear Benedict, Mrs. Winter," she said, and her condescending tone made Jane bristle. "Whatever the privations of his past, he is heir to the earldom now and, as such, can afford new stockings."

Mama smiled at the countess. It was a smile Jane had seen before, a polite curving of the lips that in no way denoted pleasure. "There is still wear in these," she said. Her voice was carefully modulated, not a hint of emotion in it.

Say nothing more, if you have any sense, Jane silently advised the countess.

The countess, of course, did not heed the advice Jane had willed upon her. "What is the point?"

Mama's stare could have frozen the water in the earl's lake. "Willful waste makes for woeful want."

"Understood. And frugality is, undoubtedly, a virtue. At Carrow House, though, we have servants to do the mending."

"Ah, but I like to be occupied. Idle hands are the devil's workshop, are they not?"

Jane looked up at the ornate ceiling and wondered how Robert and Ben were faring with the earl. She would wager the atmosphere in the dining room was a great deal more cordial than it was in here. The earl had seemed pleasant, as warm as his wife was cold, and genuinely overjoyed to see Ben. But then, had he not been the sort of man to welcome his long lost, mentally challenged son, Jane did not think Robert would have brought them here.

Robert was compassionate and considerate, and from the first he had treated Ben exactly as he should. He'd never been condescending or mocking, like so many others had over the years. In fact, apart from that one moment on their first meeting in Bloomfold High Street, he had never reacted to Ben in any way that could be construed as objectionable. Now that Jane knew the truth of Ben's heritage, that moment of staring, which had so incensed her at the time, was far more understandable to her.

Over the weeks, Jane had watched Ben model himself on Robert, growing in confidence and stature with every day spent in his brother's company. Tonight, when both Robert and the earl had invited Ben to stay for brandy, his chest had puffed out so that Jane feared for his waistcoat buttons, and his smile was so wide it split his face. Robert had told Ben he would stay because he was a gentleman, and Ben had been beside himself with glee.

That instinctive knowledge of Ben's needs was just one of the things Jane loved about Robert.

She tensed, the smile sliding from her face. *Loved*? Surely, she meant *liked*. She didn't *love* anything about any man. She had learned not to do that four years ago, and it was not a lesson that bore repeating. She liked Robert for his kindness, his honor, and his integrity. She enjoyed his sense of humor and his conversation, the many interests they held in common. His handsome face was alluring, as was the way his broad shoulders filled his coat and the muscles in his thighs gave his breeches a good shape. Then there was the way his dark hair flopped over his forehead, drawing attention to the mischief and laughter in his deep brown eyes, the dimple in his cheek, which appeared only when his smile was genuine, and the way his kisses made her feel: warm and content, and wanting more.

But admiring these things did not mean she was in love. Did they?

Unsettled by her thoughts, Jane straightened, forced Robert from her mind, and concentrated on the conversation within this room. Mama was still darning the stocking, a slight smile on her face. Her expression could be interpreted as one of contented serenity, but Jane knew otherwise. She had just put Lady Barwell in her place and was relishing the satisfaction.

The countess, however, was not ready to concede defeat. "Idle hands are the devil's workshop." She repeated Mama's words and the sour expression on her face said they tasted bitter to her. She sniffed, contemptuously. "The Book of Proverbs, is it not?" She grinned, and Jane was reminded of a cat about to pounce on a bird. "Are you able to read your scriptures, then, Mrs. Winter?"

Jane bristled at the blatant attempt to bait Mama. Their family may never have been wealthy, and since papa's death the situation had become dire at times, but they were not heathens, and their education was as sound as Lady Barwell's.

Mama inclined her head, acknowledging the barb, but her smile did not waver. "I most certainly am," she said. "And I do. Daily. In fact, I consider the times when I read and contemplate the Bible to be golden. Although the phrase I used just now is not to be found within that holy book. Chaucer used it in his 'Tale of Melibee.' A writer of very droll prose, Mr. Chaucer. I am sure you must have enjoyed the Canterbury tales?"

The countess' expression was stony. "I haven't had the pleasure of reading them," she said, her voice low and curt, as if the words were forced out between gritted teeth.

"Oh, you should," answered Mama. "Some are exceedingly funny—if a little risqué. Although Melibee is tedious, so I wouldn't recommend it as your first one." She turned her attention back to Ben's stocking. Lady Barwell glowered at her. Jane studied the teacup she held and concentrated on not grinning.

After a moment, Lady Barwell turned her attention back to Jane. "Mrs. Frobisher," she said, her smile flickering back to life. "You are a widow?"

"I am, yes." As always, Jane mentally crossed her fingers against the lie. After telling the same tale for so many years, she thought it might have become easier, but it hadn't.

"What did your husband do?"

"Do?" Jane frowned, confused. This question had never been asked before, so she had no ready answer, and she wasn't an accomplished enough liar for something to trip effortlessly from her tongue. She cast around for a respectable profession she should claim for the dear, departed Mr. Frobisher. Before she could think of one, Mama intervened.

"My son-in-law didn't *do* anything," she said without looking up from her darning. "He was a gentleman." Jane breathed a silent sigh of relief.

The countess nodded. "I assume he left you well provided for?"

Jane's eyes widened. The question would certainly have been contemplated by her acquaintances ever since she'd first told the world of Mr. Frobisher's untimely death, but it should never have been asked of Jane to her face. That a countess could be so rude left her speechless.

Again, Mama stepped in. "My daughter is able to

manage."

Lady Barwell nodded and gave Jane a practiced look of sympathy that made the hairs on the back of Jane's neck stand to attention. "But then, you have no real cause for concern, do you?" She smiled and shards of ice seemed to pierce the air. "You are still young, and passably pretty. You must have hopes of marrying again."

Marrying again? Or rather, marrying at all. Jane had accepted the impossibility of that the day Sydney had rejected her and Mama had come to the rescue by inventing a decent but dead husband. Mr. Frobisher had saved the family from ruin, but in doing so, he had doomed Jane to a lifetime of spinsterhood. For how could she ever marry now? If she wished to wed, she must tell the groom the truth about herself and Lucy. Not only would any decent man be disappointed she had lied to him, he would probably be disgusted at her wantonness. Even if he did not immediately turn away from her, he would wonder when her immorality would surface again, and that could not bode well for a happy union.

She thought of how she might confess her past to Robert. No doubt he would listen without interrupting until she'd told him all; his good manners would ensure that. But what then?

Robert was a man of honor and integrity, the kind of man who would search diligently for his brother rather than take Ben's not-insignificant birthright for himself. Surely, such a man could no more accept Jane's dishonor than he could fly to the moon. The thought of his disappointment, the contempt in which he must hold her once he knew, caused a sharp pain in Jane's breast. She fought the urge to massage it.

No. Robert must never know.

His stepmother smiled at Jane, benignly. "You like my stepson—my younger stepson—very much, do you not?"

The question made Jane wonder if she had voiced her thoughts aloud. Her horror must have shown on her face, because Lady Barwell laughed, softly.

"I have eyes. I saw the way you look at Robert," she continued. Again, the look of practiced and calculated sympathy softened her features. "I would not be doing my duty if I didn't warn you not to set too much store by him. I would hate to see him hurt you."

That was not what Jane had expected her to say. "Why would he hurt me?"

The woman's laughter was brittle. "Oh, he will not *mean* to hurt you. He never *means* to hurt anybody." She leaned forward, as if conveying a confidence. "My stepson is altogether too charming for anybody's good. You would not be the first young woman to have her heart broken and, dare I say, her dreams dashed by him. Shall I ring for more tea? The gentlemen will join us soon."

Mama and the countess engaged in further conversation, but Jane did not hear them as the shock of the woman's words settled over her. She was hardly able to think past the pounding of her heart and the taunting, ringing voice in her head.

He never means to hurt anybody. Too charming for anybody's good. You would not be the first young woman to have her heart broken...

No! The word was so vehemently expressed that Jane looked around, thinking she must have said it aloud.

Neither Mama nor Lady Barwell paid Jane the slightest attention and she released the breath she'd held in trepidation and retreated into quieter thoughts.

The fact was Robert could, indeed, hurt Jane badly. For one thing, Jane did like him, very much, in every way it was possible to like someone. His smile, and the tormenting dimple it brought to his cheek, made her heart skip. The merest brush of his hand against hers sent jolts of electricity coursing through her, even when she felt it through her thickest gloves. She lay awake at night, thinking of him, and wondering what he thought of her. When she slept, he invaded her dreams. She looked forward to their conversations, the bright banter, the intelligent puns, the discussion of shared interests. Seeing him with Lucy filled her with warmth, and his kisses…oh, his kisses!

She had a vision of him leaning toward her, his eyes dark with desire, the warmth of his breath caressing her skin. She smelled the cologne he used, the mint of his tooth powder, the unique scent of him as he came nearer, nearer, nearer… Then, at the very moment their lips touched she heard the countess' words of warning:

You wouldn't be the first young woman to have her heart broken by him.

Could that be true? Could Robert be so callous, so self-serving, as to allow a woman to be hurt by his unthinking actions? Everything within Jane screamed that it wasn't true. He would not be so cruel. But then, why would Lady Barwell lie about it? Why would a stepmother, even one with so obviously chilled a relationship with her stepson, besmirch his good name? What could she hope to gain by it? She had nothing to gain. No reason to lie that Jane could think of.

On top of which, Jane knew her own ability to judge was flawed when it came to men. She hadn't believed Sydney was the sort of man to seduce and then abandon a woman of good birth, either, and look where that had got her.

She was still tying herself into anxious knots over the countess's words when the gentlemen came into the room. She looked up and her eyes met Robert's. He smiled at her. Nervous, she bit her bottom lip as he took a step toward her. Her heart began to pound desperately, and she felt the heat rising from her chest, through her throat, into her face.

I've seen the way you look at my stepson.

Were her feelings so obvious? They must be, if Lady Barwell had noted them on first acquaintance. And if she had noticed, then surely, so had he…Oh Lord, how could she converse with him now? What on earth could she say that wouldn't cause embarrassment to them both?

At the last moment, Ben darted past Robert and sat in the seat his brother had clearly intended to occupy. Jane tried to hide her relief as Robert smoothly changed tack and sat in a chair on the other side of the room. The distance between them made Jane feel something, but she couldn't have said whether she was happy for it or sad.

"I drink brandy," said Ben. "Not like it. But I still a gentleman."

Jane smiled and gave her attention to her brother— no, *Robert's* brother. "You didn't like it?" she asked.

"No. It like when you eat something from the garden and not wash soil off first."

That was not what Jane had expected him to say, but still, Ben knew what he had tasted, and it wasn't for her to correct him.

He went into a long monologue about how he was a gentleman now, and that meant staying with the other men after dinner and not coming into the drawing room with the ladies anymore. Jane listened and nodded encouragement when it was relevant, and spent the rest of the evening trying not to let her mind, or her eyes, wander over to where Robert sat, talking with the rest of the company.

****

Robert had been tired when he went to bed. He'd stifled more than a few yawns and every muscle was heavily relaxed, but when he got to his chamber his mind seemed to wake again. Thoughts plagued him, tumbling over each other, tangling as they fought to surface and be examined.

His father's health was worse. The earl was gaunter and more frail than he had been when Robert left on his quest, and the episodes of senility were still present. There had been more than one of them this evening, and that was a concern; to Robert's knowledge, Father had never slipped into his own world quite so often before.

But what was to be done about it? As far as Robert was aware, there was little in the way of treatment for the earl's condition. In fact, far from looking kindly on his illness, many people would call him mad, and fear of him may well become an issue. An ordinary man afflicted in such a way would likely be incarcerated in an asylum, or even a prison, where he would be shackled and beaten, bled and purged, all in an effort to reform him. Robert had considered such treatment inhumane even before he had read the works of Philippe Pinel, who insisted that madness was a disease, not a crime, and should be treated as such. Unfortunately, most people did not agree; Pinel himself had been lucky to escape prison for voicing such opinions. If society could treat a medical man in that way, they were unlikely to listen to Robert, or anyone like him.

Father's title would protect him to an extent. The king had not been imprisoned when he became ill, but lived in seclusion at Windsor. Perhaps the same arrangement could be made for Father? Carrow House and its grounds were extensive enough that his confinement would not seem like incarceration, and they had the means to hire nurses. Robert could act as his father's Regent—although he couldn't see the earl agreeing to that, which posed quite the problem. If he tried to take control without his father's consent, word would surely get out, and the very thing Robert hoped to avoid might happen. To say nothing of those who would consider the entire family tainted by madness and, therefore, bad blood. Especially when people thought of the earl's illness together with the news of Ben, thirty years old but still, in many ways, an innocent child. He knew, from things Mrs. Winter had said, that people had already accused him of being a punishment for the sins of his parents. How much worse would that be when it was known his father was also afflicted? People would assume the condition was hereditary, and the entire family would become pariahs. No respectable woman would marry Robert, nor Barnaby in years to come. No businessman would deal with them.

If either Ben or Father had been an isolated case, the only one afflicted in an otherwise hale and hearty family, it might not be so devastating. Oh, there would be some who would gossip behind their hands; there always were.

On the whole, though, most would not consider one incidence as reason to condemn the entire bloodline. But two, in two generations…

Should Ben be rejected by the Society Robert had forced him to join, if people were cruel, Robert would never forgive himself. He'd grown fond of his brother and hated the thought that anyone else might hate him simply because he was Ben.

Robert wasn't the only one who would be heartbroken at such an outcome. Janey would be too, and she would blame Robert for it. Rightly so, though the thought that she might detest him made his stomach churn, and a sharp pain filled his chest.

She had looked uncertain in the drawing room tonight. He started toward her, but she'd seemed uncomfortable, as if she'd rather he didn't. That only made him more determined, anxious to know what had overset her. If he'd done something wrong, he deserved the opportunity to put it right. Again, his stomach churned, and that pain in his chest stabbed at him. He could not, would not, be at odds with Janey, not if he could possibly avoid it.

He'd been halfway to her when Ben cut him off. His brother was eager to tell her where he had been and what he'd done, and after that, the chance to speak with her never came again. It worried him now. How could he make amends when he didn't know his crime?

He punched the pillow into the shape he wanted and resolved to tackle her about it in the morning, then closed his eyes and tried to relax into sleep. If he was lucky, she would forgive him whatever transgression he'd made, and they would cry friends again.

If he was lucky. His father's words came back to

him. *"Either you are the unluckiest man in England, or somebody has taken great exception to you."*

As far as Robert knew, he had given nobody cause to dislike him. At least, not enough that they would want him hurt or dead. He was an easygoing man, on the whole. He tried not to cause offense when he didn't have to do so, and most people parted from him on good terms. He'd bullied no one at school or University, cheated no one in business, taken no one's fortune at cards and, to his knowledge, he had never been anyone's bitter rival in love. No woman had ever interested him enough to want to be.

Again, he thought of Janey. He remembered how she'd stood in her Mama's cottage in Bloomfold and announced she and Lucy would not be left behind while her mother and brother travelled to Barwell. She'd stood, ready to defy them all, her eyes sparking bright blue, ice and fire. Her blonde hair was slightly disheveled where she'd removed her bonnet, and wisps of it shone in the sunshine that seemed to come through the window just to illuminate her. She'd been magnificent. He had been spellbound.

Inwardly he had rejoiced at the thought of spending more time with her, even as he wondered if it was prudent to do so. He enjoyed her company, but at the same time, it grew more and more difficult when, every time he saw her, all he wanted to do was take her into his arms, hold her close, feel the warmth of her against him, her soft breasts pressed against his chest, her pulse beating with his, her lips warm and full and welcoming. He wanted her slender fingers to play in his hair, sending those delicious shudders through his scalp and down his spine, until his brain surrendered, all thought retreating as his blood flowed south and made him ache with need.

Just the remembrance of it threatened his control. How did the woman do that? She wasn't even present, and she brought him close to the edge. She filled his thoughts, visited his dreams, would not let him be.

Janey like Robert. Ben's words echoed in his brain.

"And Robert likes Janey," he whispered into the empty darkness.

The truth in the statement caught him by surprise. Robert liked Janey. He had feelings for her, and they were deeper than he'd imagined he could ever feel. Although he told himself, rather more quickly than was decent, they were merely feelings of lust, not love. Love wasn't like this.

Not that Robert had ever been in love, or even close to it, but surely, it could not be like this. This torment of wondering what the other person felt, the uncertainty over every word they said, every look they gave. The need to be with them as much as one could, to spend every waking hour with them, or thinking of them, dreaming of them, wondering what they would think of the things one saw, or heard, or came upon in the course of a day.

But then, what was love, if it was not those things?

He sat up in bed and stared, wide-eyed into the darkness. Was he in love with Janey? If he was, what did it mean? Could he, in all conscience, offer for her? Would she be willing to take him? He didn't think she would reject him because he was a penniless second son; she wasn't angling after the catch of the season or expecting vast wealth.

Nor did she care for the title. It wasn't a world she was accustomed to, after all.

He frowned. Ben was the heir apparent and would become the earl when Father died. However, given Ben's disabilities, it was unlikely he would produce an heir. Which meant that, one day, Robert, or Robert's son, would take the title. How would Janey feel about that?

Most women would see it as an advantage, something in Robert's favor. His Janey would probably hate the idea.

His Janey? Was she *his* Janey? Was she *his* anything? He huffed a humorless laugh. Here he was, worrying how hypothetical futures might affect her, and for aught he knew, it was moot because she felt nothing for him at all, let alone love!

The thoughts swirled round and round in his head, taking him first this way, then that. His eyes were heavy, and there was a dragging headache behind them, and he cursed his mind for being so active. He punched the pillow once more and willed himself to stop thinking and try to fall asleep.

It was a long time before he managed to do so.

Chapter Sixteen

Robert came to with a start. The sun was just beginning to lighten the sky, and all was quiet. His eyes were heavy and his head pounded, as if someone used it as an anvil. His forehead felt hot and clammy, there was a churning roil in his stomach, and that insistent stabbing pain in his chest.

He took deep breaths, trying to tamp down the nausea and pain, but it didn't help. Nor did the water he sipped from the glass on his nightstand. If he didn't know better, he would have said he was hungover, but that wasn't possible. He'd had only three rummers of brandy last night, and he'd drunk those on a full stomach. Although, he remembered now, the drink had tasted strange at first, as if it was corked. Could it have been off?

Really, what did that matter now? All that mattered at this moment was that he felt like death warmed over. The how and why of it was irrelevant.

Fresh air would help. A slow walk in the park would clear his head and help the nausea subside, at least enough that he could eat something to settle his stomach completely.

He dressed, making himself decent, if not exactly presentable, forgoing his cravat and stock, for the thought of those things around his throat made his stomach bubble in horror. It wasn't as if anyone would see him, was it? Save for a gamekeeper, and perhaps a poacher.

There wasn't a soul about as he crept out of the kitchen, through the gardens, and across the park to the lake. The pain in his chest subsided as he walked, and he wondered if he had strained his muscles, though he couldn't think how he might have done. Nor did he care. He was simply glad the pain was fading.

A morning fog hovered, thick and white, just above the ground, and the deer seemed to float on it, their legs invisible. Above the fog, the air was crisp and clean and fresh. The first birds chirped their good mornings. In the woods, a fox barked. The lake was calm, wisps of mist floating on it, giving it an otherworldly feeling, so that he wouldn't have been surprised if a hand had thrust through the surface, holding up a sword. He smiled at the image and breathed the damp air, listening to the soft plop and splashes of ducks diving for food, and the gentle buzz of early morning insects. The island in the center of the lake stood tall and proud, the summerhouse silhouetted against the pale sky like a castle on a cloud.

Robert stayed at the lakeside for a few minutes, savoring the peace and quiet, but it didn't stop the headache, or the churning in his stomach, or the acid taste on his tongue. His muscles ached and the pain in his chest threatened to return. Since movement had helped earlier, he walked around the lake and into the woods, along the trails he had roamed as a child. Then, he had been hunting tigers in the jungles of India, or following robbers to secret dens to steal back their ill-gotten treasures. Now he chased nothing more than well-being and an end to his malaise.

The churning in his stomach grew worse. His throat

shivered a moment before he leaned against a tree and cast up his accounts. He groaned and coughed and retched until his stomach was completely empty, and all he had left to expel was air. His stomach muscles cramped, and his chest felt tight, although thankfully the stabbing pain seemed to have disappeared. His throat hurt, and his mouth filled with a bitter, burning taste. The headache still pounded behind his eyes, and all he wanted to do was go back to the house, lie in his bed, and sleep it off.

He straightened, turned, and froze. There, on the path, watching him, eyes wide with horrified concern, was Janey Frobisher.

****

Jane woke early, even though sleep had not come easily to her last night. She had tossed and turned in the big comfortable bed, first covering herself with the blankets, then throwing them aside when she grew too warm. She lay on her back on one pillow but her neck ached, so she tried two. When that didn't help, she tossed them away and lay on her front, then pulled the pillows back into use when she lay on her side. Nothing helped, and it was only through sheer exhaustion that she'd finally fallen asleep sometime after the grandfather clock in the hall had boomed twelve times.

Now it was morning, though still early if the light coming through her window was any indication. The house was quiet, just the small sounds of servants going about their duties. Jane kicked off her blankets and slid from the high bed, padded over to the window and looked outside.

It had the makings of a beautiful day. The sky was already a pastel blue and glowing brighter by the second.

The sun was still low, almost resting on the horizon, pink and purple smudges surrounding its orange ball, and the few clouds were small and white and high. Dew glistened on the grass, looking exactly like the diamante lanterns of the Fairy Queen's ball Mama had described so vividly in her stories, while cobwebs were silver lace against the dark leaves of the bushes. Deer grazed lazily in the park, beyond which, only just visible, was the shimmer of the lake.

Jane sighed. If she must lose Ben, she couldn't ask for a more beautiful new home for him. Provided his true family loved him, and her first impressions were that they would, Ben would be very happy here.

She could be happy here too, she mused. She would love being able to walk in such a garden, enjoying the peace and solitude.

That wasn't an option for the long term, of course, but she saw no reason not to enjoy the privilege while she could. After nearly a week cooped up in a coach, a walk in the fresh air would do her a power of good. She could explore the garden, clear her head of the tormenting thoughts that had kept her awake, and settle herself before she had to meet everyone at breakfast.

She slipped out through a back door into an herb garden, where the scents of lavender and mint filled the air with hope and peacefulness. Delicate flowers flumed at one end, covering a trellis and splashing their colors all around. How fortunate Robert had been to grow up here, surrounded by all this beauty and peace. He must have had a very happy childhood, for who could not, in such a place?

Thinking of him made her wonder yet again at what Lady Barwell had said. *You wouldn't be the first young woman to have her heart broken by him.*

Jane could not believe Robert was as heartless and careless of the feelings of others as his stepmother suggested. Yes, he had kissed her and touched her in ways she should not have allowed, but did that make him an out-and-out philanderer?

The countess had gone out of her way to warn Jane away from him. Why? Was it a kindness to a young woman she perceived as naive? Or was it, as Jane suspected now she'd had time to think about it, to rid herself and her stepson of an unsuitable woman, clearing the way for a better bride? If that was her plan, it was wasted, for Robert had no intentions of marrying Jane.

Which was just as well. "All these machinations and politics are too much for me," she told the deer, who startled away as she crossed the park.

She skirted the lake, which was a great deal wider than it appeared in the view from her window. In the middle of the glittering water, an island held a summerhouse, surrounded by towering and overgrown rhododendron bushes. There was a boat jetty on the island, the sister of the jetty on the shore. Near to the shore's jetty was a boat shed, and Jane imagined summer days spent languishing in a boat, parasol protecting her from the sun while Robert rowed to the island. He would take off his coat in the heat and, as he rowed, his muscles would pull against his shirt, his skin showing dark beneath the translucent white linen, calling for her to reach out and touch it…

"That is beyond enough!" she told herself. A gathering of ducks quacked and flapped their wings against the water, as if agreeing. One bobbed his head under the water, his tail end standing upright, in criticism of her. She resisted the urge to put out her tongue at the judgmental bird. Instead, she walked around the lake and into the woods beside it, where she followed a narrow footpath between silver birch trees surrounded by tall, green fern fronds, snaking tendrils of convolvulus and occasional tangles of bramble. Birds gossiped noisily in the branches overhead, and a squirrel jumped from one tree to another, making the wood creak and the leaves rattle.

Suddenly she became aware of another sound, the sound of someone coughing and retching terribly. The poor soul sounded as if they were dying.

Unsure what she might find but unable to leave an ill person to fend for themselves when she might be able to help, Jane hurried around a bend in the path, and stopped short at the sight of Robert, leaning against a tree trunk, purging everything from his stomach.

****

Robert straightened and adjusted his coat. He was mortified. He hadn't expected anybody to be here but, if someone did have to see him in this state, why must it be Janey? He had no illusions about the way this would appear to her: bloodshot eyes, disheveled clothing, and retching—she would think he'd spent the night carousing, emptying the decanter and acting the indolent aristocrat. The moment he'd returned home, she would believe, he had taken up the worst habits of the idle rich. For reasons he could not explain, even to himself, it mattered to him that she did not think that.

He took a step toward her. "Janey…"

"You poor man," she whispered, and she reached out to him. "Was it something you ate?" She took his hand and led him back along the path toward the lake.

Robert went with her, hardly aware of what he was doing. He stumbled on the uneven ground, and she tightened her grip, steadying him. Her fingers burned their imprints into his arm, warming his blood and calming the pounding in his head.

"You look terrible," she said. "Your face is so gray, and your breath..." She wrinkled her nose.

"I'm sorry," he mumbled.

"Don't be sorry." She smiled. "You can't help being ill. But you need to drink."

He gave her a weak smile. He had a feeling it was drinking something which had caused this in the first place.

That made him think of his father. The earl had drunk as much of the tainted brandy as Robert had, and he was not a strong man. Robert prayed it hadn't had so violent an effect on him, for he wasn't sure the earl's weakened constitution could stand up to it.

"I don't suppose you carry a hip flask?" Janey continued, brisk and in control. "I suppose it's not something you would carry in the grounds of your own home, is it? Is the water in the lake drinkable? At a pinch, it might help, although if you can wait until we return to the house where I can make you a cup of tea, I believe that would be better."

"I can wait," he said. His voice was low and raspy, and nothing like he normally sounded.

"All right." She smiled, sympathetically. "Let me know if you need to stop and...well, let me know." She colored and looked across the park to the house. To Robert, every muscle aching, it seemed a thousand miles away. He just wanted to crawl into bed and lie there until he died.

****

Jane didn't think she had ever seen anyone look as sick as Robert did this morning and still remain on their feet. His face was gray, which made his swollen lips look redder than if he had worn rouge. His eyes had sunk into his head, and were surrounded by blue-black circles. His hair stood up; she suspected he hadn't brushed it this morning. Hardly surprising if he felt as ill as he looked.

If she didn't know better, she would have suspected he was hungover, but she had seen him the night before and he had been sober. All he'd drunk after he came into the drawing room was tea, and she didn't believe he would then have gone on to drink his father's cellar dry when everyone else went to bed. But if he wasn't over-imbibing, it must have been something he'd eaten.

She thought of all they'd had at dinner. A beef consommé. It couldn't be that. That's what they fed to invalids to aid their recovery, so it wasn't likely to cause illness. The fish had been succulent and fresh, and the meat course had been cooked to perfection. Syllabub, fruits, the cheese and bread, all had been exactly as they ought to be. The wine had been fresh and fruity, not heavy. And none of it had had any adverse effect upon her. Since she was not as used to rich foods as he was, she would have expected it to be herself who reacted to anything bad, not Robert. It had to have been something he'd had that Jane had not.

The only thing she could think of that fit that criteria was the brandy. A memory came: Ben sitting in the drawing room, his face scrunched into a very expressive grimace. "Not like brandy," he'd said. "Like when you eat something from the garden and not wash soil off first." Last night, she'd been amused by his description.

Now, she pondered it carefully.

"Ben said the brandy tasted strange," she told Robert,

"He did?" Robert stopped and stared at her. "He said so in the dining room, too. I thought he just didn't like it."

"Well, that's true. He didn't." But now she thought about it, that didn't ring true. Jane remembered one Christmas when her father had given Ben a drink of brandy, much to Mama's consternation. "He's a young man," Papa had excused. "And it's Christmas." As Jane recalled, Ben had liked the taste well enough then. But last night... "He described the taste," she said, "and he knew it shouldn't taste that way, because it wasn't his first time drinking it."

"Did he say it tasted muddy?" asked Robert, staring toward the house, his expression thoughtful. "Bitter?"

Clearly Robert had thought the same as Ben—there was something wrong with it. Which begged another question, which she voiced before she could stop herself. "Why did you go on to drink more of it, then?"

His grin was sheepish, and Jane realized she had used her Scolding Mother tone on him, the one she normally reserved for Lucy's minor transgressions. Horror filled her. She had no right to talk to him in that way, even if his actions were foolhardy. Still, his grin indicated he had taken no offense, for which she was relieved.

"In my defense," he said, "after the first few sips, the strange taste disappeared."

"Disappeared?" That made no sense at all. "How could it disappear?"

"I don't know. It just did. One minute the brandy

was strong and bitter, and the next…" he frowned, moaned at the way the movement pulled at his forehead, and massaged his temple. "The next moment it was mellow to the point of tastelessness and…" He stopped, his eyes clouded with anxiety. "The tea we drank in the drawing room. How strong was it?"

She blinked at the strange question. Just when she thought this conversation couldn't become any more bizarre. "The tea?" she asked when he continued to watch her, clearly waiting for an answer. "It was…it tasted as tea normally tastes. Why?" What on earth did that have to do with spoiled brandy?

"It didn't taste bland? Watery?"

She shook her head. He rubbed his hand across his jaw. She heard the soft rasp of his gloves on his morning beard and wondered what it would feel like to stroke her own fingers over the stubble. Would it be rough and prickly, the way it looked, or soft and cool like the hair on his head?

Questions she should not be contemplating at any time, but especially not now, when he was clearly ill. The taste of the tea clearly worried him, though Jane could not begin to understand why it would.

"I couldn't taste it," he said, softly, bringing her back to the conversation with a jolt.

"The tea?"

He nodded. "Nor the sugar biscuits. They tasted like dust." He thought for a moment. "I think somehow, the brandy destroyed my sense of taste."

"And then made you ill? Is that possible?" Jane knew little about brandy, or any other spirits, except that they could take away a person's power of reasoning. But then, if they could take away a man's ability to control his actions, his speech and the power to remain upright, perhaps they could also take his ability to taste. But after just one mouthful?

"Thank goodness Ben didn't drink any more of it, then," she said, shuddering at the thought of Ben being as ill as Robert. "He is the world's worst patient," she explained with a smile.

Robert did not smile back. "Ben didn't," he said, his lips pressed together and his face grim. A feeling of dread crawled through Jane's chest at the way he now looked. "But my father did. And he was unwell to begin with."

He hurried across the park to the house with an energy Jane would not have believed he possessed scant moments ago. She had to run to catch him up.

"Robert?" she called to him. He was frightening her.

"I need to make sure my father isn't suffering the way I am," he replied. "He's weak from his illness. I don't know how this would affect him." He quickened his pace.

Jane picked up her skirts and hurried after him.

Chapter Seventeen

Jane followed Robert through the back door and into the kitchen. He strode on, oblivious to the shocked servants staring after him. This would cause talk and speculation in the servants' hall when they ate breakfast, Jane thought as she raced to keep up with him. She could hear them now: "Mr. Robert was out with that Mrs. Frobisher, and not a chaperone in sight! And before breakfast!"

Perhaps Jane could convince her maid of the innocent nature of the morning, and the maid could make sure everyone else knew the truth. Although whether they would believe it was beyond her control.

They went through the door into the main part of the house. Once in the hallway, Robert stopped. He still looked gray, his features haggard, but there was more energy about him now and he didn't look as if he would be sick again.

"I need to go to my father," he said. "I can meet you in the breakfast room shortly." Jane nodded. A dish of tea would be welcome, although she knew she would not eat anything before Robert returned. Having seen how sick he had been this morning, she was far too anxious for his less robust father to have any appetite.

There was nobody in the breakfast room. Jane made her way over the thick Chinese rug to the sideboard, intending to pour herself a dish of tea. Through the open door, she heard Robert's boot heels sound against the black and white tiles of the hallway.

"William," he addressed the footman. "Is my father out of bed yet?"

The footman's voice was respectful. "Not to my knowledge, sir."

"Thank you. I'll go up and see him…"

"You will do no such thing!" The countess' tone brooked no argument. Jane stiffened and instinctively took a step back from the sideboard, feeling as if she shouldn't be touching anything there. She looked to the door and saw the footman hurry past, clearly unwilling to be party to this new conversation. If conversation was what it could be called, Jane thought, and she grimaced as the countess let Robert know her opinion.

"You have not been here these last few months, but I have. While you've been running about the country on a fool's errand, I have been here taking care of my husband's health, and I won't…"

"It was not a fool's errand."

"I beg to differ. In your mad dash to play the hero, all you have succeeded in doing is bringing that boy here, where he can't possibly be of any use and merely upsets your father."

Jane stiffened, her back straightening, adding inches to her height. The hairs at the nape of her neck stood to attention and her hands balled into fists. Lady Barwell was going to apologize for that. She took a step forward, then stopped as she heard Robert, his voice low and even, and cold enough to freeze the sea in summer.

"That 'boy' is a full-grown man and almost as old as you. He is also heir to your husband's title and will one day be head of this family. You might wish to remember that."

"Don't you dare threaten me, Robert Carrow! You don't want him here any more than I do, and for far less altruistic reasons."

"If I didn't want him, I would not have searched for him."

That, Jane thought, was true. Lady Barwell's argument made no sense. And what could possibly be altruistic about rejecting poor Ben?

"You searched for him because you said you would. Had you not done so, the value of your word would have been called into question. I'll wager you never expected to find him, though. Now you have, and he has usurped your position…"

"I have never coveted the title, or anything else, and I resent the inference that I have. I hope it all belongs to my father for years to come."

"As do I." Lady Barwell's voice cracked, and suddenly Jane felt sorry for her. She'd been cold and aloof, less than welcoming to Ben and Jane's family, but it seemed she really did love her husband.

"I care for my husband very much, sir," the countess continued, echoing Jane's thoughts, "which is why I am appalled at the cavalier way in which you undermine him."

Undermine him? Jane frowned. Whatever could the countess mean? The love and concern Robert had for his father was plain to anyone with sight, and obvious in the lengths he'd gone to in order to find Ben and bring him home.

"You think bringing that boy—man—into the family will aid your father? You are much mistaken. All you have done is create more trouble for him."

"I don't follow your logic, madam." Robert's tone boded ill for the countess. Jane licked her lips, nervously, glad it was not she who faced him at this moment.

Lady Barwell was either unaware of the anger rising inside her stepson or she didn't care. "Don't be obtuse, Robert," she said, in a voice that have could have cut glass. "Not only have you brought another family member to confuse your father when, Lord knows, he is confused enough already—forgetting us, losing recognition, and unable to make sense of our presence—but you've done so with a son who is, to say the least, deficient."

Jane's cheeks heated and her eyes burned, and she swallowed hard to push down her anger at Lady Barwell's callous words. Callous, and untrue. She wanted to storm out of the breakfast room and tell the lady so, to her head. She saw herself, hands on hips and head high, boring holes through the countess with her furious stare, daring her to say such a thing again. Ben was not deficient and nobody had the right to call him that. Ben was different, but he was not deficient.

It was all Jane could do to rein in her temper and stay where she was. She wasn't supposed to be privy to this conversation, and it would be wrong of her to show herself now. Of course, Robert knew she was here, and he was probably aware she could hear them, but the countess didn't and, if she discovered Jane, it might make things worse.

On that thought, Jane stepped back, away from the sight line of anyone passing the doorway, and forced herself to stay quiet.

"Deficient, madam?" asked Robert. "There is nothing deficient about my brother."

"Of course there is! He's a—child in a man's body."

Robert laughed, but there was no humor in the sound. "Would that we could all be thus. The world would be simpler, and far happier."

"That's absurd."

"Is it? Even the Bible recommends it. '*Verily, I say unto you, except you become as little children, ye shall not enter into the Kingdom of Heaven.*'"

"For goodness' sake! That does not mean what you think it means."

"Enlighten me. What does it mean?"

Jane listened, intently. She couldn't think of an alternative meaning for the verse, either.

"We are not talking about the Kingdom of Heaven! We are talking of an earldom here on earth. One your father frets over, worrying about its future, what will become of it after his… He worries about it. Now you bring him an heir who, by nobody's fumes of fancy, could ever be capable of taking the reins."

That much, Jane conceded, was true. Ben did not have it in him to do the tasks required of an earl. He would need help, a kind of regent, when he took the title.

"I will be here, at his side," said Robert, his tone suggesting that should be obvious.

"I sincerely hope you will," answered Lady Barwell. "It will not, however, save your father from his anxieties. The worry will undermine his health and undo all my hard work."

"Your hard work?" asked Robert. He sounded incredulous.

"Ministering to him. Nursing him when he took a turn for the worse."

"Mopped his fevered brow, did you?"

The countess cleared her throat. "More than once," she said, primly. "While you were gone, I looked after him, and this I can tell you. He will not be receiving visitors today." Her words sounded as if she thought they should be final. Which probably meant she would now make her way into the breakfast room, find Jane, and know she'd overheard.

The French windows were open to the terrace. Jane moved to them, intending to hide out there until the lady had gone.

"I am hardly a visitor, Jessica," argued Robert as Jane reached the windows.

The countess' footsteps stopped. "Do you not care for his wellbeing?" Her voice had gone up a notch. "He is unwell and needs his rest."

Jane reached the doorway into the garden. The breeze coming through it billowed the curtains and riffled her hair.

"You are not good for your father's health," Lady Barwell continued. "One evening in your company and he has taken a significant turn for the worse. I know not…"

Jane did not discover what Lady Barwell knew not, because she stepped out onto the terrace and moved away before anyone saw her lurking there.

The early morning sun was warm on her face, and its brightness enhanced the colors of the flowers growing in pots and planters around the edges of the flagstone terrace. Windows gleamed. Across the park the morning mist had burned away, leaving the grass an emerald green. The lake shone silver on the horizon, the island with its summerhouse a dark silhouette at its heart.

Farther along the terrace, Jane slipped through

another open window, into the library. This room was darker than the breakfast room, the window drapes heavier, and the floor-to-ceiling shelves of books on three walls swallowed much of the light that did find its way in. The furniture was dark too—a walnut table, dark leather armchairs, a tantalus in one corner. The room had a masculine feel, and Jane suspected this was very much the earl's sanctuary, somewhere his wife never ventured.

That made her think again about what she had just heard. *Do you not have a care for his wellbeing?*

Jane pursed her lips, angry on Robert's behalf. It was plain to see he cared for his father deeply and would do nothing to put him in danger. Quite apart from that, Robert would not hurt anybody deliberately. He was not that kind of man. He was kind and caring—had he not risked his life to save Lucy? He'd shown patience and understanding to Ben, too. Indeed, it was because he cared that he'd sought Ben in the first place. How could Lady Barwell think otherwise?

Cynical thoughts invaded. Lady Barwell was a shrewd woman who knew exactly how to get her way. She'd done it to Jane last night, planting doubts about Robert's character. Now, she worked her dark magic on Robert. The woman knew he would not risk his father's health, and she used that in an effort to bar him from his father's company.

Why would she do that? Completely isolating her husband from those he loved seemed extreme. Not even the most anxious of devoted wives would go so far, surely?

Something was wrong, Jane could feel it, but she didn't know what it was. Yesterday, the countess had appeared aloof, cold, and even uncaring. Today she was so concerned that she declared her husband's own son a threat to him. She could have been two different women.

Then there was Robert's illness this morning. True, he hadn't shown the confusion the earl exhibited, but physically, perhaps the two men shared symptoms. Was it possible the only thing wrong with the earl was that he'd been drinking tainted brandy? Mayhap, over a prolonged period, bad spirits could cloud a person's mind as well as unsettling their stomach. After all, good spirits could do so, if one imbibed too much. Jane was no expert, but it made sense to her. If getting rid of the tainted brandy restored Robert's father to health…

She must find Robert and tell him her suspicions, and… No. No, she couldn't do that. Robert loved his father, and it would pain him deeply to be given hope that was then snatched away again if Jane were wrong. Jane would not cause him that sort of pain. She cared far too much for him to do that.

It would be better to discover all she could about Lord Barwell's illness first. Then, when she was certain of her facts, she could tell Robert and he could put it right. And if it turned out the earl's condition was not caused by whatever had made Robert sick, well, he would not be hurt by her conjecture.

But how was Jane to discover the facts? She wrung her hands together and paced the long room. The only sure way would be to visit the earl and learn what she could at his sickbed.

No! She could do no such thing! It would be highly improper to visit a man in his bedchamber, even if he was supposedly at death's doorstep.

But how else could she discover the truth?

"I need to know," she whispered. "I'm supposed to

be a widow. It's not so bad for a widow to enter a man's chamber." Even to herself, she did not sound convincing.

An image came to her, of Robert wearing a black armband and an expression of such grief, it broke her heart. She reached out to him, and he turned dull eyes to her, saying, *You could have saved him*, in accusation.

Jane's heart pounded. She couldn't bear to see him in such anguish. She couldn't live with the idea that she might have prevented it and instead had done nothing.

She would go to the earl now. She would discover what she needed to know, and if she was correct, things could be put right. She could make Robert happy, and Ben, and Lady Barwell too. The woman would be glad to have her husband healthy once more.

Besides, if she was careful and quick, who would know? She could be in and out before anyone was any the wiser.

On that thought, she opened the library door, checked the corridor was clear, then sneaked off in search of the earl's private rooms.

The corridor in the family wing of the house was lined with portraits of their ancestors. Here and there, Jane saw a resemblance to Robert—the curve of a smile, the creases of contentedness around dark eyes. Under other circumstances she might have dallied, studied the faces in the way she could not study him, endeavoring to somehow learn his secrets from his ancestors. Today, she had more important things to do.

Her feet sank into the deep pile carpet that made her steps noiseless. It added to the hushed eeriness of the place, and she shivered. If it weren't for Robert, her need to help him find the truth, Jane would have turned tail and fled.

At the door she thought led to the master bedroom, it took three attempts to raise her hand and knock. Her heart was in her throat, and her stomach did a funny flip-flop, like a landed fish on a riverbank. A voice in her head whispered, *Run*.

What if the earl was not fit for callers? What if he was only half dressed? Taking a bath? What if…?

Panic rushed through her. She could hardly catch her breath. Her head swam. She needed to leave, to escape and hope she encountered nobody on the way back. She took a step backward, then stopped as the door swished open, revealing an impeccably dressed man with a gaunt face and silver hair.

"May I help you, miss?" His voice was crisp, his face expressionless.

A moment passed. Jane's tongue froze, refusing to allow speech to come. Not that her brain let the words form anyway. The man looked down the length of his nose in disdain which, she reflected, was not easy considering he was shorter than she was.

The absurdity of that thought made her want to giggle. She fought the urge to do so, and the effort brought her senses rushing back. She cleared her throat and said, "I am Mrs. Frobisher. I heard Lord Barwell was unwell. I came to pay my respects and to ask if there is anything I might do to help him?" Her voice sounded clear and calm and confident, which was both a surprise and a relief.

The man's eyebrows shot up, pushing his forehead in wrinkles toward his hairline. Jane bit her lip. Why had she thought, even for an instant, that this idea would fly?

"Mrs. Frobisher?" The man let the name settle for a moment before he continued, "The lady who helped Mr.

Robert after his accident."

"Yes, my mother and I—"

"You have nursing skills, I assume?"

"Well, I…"

"Forgive me," he said and inclined his head in a sparse bow. "Of course you do, or you would not have been entrusted with Mr. Robert's care. I am not usually so obtuse. Please enter." He stood aside and held the door so Jane could move into the room. She had no choice now but to oblige.

The room was not the earl's bedchamber but his dressing room. It was small, no more than ten feet by ten feet, and contained two armoires, a chest of drawers on which was carefully arranged a gentleman's grooming kit, the mother-of-pearl handles gleaming a soft pink-white in the light from the half-shuttered window. A bathtub stood against the wall, squeezed between one of the armoires and a large packing case, and a cheval mirror was angled in one corner. A table and chair filled another corner, and on the table were pots and bottles of lotions which, Jane guessed, were a gentleman's equivalent of a lady's creams and perfumes.

This was wrong. She should not be here. She turned to make her apologies and froze, because the man looked at her as if she was the answer to all his troubles, a ministering angel who would restore Lord Barwell to health with a wave of her hand. Jane swallowed, hard.

"I am Timmins," he said. "His lordship's valet. I'm charged with his care, but I can't seem to…" He took a deep breath and steadied his voice, which had trembled slightly. "It doesn't matter what I do, do you see? What remedies I try. Nothing works. I am at my wits end, to tell the truth. And," he leaned toward Jane and lowered his voice as if imparting a confidence, "the way Lady Barwell looks at me, I'm sure she blames me. She thinks I am responsible for making my lord ill. But I am not!" Indignance mixed with anxiety on his face, and Jane knew she could not leave.

"She cannot think any such thing." She rested her hand on the man's arm, reassuring him. "Anyone can see you have done your very best for him."

The valet's bottom lip quivered, and his eyes shone with unshed tears. He patted Jane's hand on his arm, then moved away, his back to her, and spent several seconds straightening the already perfectly laid out grooming set. Jane waited for him to fully compose himself.

"Thank you," he whispered, at last. "You cannot know how much those words mean. And, having heard how splendidly you restored Mr. Robert to health, I am overcome with gratitude at your presence here."

Terror shot through Jane, so strong it almost knocked her off balance. The two cases could not be more different. Robert had been forced to bed with broken bones and painful bruises, and he was young and strong and did most of the healing himself. The earl, on the other hand, might well have been drinking brandy that poisoned him, especially if his illness was in any way like Robert's had been this morning, The sight of him in the woods had shocked Jane: his skin had been so gray, his lips garishly red, and his eyes hollow, surrounded by rings of bruised purple. There had been a cold sheen to his forehead, and the hair around his face had been damp and flat.

Yet, even sick, he'd been powerful, his shoulders broad, although stooped, the muscles in his thighs flexing against his close-fitting breeches when he fought to keep his legs from buckling. He wore no cravat, and Jane had struggled to take her gaze from the V of skin at his throat, and the smattering of dark hair on his chest above the neckline of his shirt. She wondered, not for the first time, what he looked like beneath that shirt. Was he as strong as he looked, or was it an illusion, his shoulders narrower and his chest a little sunken without the aid of clothes? Somehow, she thought not.

Which was not something that should occupy her mind, even for an instant. Her cheeks heated at her wantonness, and her scalp prickled. She thanked the Lord that Timmins could not read her thoughts.

The valet clearly thought his praise had caused her blush, because he assured her she should not be discomfited: praise should be served where it was deserved. Jane cleared her throat and changed the subject.

"I am not completely au fait with Lord Barwell's illness," she said, briskly. "What exactly are his symptoms?"

"Well." The valet clasped his hands tightly in front of his waist. "He has…" He winced. "You will, I am sure, pardon me for discussing such things with a lady like yourself…" Jane inclined her head and he continued. "He has had a great purging of his stomach. Many times. And to such a degree I am surprised he can still eat. I would not be brave enough to do so, knowing what it was going to do to me, but my lord is made of sterner stuff."

"A purging?" Jane frowned. "By which you mean…?" She felt her blush rise again as she waved her hand up and down trying to indicate the detail of her question. She wished Mama was here, for Mama never seemed to have trouble discussing such things. Jane supposed it came through a combination of the practicalities of motherhood and intimate knowledge of a husband.

"Through both ends," the valet said, and his face burned bright crimson. "He needs his gazunder more times than I care to think about, but..."

"Gazunder?" Jane was not familiar with the word. She wondered if it was a medicine Timmins had administered.

The question threw Timmins off guard. "Gazunder," he repeated. "You know, ma'am. The chamberpot. We call it a gazunder, because it "goes under" the bed, do you see? He needs it a lot. But he also casts up his accounts, if you'll excuse me for saying something so vulgar."

"A lot?" Jane pictured Robert doing the same thing this morning.

"A lot," confirmed Timmins. "Then there are the attacks. Shivering uncontrollably, sweating profusely, if you'll pardon me for saying. He's tired and weak, and who can wonder at it?" He grimaced then, as if his next words left a bad taste in his mouth. "I'm not sure if the other attacks are anything to do with it, some people do seem to suffer as they grow older, although Lord Barwell was not as old as most when they started, and all I can say is, before his illness, he never showed any sign, so they may be part of it after all. Or perhaps they were brought on by the distress of his illness, or they were going to happen anyway."

"Other attacks?"

Timmins bowed his head over his clasped hands as if praying. He nodded as if he'd come to a decision, then took a deep breath. "My lord's mind is not as sharp as it once was, do you see? That is to say, it is, when he is lucid. Unfortunately, he seems not always to be lucid. He…forgets things. Such as, who I am, who Lady Barwell is. It is most distressing."

"I can imagine. And this forgetfulness began at the same time as his other problems?"

"About three weeks later."

Jane had heard enough. The earl's physical complaints were so like Robert's this morning, it could not be a coincidence. Which meant bringing relief could be as simple as…

"Get rid of the brandy."

Jane didn't realize she had spoken aloud until Timmins protested. "I couldn't do that, Mrs. Frobisher. The earl enjoys his brandy each evening."

"I don't mean all brandy," Jane qualified, and Timmins looked relieved, then perplexed.

"What did you mean?"

"The brandy in the dining room," she said. "In the library and his study, too."

Timmins raised his eyebrows. "All of it?"

"Yes." She chewed her lip, thoughtful. "Where did the brandy come from?"

The valet looked as if that was the most stupid question he had ever been asked. "The casks in the cellar."

"Would you be able to give him brandy that did not come from his cellar?"

"I hardly think…"

The valet stopped mid-sentence when a voice from the corridor said, "Do as she says."

Chapter Eighteen

Robert reached his father's dressing room in time to hear Jane's edict. Timmins had borne a look of outraged horror and begun to refuse her request. Even now, when the order came from Robert, Timmins clearly wanted to object.

Blast the man! Robert didn't have the time or the patience for this. His head still pounded, and his brain was fuzzy with the aftereffects of his illness. He hadn't dared eat or drink anything beyond a small tumbler of water, which had not quenched his thirst nor completely taken the sour taste away.

On top of that, he'd had to deal with Jessica when he'd been ill-equipped to do so. Usually, he was unfailingly polite to her, no matter the provocation. Today, his mood had got the better of him and he had been, at the very least, acerbic. He'd watched her walk away, clearly as vexed with him as he was with her, and then he'd made his way upstairs, determined to see his father, whether she liked it or not.

The earl's bedroom door was locked, so he'd sought entry through the dressing room and stumbled upon the discussion there.

He didn't want to dwell on the fact that Janey sat in his father's private rooms, completely careless of her own reputation. Did she not realize the servants saw everything and gossiped about it all?

A wave of nausea broke over him. He didn't know whether it was the remnant of his illness or the thought that Janey could be hurt by gossip. Whatever the case, he took several deep, slow breaths until his stomach steadied, though his head still swam, making it hard to focus. Janey's face creased with concern.

"You should be resting." Her voice was quiet, but her expression was determined.

Lord, he thought, save me from managing females who throw orders at me.

"Mr. Robert," said Timmins, his hands clasped so tightly his knuckles were white, "Mrs. Frobisher says I am to destroy the master's brandy, and you tell me to obey. But his lordship enjoys his brandy—"

"He will enjoy it from another source."

"But why, when we have—"

"Timmins!" Robert's admonishment silenced the man, for which he was grateful. He knew he couldn't take much more. He needed to lie down until this sickness worked its way through him.

The valet's lips thinned, and his chin trembled, and Robert thought the man might cry.

Janey came to the rescue, her soft voice soothing even as she was being practical. "It is our belief, Mr. Timmins, that something has tainted the casks in the cellar. We wish only to ensure Lord Barwell has the best, and safest, brandy."

Timmins looked from Janey to Robert and back. "Is that what has been making him ill?" Completely forgetting himself, he sat heavily, elbows on his knees and head in his hands. "I poured him drinks from those decanters. Every day."

"You were not to know." Janey patted his shoulder.

He took a shuddering breath. "What tainted the casks? How did it get into the brandy?"

"Both excellent questions," said Robert. His legs were going to give way any moment now, so he leaned against the wall and hoped he looked nonchalant rather than weak, although Janey's expression told him she wasn't fooled. "We aim to stop the rot," he carried on. "That means buying my father's brandy from an independent source."

"Of course," said Timmins. He wiped the tips of his fingers under his eyes. "I'll buy it from the Dog and Gun over in Earl Shilton. He's the most honest landlord in the area."

"But remember—until our investigations are complete," added Robert, "we don't want *anyone* else to know what we suspect."

Timmins eyes widened. "You think somebody put something in the brandy on purpose?"

"I don't know. But I must consider it."

"No one shall hear of it from me," said the valet, gravely. "I'll not even tell his lordship, although that's so he doesn't get upset, rather than because he might let it slip." He stood and smoothed down his waistcoat. "I'd better be on my way if I'm to get to Earl Shilton and back before he needs me." He bowed and left the room.

As soon as he'd gone, Robert sagged. It took great effort not to slide down to the floor.

"Come and sit." Janey took his arm and draped it over her shoulders. Robert accepted her help, concentrating his efforts on supporting as much of his own weight as he could. The last thing he needed was to knock her off balance and end with them both lying on the floor in a tangle of limbs. She was warm and soft against him, yet strong and determined, too. The scent of her soap, so fresh and clean, made his senses whirl and his head swim, though it did seem to lessen the churning in his stomach. Her hair tickled the underside of his chin, and it was only his current weakness that prevented his body reacting in a way that would have embarrassed them both. Every cloud has a silver lining, he thought wryly.

And wasn't he a blackguard for thinking such a thing when she was merely trying to help him? Shame and self-disgust left him feeling worse than ever. He tried to stand without her aid, to put some distance between them, but found he could not do so.

"Why didn't you sit down in the first place, you daft man?" she murmured, oblivious to the direction of his thoughts as she maneuvered him into the chair. She clicked her tongue, impatiently. "Because I was standing, is that it?" She sighed. "Honor and good manners are very becoming in a gentleman, Robert Carrow, but so is common sense. You are sick, and that makes a huge difference. Now, sit."

"Yes, ma'am," he answered. He gave her a poor excuse for a smile, one which barely troubled the muscles in his face. Judging by the sidelong look she leveled at him, he would have been better not to have bothered. "What do we do now, do you think?" he asked.

"You go to bed and rest," she answered, briskly. "While I go and spend the morning with my mother, and hopefully, Lady Barwell. Who knows what I may hear in an 'innocent' conversation?"

"I meant, about the brandy." He breathed out heavily, his chest tight, his lungs full and refusing to empty. He swore under his breath. "Whatever has been done to it, it has to be deliberate."

"Yes," she agreed. "But who would do such a thing?" She looked at him then, and her big eyes seemed to see right through him to the thoughts and feelings he hid from the world. The notion was unsettling. She watched him for a moment, then one side of her mouth kicked up in a half smile. He wished he could kiss that little curve in her lip, but he knew he wouldn't stop there. He would draw her closer, tasting her, pulling her hair down from its pins until it hung over her shoulders and covered his hands...

For one wonderful moment, he thought she was going to kiss him. She half closed her eyes, her lips parted and her tongue darted out, just enough to wet them. Robert's groin tightened. His breathing shallowed and his heart sped up.

"I'm going now," said Timmins, coming into the dressing room from Father's bedchamber. Robert sat bolt upright. Janey stepped away, suddenly fascinated by Father's grooming set. "Lord Barwell is asleep," continued Timmins, who was either the most unobservant servant ever or the most discreet. "Hopefully, he won't wake until I return."

Timmins left again and there was an awkward silence. Janey stood at the dresser, stroking the mother-of-pearl backing on Father's clothes brush with the tip of one finger. Robert wished it was him she touched. He could almost feel her hand on him, gently caressing him, her soft fingers against his hard...

What was the matter with him? He was not a giddy schoolboy who could not control his urges!

Her shoulders were stiff, her head bowed. She was embarrassed and upset. He should say something, soothe her worries, make her feel better, cut through the atmosphere that had descended upon them.

In the end, it was Janey who spoke. She half turned her head and said, over her shoulder, "We need to find the culprit. For the poisoning." Her voice was low and husky. Robert didn't dare answer, for fear his own voice would give away his need for her.

She turned. Their eyes met, fleetingly. She turned away. Robert looked down at his hand resting on the arm of the chair.

"Who…" She cleared her throat. Robert's heart pounded a strange, unrhythmic tattoo at her uncertainty. Then she asked a question which doused the moment as surely as a bucket of cold water would have. "Who would gain the most at your father's demise?"

"Until a few months ago, me. I would have taken the title, the estates, everything he hadn't bequeathed elsewhere in his will. Now, it would be Ben…" Robert's voice tailed off. "Technically, it would be Ben," he corrected himself, "although until the Committee on Privileges accepts his claim, I suppose it is still me."

"That doesn't help. We know it's not you." Janey put her hands on her hips and blew out her breath, ballooning her cheeks. "Who else benefits substantially from his will?"

Robert tried to remember what his father had told him when they'd been in his study, going over the estate accounts. To be honest, he hadn't wanted to contemplate his father's passing, so he hadn't paid much attention. "I believe there are a few bequests to longstanding servants," he said. "Enough that they'll be comfortable, but certainly not enough to kill for. And a bequest to the church." He grinned. "He called that taking care of his immortal soul."

"Lady Barwell?"

Robert frowned, then wished he hadn't when the movement in his face shot needles of pain into his head. "No," he said. "She gets to live in the dower house for life, and she'll have her widow's portion, which I believe is generous, but not nearly what she has now. Barnaby, her son, is provided for, of course, but that's it."

"It's not his will that's driving this, then." Janey bit her bottom lip as she thought. Robert wanted to kiss it better, to smooth his tongue over it and taste the fullness of it. He closed his eyes and tried to concentrate on the matter in hand. "Revenge?" she went on. "Anger at some slight?"

"I don't know." He made the effort to stand, and swayed a little, although he felt better now than he had just half an hour ago. "First things first. We need to empty the decanters. Especially in the dining room, which is the one Father would use most often."

"I thought about that. The decanter in the dining room will be in full view of everybody. If we simply empty the brandy, it will be noticed. More so than the other decanters would be. Then the villain will know we've caught onto him. He'll either go to ground and be impossible to expose, or he'll redouble his efforts, putting your father in even more danger." She sighed. "I don't know how we are going to do it, but we have to find a different way to get rid of that brandy."

Robert pondered her words for a moment. She was right. If they tampered with the decanter in the dining room, it would be noticed. "I have an idea," he said, and he grinned. "Let's go down to breakfast, shall we?"

Janey frowned. "Are you up to it?"

"Eating? No. The way I feel, I don't ever want to eat or drink again. Thankfully, my idea does not include me doing either one."

****

Jane and Robert returned to the small family dining room, which was also used as a breakfast room. Lady Barwell sat at the table with a plate of bread and jam and a half-full cup of chocolate. Mama and Ben were also there. Seeing them gave Jane pause. She didn't want to worry or upset Ben, and she knew their actions would do so. But she couldn't ask Robert to change his mind without alerting everyone to his plan.

Like Lady Barwell, Mama ate bread and jam, but Ben tucked into a plate of bacon, eggs, sausage, and kedgeree. It warmed Jane to see him so enjoying his new position in life.

She went to the sideboard and poured the dish of tea she'd promised herself an hour ago, then filled a plate with bread and butter, an egg, and a sausage. She almost spooned a few mushrooms on top but thought better of it. If there was a poisoner in the house, it would be all too easy to use mushrooms for their evil purpose. She sat near to Ben and Mama and readied herself for what was to come.

Robert stood by the sideboard and made a show of rubbing his hands over his face. He was still pale and haggard, and the five o'clock shadow darkening his chin gave him the appearance of a rogue regretting the night before. He had stopped at his rooms on the way down to breakfast and donned a cravat, though it was deliberately tied in a sloppy manner.

Lady Barwell narrowed her eyes at him. "Robert? Are you well? You look even worse now than you did when I saw you earlier, if that were possible."

Robert inclined his head. "Whereas you, Jessica, look as beautiful and as poised as ever."

She stared at him as if trying to decide if he paid her a compliment or mocked her.

"I must have had more to drink last night than I thought," he went on. Mama smiled and shook her head, indulgently. Ben concentrated on his food.

Jane's mouth was dry. She sipped at her tea, nervously. Now that the plan had been set in motion, she hardly dared look at Robert, for fear she would give away their scheme. Not that she thought for a moment that anyone at this table was involved, but they'd agreed the fewer people who knew what was happening, the better, because the reactions of the others to the news might be enough to warn the villain, and that was something they were not prepared to risk doing.

Robert moved to the tantalus in the corner of the room. Jane heard the chink as he unstopped the decanter. Surreptitiously, she glanced at Ben. He continued eating, completely unbothered by what his brother was doing.

The countess, however, was horrified. "Robert? What on earth are you doing?"

Everyone turned to see him lift the decanter by its neck. He saluted his stepmother with it and gave a half grin. "Hair of the dog," he said in a gruff voice that did indeed sound as if he was suffering and in need of the age-old hangover cure.

It was over in an instant. If Jane had blinked, she would have missed it, but she had to give Robert his due; he made the whole thing look natural and accidental. One moment he was gripping the three-quarters-full decanter, ready to pour himself a drink. The next, it slipped from his grasp and fell, in a strange slow motion, to the floor. He even made to grab at it, as if he was trying to save it, although, of course, he was nowhere near quick enough.

The heavy glass bottle missed the carpet and hit the wooden floor, smashing into a hundred pieces that flew in all directions. Brandy splashed the carpet and the bottom of the wallcoverings, spattering a dark pattern across them, then running down in dirty brown rivulets. A pool of liquor spread on the floor and seeped under the edge of the carpet. Dark spots showed on Robert's stockings.

For a second, there was silence. Then Robert grinned sheepishly and said, "Oh dear."

Jane pursed her lips to keep herself from giggling, a mix of triumph at his success and hysterical relief that he'd managed it bubbling inside her.

"Oh dear?" The countess threw down her napkin and jumped to her feet. "Look what you've done! And all you can say is, 'Oh dear'?"

Robert shrugged. "Sorry."

"Look at the mess! My carpet is ruined. We'll be treading on that glass for days, the place will smell like a cheap tavern, and—and—oh!" She finished on an exclamation of furious frustration, then rang the bell for a servant.

Beside Jane, Ben began to moan, a soft hum that built quickly to a howl of distress as he rocked back and forth in his chair, hitting his hands aggressively against his head. The countess glanced at him, then at Robert, as both Mama and Jane leaned in to comfort him.

"See what you've done?" hissed Lady Barwell. Robert looked truly contrite now.

Not as contrite as Jane felt, though. She should have

tried harder to stop Robert from carrying out his plan while Ben was in the room. She knew how much he hated loud noises and conflict, and she had permitted both to happen. True, she hadn't known until she came in that Ben was here, and it was difficult to know how they could have aborted their actions without giving it all away, but that was really no excuse. Ben was upset, Mama was trying to soothe him, and Jane felt truly dreadful.

The footman, William, appeared. He looked around, momentarily startled by Ben's howling and self-flagellation. Almost immediately, though, he hid his feelings behind his professional face.

"We have had an accident," said Lady Barwell, glaring at Robert. "Please see the mess is dealt with and find another decanter." She turned back to Robert. "I don't see why your father should be deprived of his after-dinner drink this evening, simply because you are so oafishly clumsy." She turned to Mama, who was cuddling Ben. He had stopped rocking now, although he still cried. "I will be moving into the parlor while the broken glass is cleared and the mess cleaned," she said. "I hope you will be able to join me." She strode from the room with one more glare at Robert.

"Come along, Ben," said Mama, in a soft, soothing voice. "Let's get you to your chamber where we can be quiet for a while." The words pierced Jane and filled her with a renewed guilt and shame.

"I'm sorry, Mrs. Winter," said Robert.

Mama smiled and dismissed his apology with a wave of her hand. "These things happen. No real harm done." She led Ben away.

Knowing Mama wasn't angry did not make Jane

feel better. She felt sure her parent would be more than a little upset if and when she discovered the whole thing had been done on purpose—although she could not possibly make Jane feel any worse about distressing Ben than she'd already made herself.

Chapter Nineteen

Several hours later, Jane saw Robert walk into the study. He had bathed and shaved and changed his clothes, and now looked much better. Eager to find out if that meant he felt better, too, she knocked lightly on the door and followed him inside.

"I'm much better, thank you," he answered her with a smile that made his dimple wink. His cheeks held more color, and his eyes were no longer dull, the dark circles largely gone. "I slept," he said. "That seems to have done the trick. If my father has been suffering like that for some time, I am surprised he is still with us." He hesitated. "How is Ben? I hope I did not distress him too much?"

"Not at all," she said, then thought better of telling the lie. "Well, yes, but he will survive. He doesn't like to be startled, and he doesn't like loud noises, but once he realized nobody was hurt, he soon calmed." She grinned. "He thought it was funny that you were scolded. He's not used to anybody being scolded, other than himself and Lucy."

Robert grinned. "We are never too grown to be put in our places by our parents."

"That's what Mama told him." She chuckled. "Then later she had to scold him, so he no longer holds the moral high ground."

"Oh dear. What did he do?"

"He tried to climb the stairs inside one of your towers."

Robert nodded. "They fascinated me when I was a boy, too. I pretended I was a knight, holding the castle for the king and fending off attackers from the battlements."

"They're very high."

"Yes, they are. And the roof can be slippery. I shudder to think of the danger one could find up there. Something I never even considered as a child."

"Mama considered it. She had already forbidden him to go there yesterday, so he was well and truly in the suds when she caught him today."

"I will see if it can be locked up somehow, so he cannot be tempted. Where is he now?"

"Mama took him for a walk to the lake. He wanted to see the summerhouse, although I doubt she'll be willing to row him to the island."

Robert picked up the half-filled decanter of brandy and took it to the window while he spoke. "Another place I loved as a boy," he said. He looked out to make sure nobody was watching, then emptied the brandy onto the garden. "There's an icehouse under it, you know. Very clever design, really. The water in the lake ensures the temperature never rises much, so ice lasts a long time." He shook the last drops from the decanter and closed the window before returning it to the table, where glasses were arranged, ready for drinkers to use. "Another of my playgrounds. In that one, I pretended I was an explorer, discovering the frozen North."

There was a moment of silence. Both of them seemed to cast around for something else to say. Jane could not think of a thing.

"How have you spent the day?" he asked, at last.

She smiled, grateful for a question she could answer positively. "I've been productive in my enquiries. I now know which member of your staff fills your father's decanters."

Robert frowned. "The butler," he said, as if that was obvious.

Jane shook her head. "He has delegated the task to a younger man. I suspect his own legs find the stairs difficult. They are quite steep, and he is getting on in years."

Robert acknowledged that with a brief bow of his head. "He has been the butler here since before I was born. But how did you discover this? Did you ask questions? I hope you did not put yourself into any danger."

She shook her head. "I didn't. Nor did I alert anyone to what we're doing." She moved forward, her eyes on the desk in the corner of the room. The mahogany desk was highly polished, and large enough that several people could be seated around it comfortably. A small pile of books rested on top of it, and she ran her finger along the edge of the top one. "I explored the cellars and found a small niche in the wall, just off the main corridor," she continued. "I hid and waited to see if anyone would come."

He watched her closely, so he could not have missed her smug grin. "Somebody did?"

"William. He unlocked the wine cellar, went to a cask with a loose lid and filled the new dining room decanter from it. Then he took it back upstairs. Unfortunately, he locked the wine cellar again, so I couldn't investigate further."

"For which I'm profoundly grateful."

Jane gave Robert an annoyed look. "I made certain I was safe," she said. "I am capable, you know. I'm not a child."

"You are no match for a big man like William."

Jane sniffed her contempt for his argument. "I was careful."

****

Robert could tell she wasn't about to admit he was right, and he didn't want to argue, so he changed the subject. "Why does William fill the decanters? Martin has always taken his duties as butler extremely seriously. I would never have believed he would allow anyone but himself to do his job."

"As I said, he may be feeling his age."

"Possibly." Robert pulled a face. He was not convinced Martin would consider physical frailty a good excuse for not carrying out his duties for himself.

"Or," Janey continued, "he might have had no choice. As you said, William is a big man, much bigger than Mr. Martin. If he took it upon himself to intimidate him…"

If that was what had happened, it was another sign that Father's control of the estate had slipped. Things needed tightening, urgently. "I'll look into it," he promised, aiming his vow more at himself than at Janey.

"Although, even if William has usurped Mr. Martin, what he is doing makes little sense," she said. "Why would a footman wish to poison your father's brandy?"

Her naive question proved she was out of her depth and shouldn't be skulking in dark corners, trying to trap villains. "Why do you think a footman does anything?"

She thought for a moment. "Loyalty or money."

"He clearly has no sense of loyalty, or he wouldn't be giving the earl tainted brandy." Unless William was unaware that the brandy *was* tainted. That was possible, although Robert was too cynical and worldly-wise to give the footman more benefit of the doubt than that.

Janey shrugged. "Money, then. Someone paid him to do it. But who, and why?"

Her nose crinkled as she asked, and Robert wanted to kiss it. That she would pull such a face endeared her to him more than he could say. Most ladies would sooner try to fly than risk such a candid expression. All they did was designed, not to show their honest thoughts, but to display their most elegant, beautiful selves. Little did they know Janey making faces and acting unselfconsciously was more beautiful and more tempting than all their careful stillness and lack of emotive expression could ever be.

She turned and caught him watching her. He knew he should look away, pretend he hadn't been gazing at her like a moonstruck calf, but he could not. More, he did not want to.

Their eyes met and held. Time stood still. The noise of the house disappeared, until there was just him, and Janey. She was near enough to him that he could see the tiny flecks of silver in her eyes, changing them from a solid blue to a stormy gray. The scent of her sweet lavender soap filled the air. Her skin shone, the color of the summer sun at dawn, a testament to the time she'd spent outdoors, and her hair was spun gold. Her lips were parted, and he could hear her soft breathing. His own breath sounded harsh to his ears, filled as it was with want and need. His heartbeat sped and he had the strangest feeling inside him, like the buzzing of a million bees in his chest. He wanted—needed—to reach for her, to wrap her in his arms while he kissed her, long and slow, to know the warmth of her lips against his, her tongue dancing with his.

He tensed and took a deep breath. The woman was a guest in his family home. He had to treat her with respect and circumspection, if it killed him. Which, if the ache in his thighs and the tightening at the fall of his breeches were any indication, it might well do.

Thrusting his hands into his pockets, he stepped away. He thought he saw disappointment in her expression, but it was gone so quickly he couldn't be sure. Her face blanked, and she turned and looked through the window.

Robert forced his mind back to their discussion. "Where is William now? Do you know?" Not that he intended to do anything with the information. Questioning the footman was unlikely to provide him with answers, since the man could claim not to know the brandy had been tampered with, and Robert could not prove otherwise. Yet. All confronting William would do at this stage was alert the real culprit and make him—or her—harder to find.

"He went to the village," Janey answered. "Lady Barwell had a letter to post. I saw her give it to him and send him to catch the mail coach." She smiled, and the room brightened.

Without even realizing he was doing it, Robert took two steps toward her. "What would I do without you?" he murmured. Her eyes widened, filling him with horror. He made her uncomfortable. He had to salvage the situation before she ran from him in fear and disgust. "You are cool and calm in a crisis," he continued, those being the first words he thought of. "Levelheaded and resourceful, with intelligence to spare. If you hadn't worked out what made me ill and what it meant for my father, he would still be in mortal danger. Well," he clarified, "he still is in danger, but we may be vigilant on his behalf."

And now he was rambling.

Her smile fell away and the light in her eyes faded. Suddenly, the room seemed colder and darker. "I should go," she said.

"Go?" he repeated, stupidly.

"Yes. Go." She used a hand to indicate him, then herself. "We are here with no chaperone. And unlike earlier, when we were in your father's rooms…there is every chance of someone coming in here and finding us together. With no chaperone."

"Janey…"

"I should go."

She all but ran from the room. The door clicked shut behind her with a strange finality. Robert rubbed the back of his neck, bewildered. That she had been upset, he had no doubt. He just didn't have the first idea what he'd said or done to make her so.

****

It took everything Jane had to walk away from the study and up the stairs to her chamber with her head held high and a look of serene contentment on her face. Inside, she was breaking, the pain in her chest harsh and the lump in her throat choking. Hot tears gathered behind her eyes, and she blinked them away, furiously. For one glorious moment she'd thought he was going to declare that he cared for her.

What would I do without you?

Her heart had done a strange pitter-patter. He'd moved forward, and she thought—hoped—for the second time in a few minutes, that he was going to embrace her, kiss her. His eyes had darkened from that deep brown to black and his gaze lowered to her mouth. She wanted him so much, she could almost taste him on her lips, smell him on her skin, and hang the consequences. It seemed she had learned nothing at all in the last few years.

The first time, when Robert had pulled back from her again, she'd been disappointed but decided it was for the best. Anyone might have come upon them. It was, she had realized, a good thing he was capable of rational thought in that moment, because she most certainly had not been. She'd had to turn away, to stare out of the window so he wouldn't see the need for him in her eyes. She didn't want his disgust, or worse, his pity.

But then, the second time…

What would I do without you?

She'd thought…it didn't matter what she'd thought, because those thoughts were wrong. It wasn't Jane he wanted, *per se*. He wanted someone, anyone, who possessed a calm demeanor and a quick mind in this time of trial. That had hurt. The pain of it had been far, far more than it should have been. Which was why she had had to leave quickly, before her wretched tears began and embarrassed her even more.

Levelheaded and resourceful, and with intelligence to spare. Those were the qualities Robert admired in her. *Cool and calm in a crisis.*

His words were meant as compliments, she knew that. They were high praise, an acknowledgement of her worth in a world that too often dismissed her. They should please her, make her proud.

And they did. Of course they did. They were, after all, everything a woman like her could hope to hear from a man such as Robert Carrow. She didn't want anything more from him. She was more than satisfied. More than happy with what he had said.

Finally, Jane reached her chamber. She went inside and carefully locked the door, then crossed the room to her bed. She managed to sit down demurely, before the first tears finally fell.

Chapter Twenty

A week passed. The earl made a good recovery and seemed stronger every day, although he tired easily, and his face still had the grayish hue of lingering illness. As far as Jane knew, there had been no more lapses of memory or coherent thought, either, and she began to hope all would be well from now on. She knew Timmins went about every day, making sure the decanters were filled only with the brandy he bought in Earl Shilton, and that nobody had tampered with them.

For his part, the earl reveled in Ben's company. The pair of them were frequently found, heads together, grins wide. Ben giggled a lot, and Lord Barwell encouraged that. This morning, they sat together at the breakfast table, both eating heartily as they shared a joke only they understood. Mama watched them, wistfully. "I should have investigated further," she murmured. "They've missed so much because I didn't."

"You weren't to know," Jane answered. "It was better to err on the side of caution and keep Ben safe."

"That's what Lord Barwell said." Mama took a deep breath and exhaled heavily. "I'm glad they're happy together now."

"Not everybody shares your gladness," said Jane. She gave a tiny nod to the far end of the table, where Lady Barwell sat, glaring venomously at her husband and Ben.

"I feel sorry for her," whispered Mama. Jane blinked. Mama spooned jam onto her bread. "Don't be too quick to judge her. Learning about Ben must have been a shock."

Jane thought about that. She had been shocked and upset to discover the truth herself, but it hadn't really had a negative effect on her. True, she no longer had a blood brother, but Ben remained as close to her as he'd ever been, a brother in all but name. They'd had to leave Bloomfold because of the revelation, but after Mr. Turner's lies, Jane would have had to leave there anyway. The future for her and Mama was uncertain, and that was a worry, but in the meantime, they were hardly living in uncomfortable or reduced circumstances.

It must have been much harder for Lady Barwell. The countess had had to welcome this young man into her home and her life, knowing he would one day be the head of her family, with power over her. Not that Jane believed for an instant that Ben would exercise his power malevolently; it simply wasn't in his nature, and besides, Robert would be on hand to ensure Ben did as he should. However, Lady Barwell could not know these things, and she must be more than a little anxious for herself and her son.

True, Jane had heard the countess make disparaging remarks about Ben, calling him deficient. The memory of that conversation still made her bristle. However, she could also see that Mama was correct; Ben must have been a shock to the woman.

The countess might feel some discomfort in Ben's company, too. Growing up with Ben, Jane had never thought of him as anything but her big brother, but she knew there were many who were wary of him, who gave him a wide berth, much as they might a stalking tiger or a ravenous wolf. She'd been taught to pity them their lack of understanding.

Now, Jane resolved to try harder to befriend Lady Barwell. Mayhap she could help her see that Ben was no threat to her or anyone else. She should talk to Robert, too, ask him for his help in this matter. She made no doubt he would wish to put his stepmother's fears to rest.

Thinking of Robert made Jane smile. They'd spent much of the last week together, although they were rarely alone, which was a good thing, considering how she'd made a fool of herself in the study last week.

What would I do without you?

Jane had completely misinterpreted his words. She'd thought—wished—he was saying that he cared for her. In her fevered imagination, she'd heard him declare his undying love for her before gathering her into his arms and kissing her the way he had in the inn at St. Albans. She'd all but tasted his lips on hers, strong and firm, his kiss warm and filled with desire. The air had been redolent with the scents of him: the morning coffee he'd drunk, the woodsy cologne he wore, the crispness of his linen shirt and the starch in his cravat. She'd known the soft wool of his coat would be warm beneath her hands, and his strong, steady heartbeat would pulse through her fingertips. In that instant, she fancied she heard him growl as he pulled her closer, his hand on the back of her neck sending shivers along her spine and making parts of her ache in delicious and indescribable ways. The sensation of her hair, tumbling heavily down over her shoulders, joyously freed of its pins, had been so real she would have sworn it had actually happened. There'd been a jellylike sensation in her knees, a longing ache deep in her stomach...

And then the fantasy had burst like a soap bubble. He'd meant nothing by the comment, nothing more than friendship and gratitude for her gumption.

Cool and calm. Levelheaded. Resourceful. Intelligent. The compliments he'd handed her still made her want to weep, a whole week later.

Which was silly. Hadn't she wished a man might see her value? She had been so angry that Sydney saw her only as a young virgin to deflower, and the likes of Mr. Turner saw her as easy prey, while the gossips saw her as entertainment over their cups of tea. She should be glad Robert saw her properly, as a person he respected as his intelligent, levelheaded equal.

She *was* glad. She truly was.

As if her thoughts conjured him, Robert came into the room. He looked well, countryside color in his cheeks. His hair was tousled, small curls falling onto his forehead where the wind had caressed them, then dropped them and let them fall where they may. The light from the window created pinpoints in his eyes, and his black coat made the white of his shirt and cravat shine. His buff-colored pantalons were tucked inside black boots, which gleamed. Jane licked her lips in appreciation of the sight he presented, then turned her head quickly and said something inane to her mother when he looked her way.

He helped himself to breakfast, sat, and gave everyone his greetings. Jane mumbled a hello in return. Her cheeks heated and she concentrated her gaze on her plate.

"Did you sleep well, Mrs. Frobisher?" asked Lady Barwell.

Startled, Jane looked up. The countess was rarely solicitous, and her expression of a moment ago had indicated she felt anything but friendly this morning. "Yes, I thank you," she replied, bracing herself for whatever comment came next. It would not be complimentary, Jane knew from experience. She also knew it would be couched in words that pretended a friendly concern, and would be accompanied by a smile that didn't reach the lady's eyes.

The countess opened her mouth to deliver her blow, but before she could say anything, Ben called across the table, "Mama?"

Lady Barwell winced. Ben could not accept Mama was not, in fact, his mother. He continued to call her that, something the earl not only allowed but actively encouraged. Unfortunately, Ben also could not comprehend that Mama could be his mother and Lord Barwell his papa, excepting they were married and, therefore, they must be in love. Lady Barwell was an irrelevance to him, just someone in the family, like Jane or Robert or Lucy. Daily, they explained the truth to him, to no avail. Jane sympathized with Lady Barwell's dismay at this constant disregard of her position by the heir apparent.

"Mama?" repeated Ben. He looked joyful, his eyes sparkling, grin wide. "Papa say I go with him and Robson to Leicester, see horses at the…" He looked to his father for assistance.

"The Haymarket," responded the earl. His own smile was as broad as Ben's.

"Haymarket," repeated Ben. "That all right?"

"We will be back for dinner," said the earl. "Robson, my head groom, wants me to look over some horses he heard of. I thought Ben might enjoy it. We'll take good care of him."

Jane smiled. The earl was a good man, considerate and kind. He could simply have taken Ben with him today and told Mama she had no right to gainsay him, just as Robert could have taken Ben from them at Bloomfold and left them behind. Instead, both men had shown care and respect to Jane and her mother and acknowledged their importance in Ben's life.

"I have no doubt you will," Mama answered the earl. "I look forward to hearing all about it when you return."

"You will be careful," said Lady Barwell, anxiously. "You've been very ill."

"I am not an invalid," said her husband. His tone was calm and friendly, but his teeth were gritted. He'd made it clear, several times in the past week, he hated to be mollycoddled.

"I didn't mean to imply that you were." Lady Barwell's return smile was strained. She looked as though she'd sucked a lemon dipped in vinegar.

"Lucy asked me to take her to Earl Shilton," said Mama, defusing the tension a little. "She heard there is a ruined castle there, and nothing will do but to discover if there is also a princess who's been asleep for a hundred years."

"Will you be taking the trap?" asked Robert. He poured himself a second cup of coffee.

"No, not at all." Mama laughed. "Earl Shilton is but a mile from here. The walk will do us good." She sipped her hot chocolate before adding, "there have been so few sunny days this summer, it seems a shame not to make what we can of this one."

"Quite right," said Lord Barwell. "Come, Ben, we

must away if we're to get to Leicester in good time." He put his napkin onto his empty plate and stood. He hesitated for a moment while his legs unstiffened, limped the first two steps, then strode from the room, his gait strong and sure. Ben trotted after him like an eager puppy.

Mama excused herself too, leaving Robert, Jane, and Lady Barwell at the table. There was a moment of silence, which Robert broke.

"As Mrs. Winter doesn't need the trap, I thought I would use it to tour the estate. Would you care to come with me, Mrs. Frobisher?"

Jane looked at him, startled. His eyes seemed to plead with her to say yes. It might be a good idea at that, for it would give them an opportunity to clear the air between them. Although they'd been friendly enough since that moment in the study, there was also an awkwardness between them that should be addressed. Being alone with him, away from the house, meant they could talk, and perhaps return things to how they had been.

"I would be delighted," she said. "I'll change my dress and join you presently."

She stood as Lady Barwell sighed. "Everybody is so busy, out and about," said the countess. "I will be alone. What shall I do, I wonder?"

If she thought Robert would invite her to join them, she soon learned she was mistaken. Quite apart from the fact that the trap only seated two, the iciness of his smile said everything. "You could take Barnaby and go with Lucy and Mrs. Winter to the castle," he said.

Lady Barwell gave him a withering look. "Barnaby does not enjoy going out."

Robert barked a laugh. "Of course Barnaby enjoys going out. He's a boy."

"He prefers to stay indoors," insisted the countess.

"He needs to go out. It's not good for a child to be shut inside the way he is. Besides, Lucy will be there. With her to play with, Barnaby will love it."

The countess gave a contemptuous sniff. "Thank you for your opinion," she said. She stood up sharply, making her knife rattle against her plate, and stalked from the room.

Jane gave Robert a nervous smile. "I will be ready in twenty minutes," she said. He stood and bowed, and Jane retreated to her chamber.

****

In fact, Robert noted, she was changed and ready in less than fifteen minutes. She came downstairs wearing a sky-blue dress with a royal blue spencer and matching hat decorated with silk flowers in shades of blue and cream. The style of the dress was from three or four Seasons ago, and the gloves she wore had clearly seen better days, but nonetheless, she looked stunning. Proudly, Robert offered her his arm and walked her to the trap in the driveway, a picnic hamper strapped to the back. He handed her into the seat, then climbed in and walked the pony sedately over the gravel driveway and toward the estate, which was bordered on three sides by the hamlets of Elmesthorpe, Stoney Stanton, and Barwell. The earl owned several properties within the hamlets, as well as in the nearby village of Earl Shilton, but today Robert wanted to concentrate on the tenants at the farms. Last year, there had been no summer at all, and this year had been only marginally better. Robert wished to make sure the tenants were able to cope with the hardships and that there wasn't anything they needed.

Sitting beside Janey was sweet torture. The seat of the trap was not wide, and the hem of her skirts brushed the tip of his left boot. He fancied he felt the warm fabric caressing his toes, though he knew that was impossible. His thigh leaned against hers, both innocent and sensual, and he had to force himself not to reach his arm around her shoulders and pull her closer. That way lay madness, to say nothing of the slap she would probably give him.

Janey seemed oblivious to his struggle. She was cool and calm, her hands resting demurely in her lap as she watched the passing countryside with a look of serene contentedness.

If only that serenity could be passed on! What on earth had possessed him to suggest this outing? It had seemed a good idea when he first thought of it, a way of spending time with her, regaining the amity they'd shared, and putting the awkwardness of the past few days to rest. But now she was here, he had been struck dumb. Wrack his brains though he might, he could not think of a single sensible thing to say.

Thankfully, Janey could. She asked questions about the land and its uses, the people who worked it, the benefits and difficulties of the farming methods they employed. Her questions were intelligent and interested, making him feel easier, the tension of the last week disappearing.

They met with the tenants. Janey was wonderful, charming them with her interest in them and their lives, and the empathy she shared over their worries and troubles. One or two of the older men gave Robert a surreptitious wink and a nod of approval, and old Joe Eatough, invoking the privilege of being in his eighties and having known Robert since birth, even went so far as to nudge him and nod, while murmuring, "She'll do, lad. She'll do."

At first, Robert wondered if he should deny their implications, although doing that would likely draw Janey's attention to them, something he was loath to do. He didn't wish to make the situation between the two of them awkward again, and the conversation his denial would lead to might do just that. So he said nothing and let the men surmise what they may.

He did wonder, though, what it would be like if Janey did become the lady of the manor, so to speak. Ben might be the next earl, but he would need Robert to help him run the estate, and Robert's wife must take on the duties that normally fell to the countess. Janey would play that role to perfection. In her care, the people of Barwell would thrive.

He was pulled from his woolgathering as they made their way back along the lane from the hamlet of Stoney Stanton, between fields of sheep on one side of the road and woods on the other. He could see, from her expression, that she'd asked him a question.

"I'm sorry," he said. "I didn't hear what you asked."

Janey blushed. Her cheeks were a soft, rose-petal pink that made her eyes shine bright blue and turned the curls around the edge of her bonnet into spun gold. He looked at her and could not look away.

"It doesn't matter," she answered. "I was prying. Forgive me."

"No, please ask. I genuinely didn't hear your question." She continued to hesitate, and he smiled at her. "Please. I would like to answer you, if I can."

She studied him for a moment longer, then stared at

the pony pulling them along the road. "I said, I couldn't help but notice a tension between you and Lady Barwell."

Robert nodded. There had always been a tension between himself and the present Lady Barwell.

He hadn't begrudged his father the happiness and companionship of a new marriage when he'd heard the news. Robert had been at university at the time and hadn't even known his father was in the market for a wife until he'd read of the wedding in the Society pages. He hurried home to congratulate the pair and to get to know his new stepmother, a lady he'd never met, nor heard of.

Things went wrong from the start. Robert and Jessica had disliked each other on sight. To be fair to Jessica, Father had not given her all the facts of his life before making his vows, and he'd completely neglected to mention Robert's existence to her.

"Why wouldn't he tell her?" asked Janey, shocked at the earl's omission.

Robert shrugged. "He thought she knew. The family details are in Debrett's, and of course, the *ton* knew of me." He smiled, grimly. "However, Jessica was not a member of the *ton* before her marriage."

"One would never guess now."

"One would never have guessed then, either. Not that it would ever have mattered, provided she makes Father happy."

"Does she?"

Robert hesitated. He thought no, not really, but he was honest enough to own his personal feelings could affect his judgment. "He has never said she makes him unhappy," he said at last.

Janey was silent for a moment. Her expression told

him she was thinking, assimilating the information. She had a quick mind and the ability to see things from angles no one else had noticed. It was one of the things he loved about her. So many of the ladies he had met could only be described, if one was being kind, as vacuous. They had pretty faces and coy ways they learned from their mamas, but underneath there was nothing. Their conversations consisted of ribbons and bows, and catty remarks about their rivals. Janey's intelligence was like a breath of fresh air.

On top of which, she was beautiful and goodhearted. She cared deeply for Ben, was a wonderful mother to Lucy, and seemed at ease with everybody. She had fitted well into the earl's privileged household but was equally at home talking to the tenants.

She was also perceptive. "So," she said now, "she married your father, expecting to bear his heir, only to discover that wasn't the case. That must have disappointed her."

She was right, of course. He supposed most ladies who married a title would like to think their sons would continue the line. Jessica would certainly have enjoyed being the mother of an earl, and the influence it gave her.

"And with Ben's arrival," continued Janey, "your youngest brother isn't even second in line."

"No," said Robert.

A new sympathy for Jessica moved through him. She'd been given a wooden penny when she expected a golden guinea. Not only were her stepsons a shock to her but knowing her own son was unlikely ever to be the earl must leave her insecure about her own future. Robert decided he would attempt to build a bridge to her, let her know she would always be accorded the honor and status due to his father's wife, no matter who wore the coronet.

But enough of his family's tribulations. It was a beautiful day and he had a beautiful woman at his side. He should concentrate his attention on her while he had the chance. So he changed the subject and asked, "would you like to take a trip out onto the lake? See the summerhouse?"

"I think that would be lovely." She smiled.

By the boathouse the sun shone on the water, making it glisten like diamonds in a tiara. The trees were a glorious mix of greens and browns, light and dark, with here and there a splash of deeper color as the first golden leaves of autumn fluttered on the soothing breeze. The island looked closer than it truly was in the clear sunshine, the summerhouse windows catching the light and bouncing it back so he had to squint to look at it.

He helped Janey down from the trap and led her to the boathouse door.

****

Jane enjoyed the ride over the placid lake. Robert removed his coat so he could row, and his muscles flexed beneath his linen shirt with every stroke. His shoulders were broad, his chest muscular, and with every oar stroke his thighs tightened under his pantalons. His hat sat beside him on the seat and the wind ruffled his hair, giving him a rakish look that suited him far too well. She blushed and tried to push away thoughts of running her hands over that hair, smoothing it, reveling in its cool softness.

At the island, he handed her out of the boat and onto the jetty, then led her along a path that cut through waist-high grasses and multi-colored wildflowers to the small mound in the middle, on which perched the summerhouse.

It was a large building, the stone walls of which had once been a bright white but which were now a grimy gray, the paint chipped. The windowpanes had the chewed appearance of wood left exposed too long to the ravages of wind and rain. The windows were spotted with dust and rain marks, and the place had an unloved, unused air.

"When my mother was alive, we picnicked here most weekends in summer," said Robert. "She had the icehouse built under it. The water keeps the temperature down in the hottest weather, and we didn't have to row the ice across for those meals." He grinned. "It can be heavy in the boat, and dashed slippery when you try to lift it out. Of course, it had to be rowed over to the mainland when we needed it in the house, but to be honest, we rarely had need of ice over there. My parents were not ones for formal parties."

"Just picnics," she said.

He laughed. "Just picnics."

"I am intrigued. Show me this icehouse."

He took her through the large room that made up most of the summerhouse, with its chairs and tables, gray with dust and disuse. To one side was a small dais where an orchestra might have sat, and there was a space on the floor that would have been ideal for dancing. Thickly coated cobwebs decorated the walls and ceilings and joined chair backs to table legs. Cricket bats and a pell-mell set lay incongruously on a table, ready for play.

At the rear was a small hallway that led, she presumed, to other rooms, and a second, less opulent corridor, which Jane assumed led to the service part of the summerhouse—the kitchens, the pantries, and other servants' rooms.

Halfway along this corridor, he stopped by a thick, wooden door, gray with age but sturdy and solid. Even through the wood, Jane felt the drop in temperature. Robert used his handkerchief to wipe grime and cobwebs from the dull brass door handle before he turned the key in the enormous lock. The heavy door creaked its protest when he strained to pull it open. A blast of ice-cold air hit Jane squarely in the face. She flinched and coughed.

"Sorry." He grinned. "There's been no need of ice for some time. Are you sure you wish to go down there?"

She shrugged her shoulders, uneasy, though she could not have said why. "It's not absolutely necessary." She shuddered and peered down into the impenetrable darkness.

"It's ideal for storing ice, but not a friendly place to visit." He closed the door. "Now, let me give you a tour of the rest of the island." He chuckled. "It should take us, oh, I'd say, four or five minutes to see everything."

Chapter Twenty-One

The path led away from the summerhouse toward the jetty, but a small spur branched off and wound its way through rhododendron bushes that grew lush and thick over the island. Some of the bushes were small, no higher than Jane's waist. Others were taller than Robert, and darkened the path.

"Looks as if the gardeners haven't been here for a while," said Robert as he pushed past the robust plants. "I'll send them over before these bushes kill everything else on the island."

They pushed on, single file along the narrow path. Once or twice, the foliage on this side of the island blocked Jane's view of the summerhouse and the shore, leaving her disoriented, unsure of her direction. The overgrowth hid the sky, unnerving her. She tried to hide her unease, but kept Robert firmly in her view. The scent of the flowers was overwhelming, sweet yet spicy, and to Jane, nauseating. She tried breathing through her mouth to mitigate the powerful effect the perfume had on her, and was relieved when they returned to the summerhouse. Dust coated her boots and tinged the hem of her skirt. She could not imagine the present Lady Barwell spending her days here.

"There you have it." Robert smiled. "Carrow's island." He chuckled. "I may still have the treasure map I drew of the place when I was nine."

"Pirate treasure?"

"Is there any other kind? Father pointed out Barwell is a long way from the sea, but I told him that was the genius of my pirates. Any Tom, Dick, or Francis might find treasure buried near the coast, but who would think to look here?"

Jane nodded sagely. "Truly cunning pirates."

"Precisely." He gave a small bow of acknowledgement.

Jane stepped back into the summerhouse and studied the furniture, dusty and disused. Some of it would never be used again, the wood splintered and cracked, or broken apart, chair legs broken, table tops gouged. Other pieces looked more robust, needing no more than a cleaning and, perhaps, a fresh coat of paint.

Jane looked toward the plusher of the two corridors that led away from the ballroom. "What's down there?"

Robert's smile grew wistful. "Just one other room. A resting chamber. My mother used to rest in there when the rigors of a day here grew too much for her. She was ill for a long time, and though she enjoyed spending time on the island, socializing, or even just being with the family, it left her weak. Father had the extra chamber added so she had somewhere quiet when the need of respite arose. Before then, the summerhouse was just this room, the kitchens, and the icehouse."

"I'm sorry," whispered Jane. It seemed inadequate for the wealth of pain she heard in his voice, but what else could she say? That he had loved his mother was evident. He clearly missed her. Jane knew, from the way she still missed her father, such a loss didn't lessen. It simply became easier to bear.

"It's a beautiful room. Or, at least, it was." Robert

frowned. "I wonder if time has wrought much damage in there." He bowed and held his arm for her to take. "My lady?"

The door to the resting chamber was covered with more thick cobwebs, the handle dull and the keyhole all but obscured. It was plain nobody had visited for a long time, possibly since the lady it was built for had died. Jane was uneasy about disturbing it.

Robert, however, had no such qualms. He reached up, grabbed at the cobwebs, and pulled them from the door as if he was tearing open a curtain. The remains hung loose on the hinged side of the frame, with just a few threads clinging stubbornly to the main body of the door. He clapped his hands together, clearing gossamer and dust from the palms of his leather gloves, then turned the handle and pushed the door to open it.

At first, nothing happened. Jane thought it must still be locked, but Robert leaned on it heavily and shoved, and it gave with a groan, followed by a scraping sound as the warped bottom dragged across the floor.

"They can rehang this and oil the hinges when they come to deal with the rhododendrons," he said. He gave one last push, and the door opened fully.

The chamber was about half the size of the main room of the summerhouse. It had a dry smell, a little stale but not musty or unpleasant. The windows were smaller than in the main room, their angle and design subduing the light and making the room shaded and restful. The grime on them now made the room even darker, but not in a sinister way, like the darkness of the icehouse. This darkness was restful, comforting, inviting even. Holland cloths covered the furniture, protecting it from the dust and old air. Robert pushed one of the cloths back to reveal a plush, blue velvet day bed, with matching cushions resting on it.

Jane ran her fingers over the beautiful upholstery. Even through her gloves she could feel the depth of the material. No expense had been spared for the late countess's comfort. "It's beautiful," Jane murmured.

"My mother's favorite color." Robert's voice was low, reverential. Jane felt as if she intruded on his private thoughts. Then he sighed, heavily, and peeled back another cover, revealing a small table made of polished, dark wood, a leather inlay in the top, the exact shade of blue of the bed. Under the tabletop was a narrow drawer. "She would sit here and write letters," he explained.

Jane stepped back to give him space to relive his memories, but her foot hit a brass doorstop. She tripped and struggled to stay upright, windmilling her arms and leaning forward to balance herself. Robert grabbed her shoulders to steady her, and the combination of his pull and her leaning propelled them both onto the day bed. Unable to stop the fall, Jane landed on him, knocking the breath from both of them. Her breasts pressed against his chest and her skirts wrapped around his legs, their faces mere inches apart. She stared down into his dark eyes and could not look away.

Her heartbeat raced, so strong and loud she thought he must hear it. Every nerve in her body was on edge, and her skin prickled. Her cotton shift rubbed against her, bringing her nipples to sharp, deliciously painful points, and there was a warmth between her legs that made her want to press herself against him, against the growing hardness of him.

She wasn't sure which one of them moved but, slowly, the space between them diminished until she could feel his breath on her cheek. His eyes softened, dark lashes shading them as he concentrated his attention on her mouth. She smelled the wind in his hair and the lake on his skin, the fresh, outdoorsy smell of him drawing her in.

The first touch of his lips on hers was soft, barely there. She wanted to hold him to her, to press her lips to his and make him kiss her properly, the way he'd kissed her before. She wrapped her arms around his neck and pulled him closer, and he smiled against her mouth, before he deepened the kiss. His hands slid across her back and over the nape of her neck, his fingers warm and slightly rough against her smooth skin. Her spirit soared as she realized he had removed his gloves. Deftly, he undid the ribbons on her bonnet, then swept his hand through her hair. Pins scattered. Her hair fell, heavy and thick. He slid his fingers through it, slowly, with the slightest of tugs.

"Beautiful," he murmured. Jane gave a tiny moan in response.

His lips nipped at her jawline. She touched his chest and felt the erratic beat of his heart. Her own gloves disappeared, though she was not conscious of removing them.

Slowly, unsteadily, she unbuttoned his waistcoat and pulled his shirt clear of his trousers, then pushed her hand under the linen and caressed his warm skin. A muscle jumped, and he groaned. When she rubbed her palms over his nipples, he bucked his hips.

"You're killing me," he whispered, and he flipped them over so that she lay on her back and he was beside her, gazing down at her.

Then, somehow, they were both naked, clothes

discarded in a breathtaking rush. The cool air stroked her skin, making her nipples pucker and sending shivers through her belly and down to her very core. She eyed him, greedily taking in every detail. The smattering of dark hair at his throat spread, as she had thought it would, over his powerful chest and down to his flat stomach before gathering into a narrow line that led her eyes down to his impressive manhood, standing proud and hard and ready.

A shudder of fear went through her as she remembered the last time she'd been intimate with a man. The only time. Sydney hadn't undressed. He had merely unbuttoned his fall, lifted Jane's skirts, and thrust himself into her, hard and sharp. She had cried out in pain and was sore for days. Tense and stiff, she waited for a repeat of that experience.

It didn't come. Instead, Robert slid his hand along her thigh, stroking her leg, almost worshipful in his touch. He circled her core, making her nerves quiver, and a soft moan escaped her before his mouth claimed hers again. Still his hand roved over her, making her ache, driving her to distraction. She wrapped her arms tightly about him and pulled him closer, until her breasts mashed against his chest and the slick warmth of his skin set her afire.

Finally, finally, he touched the little nub of nerves at her center, and she nearly shot off the day bed. She ached, but it was wonderful. She wanted but she didn't want, hot and cold, outside herself looking in, but at the same time she was here, part of it. She wanted him to stop. She wanted him to go on forever.

And then she shattered. Her muscles turned to jelly and her bones to water. She saw stars.

"I've never…I never thought…" She didn't know what she meant to say, and she couldn't have said it anyway. She just lay still in the afterglow and wished this moment could last forever.

****

Robert held her while she came apart, loving the feel of his rough hands against her silky skin. He had never been with a woman so responsive to his touch. Her pleasure gave him pleasure, and the anticipation of what came next made him so hard it was painful. Her heart beat, fast and loud, her breath caught, and her muscles quivered, filling him with male pride. *Mine,* he wanted to shout. *I did that.*

Her breathing slowed and her heart steadied. He drew little circles on her skin with the tip of his finger and leaned in to kiss her again. He licked her lips and just like that, she took off again. Her nipples hardened, inviting him, and she writhed and twisted as the ecstasy built once more within her.

When she was nearly at the peak again, he entered her. She held him, arms around his shoulders, legs around his hips, and met him thrust for thrust, drawing him deeper, higher, further until, with a scream, she came again.

He wanted to stay buried inside her, enjoying the quivers and shudders of her body. But his own peak was nearing, and he pulled out, spilling his seed onto the Holland cloth before collapsing beside her.

"I didn't know it was like this." She closed her eyes and settled against him, her head on his chest. He put his arm around her and pulled her closer.

It took a minute for her words to sink into his sex-addled brain. *I've never,* she'd said. *I didn't know it was like this.* He frowned. Had her husband never taken care of her needs before his own? Robert knew some men were selfish lovers, thinking only of their own satisfaction. Had Janey's husband been one of them?

Uncertain if he should broach the subject, he tried to put it from his mind and concentrate on the wonderful feeling of her, soft and warm in his arms. But her disjointed phrases haunted him, and he had to know.

"It wasn't like this? Before?"

For a long moment, she lay silent and still. He began to think she'd fallen asleep. Then, finally, she said, "No. Last time, it hurt."

He looked down at the top of her head, at her curls falling across his chest. He wanted to put his hands into that lovely mane, feel it flow over his fingers. And he would do that. Soon. Right now, though, he needed to know what she meant. "It hurt?"

"Yes." She gave a little huff. "The first time does hurt for a woman, I'm told."

The first time? Had her husband bedded her only once?

"Even if the man is gentle, Mama said, it hurts," she continued.

Even if the man is gentle? Robert's jaw tensed. Every other muscle within him stilled. Surely, he had misunderstood. Janey's husband could not have… He swallowed and forced the question through gritted teeth. "He was rough?"

A moment of silence. He thought she would not answer. Then, "Yes."

Robert saw red. He wanted to go now and find the bastard who had treated her like a strumpet, and tear him limb from limb. He wished the man was not dead so he could kill him.

"He said I deserved it, that I made him do..." She took a deep breath. "We didn't take our clothes off. He pulled up my skirt and..." Her cheeks reddened and she turned away, but not before he saw the tears.

Robert's jaw was so tight his teeth clamped together. A muscle twitched in his cheek, and he had to make a conscious effort not to explode. Damn the man! If he'd been anyone other than her husband, it would have been rape. Hang that! Robert still called it rape, even if the law said what a man did to his wife was legal. He wanted to go and dig up the blackguard's remains and shoot him. He wanted to hang him from a tree as a warning to others to treat their wives well. He wanted...

Most of all, he wanted to comfort Janey. He held her closer and kissed the top of her head. "You didn't make him do anything," he said. "You deserved to be treasured, loved. Never let anyone tell you otherwise."

Her shoulders shook. He simply held her while she cried.

****

The sun was low in the sky when they drove back to Carrow House. Jane sat next to Robert in the trap and wondered if their time in the summerhouse had affected him as much as it had her. Probably not. His tanned face glowed in the early evening light, the beginnings of a beard shadowed his jaw, and his eyes watched the road, steady and relaxed. He did not look like a man whose life and feelings had been upended the way hers had been.

Perhaps men always felt differently after it had happened? Sydney certainly had. Before, he'd spoken such loving words to her, promised her so much. Then after...after he was finished, he discarded her. Was that how it was for every man?

Jane hoped not. Today had been the best experience of her life, for all she now felt that every nerve was stretched taut with the fear that the world and his wife would know what they'd done, that her face shone so red and guilty that even someone as unaware as Ben would know her for a wanton. Even now, her heartbeat was fast and erratic and there was a strange, tingling churning in her stomach and chest. She wanted it to go away, to let her return to her normal, sensible self. But at the same moment, she wanted it to stay forever, to help her relive those moments in Robert's arms, his skin against hers, his lips sending hot shivers through her.

What would happen now? Would they remain friends? Would he discard her as Sydney had done, ridiculing her and calling her names? Or would they be closer, their feelings growing deeper?

Indeed, did she want that? There were so many other considerations, other people who would be affected. It could be, would be, a terrible tangle. And yet…if only this day, this time with Robert never had to end.

They pulled up at the stables. Robert handed the reins to a groom and told the head gardener he wanted the island cleared at the earliest convenience, then walked with Jane, his hand resting lightly at her back. An innocent gesture, but Jane felt his heat on her skin as if all the layers of clothing between them had simply vanished. Contentment filled her.

In this companionable silence, they entered the house and found Lady Barwell standing in the hall, her back ramrod straight and a malevolent smile on her face that instantly drained the happiness from Jane and replaced it with dread. In the countess' hand was a letter.

"Did you have a good ride?" she asked, her voice sickly sweet. Jane's heart stuttered as if the woman's venom had pierced it.

"Thank you, yes," said Robert. A glance told Jane he, too, was wary of his stepmother.

"What about you, Mrs. Frobisher?" The countess's smile widened. "Or should I call you Miss Winter?"

Everything within Jane stopped dead. She couldn't move, couldn't take a breath. Her eyes, fixed on the woman's smug expression, could not blink. Even her heart seemed to hesitate.

Robert said something, though Jane did not register his individual words. She heard in his tone that he was angry, but whether at Lady Barwell or at Jane, she could not have said. Lady Barwell stared at Jane, and completely ignored Robert.

It was a bluff. It had to be. Lady Barwell did not know of Jane's past. She was merely fishing, and if Jane didn't take the bait, she would fail. For how could she know…?

Lady Barwell held up the letter. "I saw through you from the first," she said. "I saw you'd set your cap for my stepson."

"I did not…" Jane whispered.

"Jessica, you go too far." Robert's voice was as sharp as a dagger.

"On the contrary, Robert. A woman knows when another woman has a man in her sights. Naturally, as your stepmother, I was concerned and wanted to know more about her. You have a position to consider. I needed to know she was suitable."

Jane's blood roared past her ears, and she trembled. Her face burned, and the skin along her hairline prickled.

Nausea threatened to overwhelm her.

"So I sent to Dorset to make enquiries," continued Lady Barwell.

"You had no business doing so," countered Robert.

"On the contrary," replied the countess, and her grin made Jane flinch. "Considering what I discovered, not only was it my business, but it is my duty to expose her lies and subterfuge."

No. No. No. Was Jane never to finish paying for her one indiscretion?

"Our Miss Winter has always had ideas above her station," Lady Barwell went on. "I have learned there never was a Mr. Frobisher. Just a lightskirt who thought she could trap the son of the local magistrate. It didn't work, though, did it, Miss Winter? You were forced to quit your home in disgrace, and your family, including my husband's eldest son," she put her hand to her chest as if to hold in horrified sorrow, "shared your shame."

Jane wanted to shout that it wasn't true, but she couldn't. It *was* true. At least, in part. She hadn't tried to trap Sidney, but she had let him…

"You scheming little harlot."

There was no escape. Everywhere she went, no matter what she tried to do, how perfectly she behaved, it was always there. *Harlot.* It was as though it was etched into her face for the world to see and know. *Harlot.*

Robert stared at the countess. His jaw was clenched, his mouth a thin line rimmed with white. He knew. There was no room for doubt. Not after today. Not after she'd lain in his arms on his mother's day bed, and they…

This time there was no excusing her behavior. This time, she wasn't a naïve girl who believed she'd been promised marriage. This time, she had undeniably played the wanton. The harlot.

"I hope you are wiser than to let her lift her skirts for you," Lady Barwell said to Robert, a satisfied gleam in her eye. "She will force you to offer, like she tried to force poor Mr. Greening. And while we can prevent her success in that, it would be unpleasant, and that would disappoint your father. Should he suffer a relapse because of this…"

If Robert's jaw tightened any more, it would smash. Fury sparked from his narrowed eyes, and his lips pressed together until they all but disappeared. A spot of angry red marred his cheek, his shoulders tense and his hands fisted. He stared at his stepmother.

He cannot even bear to look at me.

From a room nearby, Jane heard Ben giggle, and Mama told him to come with her. A door handle rattled.

Jane could not face them. She could not bear to see the bewilderment in Ben's eyes, or Mama's disappointment. Not again.

On a sob, she ran for the stairs. She thought she heard Robert's boots on the tiles behind her, but she didn't look round. She ran, and she didn't stop till she reached her chamber, where she locked the door, threw herself on the bed and cried her heart to pieces.

****

Robert tried to chase after Jane but she was too quick. His legs were not back to full strength yet, so even though he took the stairs as quickly as he could, by the time he reached the corridor he heard her door slam shut and the small click of the key turning in the lock. Although, even if she hadn't locked the door, he could not have followed her inside. Not without implying he thought her what Jessica had called her.

But oh! How he longed to comfort her. To take her in his arms and hold her until her tears stopped and her fears faded. He wanted to tell her that her past did not condemn her. Not to him. Not after what he had learned in the summerhouse…

Greening—Jessica had given a name to the villain who'd done Jane so much harm. The man had raped her—that much was obvious. Taken her innocence, and when he'd got what he wanted, refused to honor the promises he'd doubtless lured her with. Although Jane should be grateful he'd done that last part. Otherwise she would have been doomed to a lifetime of misery with such a man, a man who had obviously refused to acknowledge his daughter and who'd had his victim's family hounded and exiled to boot. And who disclosed his version of the story to anyone who asked, with not a care for the lady's reputation or wellbeing.

The man should be horsewhipped. More than that. He should be pummeled until he crawled in the dirt like the pathetic little insect he was. Robert clenched and unclenched his fists. He wanted to ride hotfoot to Dorset and face down the toad. Only the thought that it would do more harm than good to Janey kept him from doing so.

With a growl of frustration, he strode back along the corridor and charged down the stairs. His temper burned, and if he saw Jessica again now, he'd throttle her! She had made enquiries? She had made *enquiries*? How dare she? What right did she have to send to Dorset, or anywhere else, to investigate a woman who had done her no harm? A woman who'd suffered enough already. Janey had been ill used and abandoned, moved halfway across the country and forced to begin again, yet Robert had never seen a trace of bitterness in her at her lot. She had not given away the baby, as many women would have, putting it behind her and pretending it had never happened. Instead, she had brought up a delightful child with love and patience. Time and again, Janey had proved herself to be honest and bright, caring and giving, gentle and kind, beautiful on the inside as well as outside.

In short, she was everything Jessica was not.

Robert would not be responsible for what he said or did if he saw his stepmother now. Nor, he realized, could he face Jane's mother, or his father. Not until he had calmed down and worked out what to do next.

Looking for solitude to order his thoughts, he slipped outside and walked through the gardens toward the park. Twilight gave way to dusk, the sapphire sky darkening at the edges. The trees were silhouettes and the color leached from the landscape. It suited his mood.

A rustle in the trees stopped him. He peered at the wood but saw no one. "Who's there?" he demanded. He generally turned a blind eye to poachers, reasoning that people must feed themselves somehow, but tonight he was likely to put the fear of God into the man.

It wasn't a poacher that stepped out from the trees, however, but one of his father's workers. Robert had seen the man once or twice, receiving orders, usually from the countess. He couldn't remember the fellow's name and didn't think he'd been employed here long.

"Begging your pardon, sir," said the man. He touched his forelock in a ridiculously subservient way. "I've been sent to fetch help. It's Mr. Willis, sir."

The head gardener. "What about him?"

"He's had a mishap, sir. Over on the island."

"The island? What was he doing there at this time of day?"

"He was clearing the bushes, sir, and—"

"Oh, for crying out loud! I didn't mean he should do it now." Why on earth had the man started such a long and arduous job at this end of the day? Did he have no sense?

"No, sir. But, thing is, he's had a fall and I can't lift him, not on my own. I'll get one of the grooms…"

Robert sighed. "I'll help you. Where is he?"

The man bowed. "Thank you, sir. This way, sir."

They rowed to the island and the man led Robert toward the summerhouse. "He went in to fetch summat," said the man, "and he fell down the steps. I think he broke his leg."

Robert shook his head and rolled his eyes. This got more and more farcical. Not only had Willis come to the island as it grew dark, but he had then seen fit to go into the icehouse. He must have left his wits in his Sunday coat. He was going to get a good piece of Robert's mind, broken leg or no.

He stepped through the icehouse door and put his foot on the first step. "Willis?" he called into the dark, then half turned to the man behind him. "Do you have a lamp?"

The man shoved Robert hard. Startled, Robert swayed for an instant, pushing out his arms in a vain attempt to keep his balance. He took an instinctive step forward, trod on air, and tumbled down the steps, landing face first against the cold, hard floor. His nose hurt from the collision, making his eyes water, and his cheek stung, as did his hands, though his gloves had shielded them from the worst of the impact.

The light disappeared completely as the door at the top of the stairs clicked shut. The lock scraped, loud and terrifying, and Robert was left alone in the freezing dark.

Chapter Twenty-Two

Jane woke with a stiff neck. Her eyes were swollen and hot, and her cheeks itched. No light came through the window, which told her it was late. Plainly, nobody had come to find her for dinner. Had they decided she wasn't fit to sit at table with them now they knew the truth? She couldn't think Mama would agree to that, but then, what could Mama do? She was a guest, and if she offended her hosts, she might be forced to leave, without Ben. Indeed, for all Jane knew, she had already been asked to leave and take her harlot daughter with her.

On that thought, Jane sat up. The pain of movement shot through her temples like a bolt and she groaned, closing her eyes. Sparks of red and orange sparked across her eyelids, but she couldn't let that stop her. She needed to know what had happened to her family while she had been hiding in here, wallowing in self-pity.

Lady Barwell had delighted in brandishing her letter, exposing Jane's scandal. Worse, Robert had been disgusted. He didn't even look at Jane while his stepmother delivered her news. All Jane had wanted at that moment was for him to take her in his arms, shield her from her shame, and tell her it mattered not one jot. He hadn't done so.

Because it did matter. It mattered that Jane had been a stupid girl with no morals and ruined herself. It mattered that Lucy was illegitimate. If that became known, the child would never be welcome anywhere, her life in tatters before it even started. And it mattered that Jane and Mama had lied to Robert. Oh, they'd only told him what they told everyone else, but that was a poor excuse. Robert wasn't everyone else. He'd deserved the truth.

What would he do, now he knew?

He had so much power. He could take Ben from them and forbid Jane, Lucy, and Mama ever to see him again.

Jane massaged her temples and tried to ease her fears along with the roaring ache inside her skull. Robert *could* take Ben from them, but she didn't think he would. In the weeks since they'd met, it was obvious Robert had come to care for Ben. He wouldn't hurt him by taking away the only family he'd ever known, no matter what that family had done.

Nor did she believe Robert—or his father, for that matter—capable of being vindictive toward Mama, no matter the disdain they now had for Jane.

Lady Barwell, of course, was a different kettle of fish. Her cold, cruel streak had been evident in the glee with which she'd denounced Jane. She'd not even attempted to mitigate the calamity by speaking to Jane privately. No, she'd denounced her loudly and with as much fanfare as possible.

The woman wanted Jane removed from her home. Indeed, Jane was surprised not to have been ejected already. But where was she to go? What would she do?

She might find a position as a housekeeper, or a companion, she supposed, if Lord Barwell's family were prepared to be discreet. Fresh tears fell as she dismissed those possibilities, for who would employ a woman with a lively child? To gain a position, Jane would have to leave Lucy with Mama. Her heart cracked at the thought, and she massaged her chest with the heel of her hand, trying to ease the pain.

Such a tangle. Such a heart-wrenching mess. And the worst thing was, Jane had only herself to blame.

She got up and used the cold water in her basin to clean her face and soothe her eyes. While she tried to make herself presentable, she heard hurrying footsteps in the corridor, then Mama called out, "Benedict Winter, come here this instant! What have I told you about going up those stairs? That tower is not safe!"

"I not Ben'dic' Winter," said Ben, defiantly. "I Ben'dic' Carrow."

"I don't care if you're the king of England," Mama said, sternly. "Get. Down."

Jane smiled, despite herself. After thirty years, he hadn't learned back-answering Mama would get him nowhere. Plus, hearing the exchange made her feel better. If Mama had heard of Jane's unmasking, she would have been here, comforting her daughter, not chasing Ben. If she hadn't yet heard, then things may not be too dire. Perhaps Mama would be able to stay here, and only Jane would be forced to leave.

Outside her room, she heard the sound of Ben's shoes, scraping on the tower's stone steps before shuffling on the wood floor of the corridor. A heavy door closed, presumably cutting off his access to the tower, and then Mama and Ben moved away, their voices growing fainter as Mama scolded and Ben complained.

Jane blinked back fresh tears. She would miss her family so much when she went. And she would miss Robert, though she knew he would not miss her. On the contrary, he would look upon her departure with relief, and that was devastating. Even though she would never see him again, she did not want him to think badly of her.

For a few moments, she let herself remember today. Their lovemaking in the summerhouse had been one of the best things that had ever happened to her, and knowing it would never be repeated caused a sharp pain in her chest that made her gasp. Deliberately, Jane went over every moment of it, committing it to memory, keeping it safe, so that, in the long, lonely times ahead of her, she would have it to remind herself of a day when, for a short while, she had been truly, truly happy.

****

Robert had no idea if he'd been trapped in here for thirty minutes or several hours. The darkness was absolute, no chink of light from anywhere. Not that he would have expected any, even if there was a way for it to penetrate the thick, underwater walls, for it had been growing dark when he got here and must be full night by now.

How could he have been so foolish? He should have known Willis wasn't stupid enough to begin a job this big at the tail end of a day. But it hadn't occurred to him that one of his father's servants would turn on him like that. He could not, for the life of him, think of a reason why the man should have done so.

It might well be the end of his life, he thought, staring into a darkness so complete it hurt his eyes. The temperature in here was wintery, as it was designed to be. He'd stopped feeling the cold air on his skin, and the tips of his nose and ears had gone from stinging to heavy and numb. The soles of his feet felt as if wooden blocks had been placed into his boots, and his fingers and toes ached. They didn't want to move when he reminded himself to flex them.

When he'd first been locked in, he'd scrambled up the steps and pounded at the door, yelling until his throat hurt. There'd been nothing but silence from the other side. Desperately, he'd rammed it, but the door was thick oak, designed to hold in the cold air, and all he managed to do was hurt his shoulder.

Now he shivered. His teeth rattled, and he clenched his jaw to stop them as he paced across the chamber, swinging his arms around himself vigorously, both to keep his circulation going and to avoid colliding headfirst with the rough wall. His fists had stung at first where they'd collided with the stone, but the pain had disappeared now, anesthetized by the cold. His muscles felt heavier and heavier, each step an effort, as if he waded through thigh-high mud, when all he really wanted to do was sit down and go to sleep, and…

No! That's how people died in the cold. And whatever happened here tonight, Robert was determined he would not die. Not until he got back to the house and saw Janey again.

Janey. She'd been devastated by Jessica's vile words. The look of horror she'd thrown at him before she ran…did she think it would change how he felt?

Of course she did! And with good reason. Many people, on learning such a thing about her, would have judged her as Jessica had. Most of the ladies in Society would cut her, while the gentlemen would think her fair game.

Hah! Ladies and gentlemen? Not one of them was worthy of the name. His Janey was worth more than all of them combined.

He wished he hadn't left her alone after Jessica's ambush. Instead of walking away and leaving her to her privacy like the coward he was, he should have knocked on her bedroom door and made her speak with him. She needed to know that he didn't care what Jessica said. Whatever had happened to her in the past, whatever others might say or think, it didn't matter, because Robert loved her as much now that he knew the truth as he ever had before.

No, that wasn't right. He didn't love her as much now as he had before. He loved her more, much more, now. Then, he had loved Janey, the widow with so many responsibilities, the loving mother and protective sister, the intelligent woman with a keen sense of humor and eyes that sparkled with her zest for life.

But there was so much more to her than those things. To start, there was the strength that had pulled her through when she was raped, for Robert had no doubt that was what happened. It was the worst thing that could happen to a woman and she still live, but Janey had not only survived it, she'd managed to put it behind her when many women would have gone into a permanent decline. Not only that, but when her violation resulted in a child, Janey hadn't taken the easy way out by leaving the baby girl to an uncertain future on the church steps but had opened her big heart and loved her.

Janey Frobisher...Winter, he corrected himself, was a wonderful, incredible woman, beautiful through and through. And Robert had to live long enough to tell her that.

The thought renewed his resolve. With a huge effort, he moved from the wall where he had been leaning, on the verge of giving in to the lethargy, and stumbled around the floor, beating his hands against his upper arms to restart his sluggish circulation.

After several circuits of the room he finally found the steps that led to the door. Slowly, on all fours, he climbed, his hands and knees protesting each time he put his weight on them, his muscles groaning at each movement. After what seemed like hours, he reached the reinforced door at the top and tried to think what to do next. Breaking the door down had been beyond him when he was at full strength; it would be impossible now. But there had to be something he could do. He refused to simply sit there and give up, not while there was breath in his body. He leaned against the door, rubbed his eyes with the palms of his hands, and prayed for inspiration.

****

Jane must have fallen asleep, because when she came to, it was fully night and the only light was from the moon. It coated everything lemon-blue and threw shadows that made everyday objects grotesque and menacing.

The house was quiet. Everyone must have retired for the night. She moved, and the ropes under the mattress squeaked. It was probably little more than a whisper, but it sounded deafening to Jane. Carefully, she climbed down, straightened her dress, and tidied her hair.

The air was chill. She shivered and wrapped her shawl around her shoulders. Then her stomach growled, reminding her she hadn't had dinner.

It wouldn't take long, she thought, to go to the kitchens and find something to eat. She didn't need much: bread, a piece of cheese or ham, a cup of milk. At this time of night, she was unlikely to encounter anyone, so there was little chance of further unpleasantness.

She left her chamber, then gasped, alarmed by the wraithlike figure at one of the corridor windows. Moonlight drained his color, leaving him looking pale and lifeless, and scary. Jane put her hand on her chest, as if that could still her racing heart.

"Ben?" she whispered.

He looked around, gave her a blank stare, then turned to look out of the window again. His nightshirt reached his ankles and his feet were bare, and his hair stuck up in clumps as if he'd been running his hands through it.

"Why are you here?" she asked. "Shouldn't you be in bed?"

"You not in charge of me," he said, belligerently.

Jane raised an eyebrow, shocked by the anger and defiance in his voice. "No," she agreed. "I'm not. But I am your sister, and—"

"You not my sister." His bottom lip came out in a pout that signaled a brewing tantrum.

"I love you as if I was your sister," she answered, carefully. "Aren't you cold?" She shivered dramatically and pulled her shawl tighter to reinforce her words.

"No."

There was a pause. Jane tried to think of a way to coax him back to his bed.

"I am man," he said, at last. "People not tell me what do."

Jane made a small noise, acquiescing. "I suppose not."

"Not you. Not Mama."

It made sense now, as Jane recalled the argument she'd heard when Mama caught Ben climbing the stairs to the tower. He must still be smarting from the scolding he'd received.

"Mama worries for you," Jane said.

"She not my Mama." Oh dear. This was not going to go well. "I tell Robert. Robert will tell her, don't tell Ben what do. Soon as he come home."

Jane frowned. "As soon as he comes home?" Ben nodded. "He went out?"

Ben looked at her as if she was a simpleton. "She say you go with him, but I know you not." He paused, then said, "She say I go in tower. Give me mission."

Now Jane was completely lost. "Who? Who gave you permission, Ben?"

"Lady Barwell. She say I grown man, not worry what Mama say."

Lady Barwell was trying to undermine Ben's relationship with Mama? Did she hope to be rid of her next? Jane must warn Mama, before it got out of hand. Perhaps she could persuade Robert to tolerate her company, too, at least long enough for Jane to enlist his help on this, should she need it.

Thinking of Robert reminded her of Ben's words. "Robert went out?" she asked. Ben nodded. "And Lady Barwell said I went with him?"

Ben nodded again. "You not come dinner. She say you out." That explained why nobody had looked for her. "She wrong. I see him go. You not there. I watching till he come home, then I say, tell Mama I am man."

Jane looked out of the window. The grass was silver in the moonlight, the flowers and bushes dark shapes around it. Beyond the park, the woods were a mass of darkness and, in the distance, the moon shimmered on the lake's surface.

If Robert had gone out, surely he would have used

the front door? Why would he go into the garden at night? And having done so, why hadn't he returned?

A strange shiver skittered up her spine and a sense of foreboding came upon her. She swallowed and told herself to stop being so fanciful. This was Robert's family home. He could wander the grounds if he wished. And yet…

"You saw him go?" she asked, trying not to sound anxious. Ben would pick up on her feelings, and she didn't want him any more agitated than he already was. "Where did he go?"

"On water."

What? Confusion frightened her. Why on earth would he be in the water?

"Robert was in the water?" she asked, her voice as calm as she could make it.

Ben rolled his eyes at her. "Not *in* water," he said, exasperated. "On. In boat."

In a boat? Had Ben seen them when they'd rowed to the island? "I was with Robert in the boat," she admitted. "But we came back."

"No!" Ben's frustration was plain. "You not there! Robert and man."

Robert had directed his head gardener to clear the island. Perhaps he'd gone back out and taken him to show him what needed to be done. If he had, though, it would have been hours ago. They wouldn't be there now, unless something was wrong.

Had they lost their boat and been unable to return? Had one of them been hurt? She remembered Robert talking of the near-miss accidents he'd had in recent months. Had his assailant caught up to him?

Jane needed to know he was all right. She needed to

go to the island and find him. Now. But she should also sound the alarm so that others might look for him, too. She could bang the gong in the hall to wake the household.

But what if she was wrong? What if there was an innocent explanation? She would have raised the hue and cry for nothing. People would be angry at their lost sleep, Robert would be embarrassed, and Jane would be even more unpopular than she was already.

Far better to be discreet about it for now. Although, if he was on that island, and hurt… She should alert someone, just in case. Someone discreet and understanding, someone who would help with the search but not make an entire opera out of it until it was necessary.

"Ben, listen," she whispered.

He turned and stared at her, his eyes big and dark in the moonlight.

"I know you don't want me telling you what to do, but would you do something for me if I asked you?"

He narrowed his eyes, warily.

"Please, it's very important."

He thought for a moment, then sighed. "Kay."

"Would you go and wake Mama and tell her what you told me about Robert in the boat?"

He glanced away, guiltily. "I in trouble?"

"No, no, Sweetling, you are not in trouble." *But Robert may be.* "But it's very important Mama knows what you saw. Can you tell her? Please? Tell her I've gone to the island to see if Robert is all right."

Ben gave a reluctant nod. "Yes," he agreed, and he ambled off to run his errand.

Jane raced back to her own chamber, found her coat

and boots, then hurried down the stairs and out of the house. She ran to the lake.

The night air had a cruel bite. It made her nose sting and her eyes water as she hurried across the park, startled deer scattering before her. Her hem grew heavy in the damp grass. An owl hooted, a lonely sound. Small clouds scudded against the sky, crossing the moon but never blocking it completely. She was thankful for that; she didn't think she would get far without its light.

The rowing boat was tied to the jetty at the shore, and it bobbed gently with the tiny swell of the water. Jane looked around, puzzled. If Robert and his man were on the island, why was the boat here? Were there two boats?

There must be, she decided, and she climbed gingerly into this one, released the mooring rope, and used one oar to push off, the way she'd seen Robert do earlier. She tried to row, but the oars were heavy and difficult to control. She stroked the water with one and the boat turned to the left. She used the other oar, and it turned back to the right. How had Robert made it look so easy? She gritted her teeth and tried again.

By the time she had mastered the oars and managed to travel in a more or less straight line to the island, she was wet and cold, and her shoulders hurt from the unaccustomed pulling through the heavy water. There was a musty smell to the lake at night, a mix of wet weed and mist, the old varnished wood of the boat and the damp wool of her coat. She coughed the smell away, and it sounded inordinately loud.

Finally, the boat bumped hard into the jetty on the island and she had to grab the mooring post to stop herself bouncing away again. Jane tied the boat to the post as well as she could, her cold fingers slipping on the uncooperative wet rope. Then she scrambled out of the vessel in a most inelegant fashion, stood on the jetty, and looked around.

She saw no other boat. Which didn't mean there wasn't one; it may have drifted from its moorings and left the men stranded. On that thought, she checked her knot once more before she walked along the jetty and onto the island itself.

There was no sign of life. No sound, nothing to say anyone had been here. Jane shuddered in the silence, then scolded herself for letting her imagination run wild. "You'll be seeing ghosts next," she muttered, but she still jumped when the breeze rattled the rhododendron bushes.

It was late and it was cold, and Robert was a sensible man. He would know rescue was unlikely to come until morning, so he would hardly sit out in the open on the off chance someone would come sooner. He'd take shelter, somewhere dry where he could sleep. Which meant he had to be in the summerhouse.

Jane pushed through the bushes. The moonlight struggled to penetrate here, and the uneven path was dark and dangerous. Sharp twigs scratched her skin and tugged at her coat. Several times, she stumbled.

After an eternity, she reached the summerhouse. It stood, dark, imposing, menacing even. There was no light from within it, no movement, no sign of life at all.

"Hello?" she called as she stepped inside. No one answered. "Hello?" There was the slightest echo in the room. She swallowed, hard.

Tiny footsteps scampered across the floor, and she was grateful she couldn't see whatever she heard. If she came face to face with a rat, she thought she might turn and run back to the boat, leaving Robert to take his chances.

Thinking of him and the trouble he might be in helped overcome her fear. She could just make out the shapes of the furniture around her. The building's stale smell was stronger now, as if the night enhanced it. Nothing moved. Jane sensed no other human in here at all.

She glanced at the small corridor that led to his mother's resting chamber. Darkness enveloped it now, hiding all but the first few feet of the hallway, but in Jane's mind she saw the chamber itself, with its velvet day bed, and the memories of what had happened there, when Robert held her, kissed her, and made her feel precious and loved. Had it really been just a few hours ago? So much had changed since then, it seemed as though a lifetime had passed since she had lain in his arms on what had been the most perfect day of her life.

Before it became the worst.

She swallowed the lump in her throat and blinked back hot tears. What was done was done, and no amount of wishing would alter it. Better to put it behind her. She took a deep breath and straightened her shoulders, turned to leave, then stopped when she heard the tiny scratching noise again. Her eyes widened, her throat dried as she looked around, half afraid of what she would see. There was nothing. No hint of movement.

She'd thought it was the footfall of a tiny animal, but now she wasn't so sure. The tapping was too even, too rhythmic. Rats and mice scurried, then stopped, then scurried on again in a much more random way.

"Hello?" she called softly. Nobody answered, but the scratching continued. She cocked her head and moved forward, listening intently, trying to follow it.

She reached the door to the icehouse and stopped. The noise was definitely coming from behind there. Jane put her ear to the wood, then rapped on the panel with her knuckles. The scratching stopped.

"Hello?" she called again, louder.

"Janey?" The voice was muffled but unmistakable. "Janey?"

"I'm here!"

"Can't…out…locked…"

Jane pulled at the door, but he was right—it was locked. There was no key in the lock, nor could she see one on the tables around the room. Her first thought was to race back to the house and fetch someone with a key. But what if there wasn't a key? Or, if there was, nobody knew where to find it? Why was the door locked anyway? It had not been locked before.

She remembered the icy air that had rushed her when he pulled the door open earlier. The cold had been a shock to her then, in the warmth of the day. Now it was the dead of night, and Robert had been trapped for hours, if Ben was to be believed. He said Robert had not come to dinner. Did that mean he'd been there since then?

"It's always freezing cold down there." That's what he'd said. People died in the freezing cold. Robert could be dying, right now.

There was no time to wake the household. She had to get him out of there, and she had to do it now. But how?

When Ben had accidentally locked himself in the pantry, Mama had broken the lock, and the door had opened. Perhaps the same would happen here. But breaking such a sturdy lock would take something big, something like…the doorstop! Jane ran to the resting chamber and found the heavy brass doorstop she'd tripped over earlier.

It took several blows, putting her entire weight behind each one, to break the lock. At last, though, the handle broke and clattered to the floor, and Jane was able to pull the heavy door open. Robert staggered two steps out of the icehouse, then fell to his knees, shivering uncontrollably, his teeth chattering. The end of his nose showed dark against the rest of his face, and ice crystals in his hair sparkled in the meagre light. His coat was stiff and cold, and he held his hands as if he could not move the fingers.

Remembering the tales her father had told of ice storms at sea, Jane knelt beside him and put her arms around him, hugging him tightly to push the warmth of her body into him. He hugged her back, though it clearly cost him a great deal of effort to do so.

They stayed on the summerhouse floor for an age. Her knees hurt where they pressed into the stone, and the tension in her arms made her shoulders ache, but she did not let go. The ice in his hair melted and ran down her face, and her own clothes were soaked, and still she held on, until, at last, his shivering lessened and his breathing evened.

"Thank you," he whispered, over and over. "Thank you."

She eased back and stared at the broken icehouse door. Somebody had locked him in. They'd tried, again, to kill him. And if it hadn't been for Ben's petulant mood…

Jane shuddered. Who could be doing this?

Chapter Twenty-Three

Robert clung to Janey as feeling returned to his fingers and toes. First, they felt wooden, then they tingled, and then as if he had been stung by a thousand bees. His nose pinched and his eyes watered, though he couldn't be certain there weren't real tears in there too, along with the effects of the cold.

He'd truly thought he would die tonight. As his strength ebbed and even lifting his pocketknife to scrape ineffectually at the door became more effort than he could manage, he'd known there was only one realistic outcome.

Nobody knew where he was. Or at least, nobody who was minded to rescue him. He'd supposed his family would miss him when he didn't turn up to dinner, although they might not have been unduly worried. It wouldn't be the first time he'd missed a meal with them because he was out, in the stables, with tenants, in the village. And even if someone did raise the alarm, they would not know where to search. By the time anyone checked the icehouse—if they ever did—Robert would have been long dead.

He wasn't frightened of dying, but he wasn't in a hurry to embrace it. He certainly didn't want to do it before he got the chance to see Janey one more time, to tell her how he felt and what she meant to him. She was his lifeline, the woman he loved. And now, like a miracle, she was holding him, warming him, saving him. He should say something. Tell her.

He opened his mouth to try. The words stuck in his throat as if they were still frozen there. The what-ifs of telling her terrified him as much, if not more, than the damned icehouse had done.

What if she didn't return his feelings?

What if she thought his declaration of love, at this time, was merely gratitude for her having saved him, literally, and not to be taken seriously?

What if he couldn't make her see she was the reason he'd clung on for so long, after hope of rescue had faded?

What if the scene Jessica had engineered had given Janey a disgust of his family, including him?

Oh, for goodness' sake! He was nothing but a coward, inventing reasons to avoid putting his heart on the line, when instead he needed to step up, be a man, and take his chance. True, she might say no, back away and reject him. But she might not. And if he didn't try, he would regret it for the rest of his life. On that thought, he opened his mouth to speak.

Janey beat him to it. "You might have died in there," she whispered. She held him a little tighter, as if clinging to him would keep him safe. It certainly felt to him as if it might.

"I think that was the idea." He shuddered, partly at the cold that still wracked through him, but mostly at the idea that whoever wanted to kill him had almost succeeded this time.

"Who can be doing all of these things to you?" She pulled away so she could look into his face. Immediately, he missed her nearness. He wanted to pull her back into his arms and hold her until she could not doubt the strength of his love for her. But now was not the time. Now was the time to address the other thing that had occupied his mind in the long, dark hours in the icehouse: the dangers that had faced him, and his father, over the past few months.

"I had some thoughts about that," he said. With some effort, he crawled to one of the tables and used it to steady himself as he stood. Hot pins pierced the soles of his feet as they took his weight, and he leaned heavily, gratefully, against the solidity of the table. He stomped from one foot to the other, easing the pain a little as blood started to flow again.

Janey watched him, carefully. "What did you think?"

He rubbed the palms of his hands together. The leather of his gloves made the friction less than he truly needed, but he still didn't have the strength in his fingers to pull the gloves off. His ears ached, inside and out, his neck was stiff, and his nose tingled and stung, but he was alive. And if he intended to stay that way, he needed to deal with this. Now.

"The attackers I encountered on my travels," he said, counting down his points on his aching fingers, "William, poisoning my father's brandy. The servant who lured me here and locked me in. They have nothing to gain from their actions, excepting that somebody paid them. While I do not deny they should face justice for what they tried to do, they are not the real enemy here. The real enemy is the person who paid them. That person had the means to pay for not one, but several attacks, and knowing that reduces the number of suspects significantly."

Janey's brow creased. Robert knew how she felt.

He'd asked the same questions before, but had found no answers. Strange how facing death had suddenly made everything so clear.

"Once I knew my assailant also had my father in their sights, it became easier to fathom, although, even then it took a great deal to convince me I could possibly be right."

Janey looked bewildered, and he smiled, although the movement made the muscles in his cheeks hurt. Dear Janey, so kind and caring. She would never understand the malice residing in some people's hearts. He hoped she never had to.

"It had to be someone who benefited from my demise," he continued, "and my father's. Someone who had funds enough to reach across the country, to employ assassins in various different places, and yet be close enough to be a threat to us at home. A footman could not do all that. Nor a coachman or a gardener. But a countess could."

In the dim moonlight, Janey's eyes widened, and she gasped. "Lady Barwell? You think…?" She shook her head in disbelief. "Why would she?"

"It was something you said that made me realize. You felt sorry for her because she'd expected to be the mother of an earl, only to discover I was ahead of her son." He shrugged, then groaned at the ache it caused. "And now, Barnaby is not even the spare."

Janey stared at him in horror. "Are you certain?" She huffed a humorless laugh. "Of course you're certain. You would not say so otherwise." She stood, took a few paces, turned and paced back, her hands clutched together at her waist. "I do not like the woman, but—to seek to have you killed simply to move her son up the line of succession…could anyone stoop so low?"

"They could." He gritted his teeth at the grim thought. "She kills me, Barnaby moves to my place in the line. If she then kills my father…" He shuddered. "It would be easier for her to keep a rein on her son, who is still a minor, and until Barnaby came of age she would have complete control of the earldom, and all that goes with it."

Janey covered her mouth with her hands, appalled. Robert understood; he hadn't wanted to believe it either, but it was the only thing that made sense of all that had happened. He remembered now, Jessica had been most put out to learn her new husband already had a son and heir. Damn his father! Why had he not told her about his family while they were courting? True, the information was easily obtained, but that didn't mean the earl shouldn't have ensured his wife-to-be was aware of it. If the foolish old man hadn't allowed a pretty woman to lead him by his…

"Killing you makes no sense now, though," said Janey, dragging him from his thoughts. "You are not the heir. Ben is."

"Ben will be no match for her." He ran his hand through his hair. It was still damp, but the ice crystals had gone. "Until we can prove her involvement, we need to keep him safe. Ensure he doesn't suffer any 'accidents.'"

Janey nodded. "Luckily, he's not a risk taker, so it shouldn't be too onerous a task. The only times he really gives us cause for alarm is when he sneaks up to your tower. It doesn't matter how many times Mama forbids it. He has a real bee in his bonnet about it, and—" She stopped and stared at him, though he doubted she saw him at that moment. *"She say I can go in tower,"* she whispered. *"She give me mission."*

"Say what?"

Her eyes focused on him. Even in the dimness, he could see the fear in them. "Lady Barwell gave Ben permission to go into the tower."

He cursed, then apologized for his language. "As soon as it's light, I will have the door nailed shut."

Janey shook her head. "That may be too late. Ben was awake. It was he who told me where you were. I told him…what if he didn't wake Mama as I said he should?" Her expression changed from frightened to terrified. "Lord, Robert, what if he sneaks up there while there's no one to stop him?"

"Let's go," said Robert. Ignoring the dull ache in his feet, he limped out of the summerhouse and toward the jetty.

****

Ben was not in his room. Jane had hoped and prayed he would be, while Robert rowed across the lake as fast as he could. They raced through the park, though she could hear in his labored breathing and stumbling footsteps that Robert struggled. It would take time for the effects of the icehouse to leave him completely. If he had died…

Jane had shoved the thought aside. This was not the time to wrap herself in might-have-beens. The very idea of a world where he no longer existed threatened to overpower her, and a tear ran down her cheek, hot against her cold skin. She had brushed it away roughly.

Now tears threatened again as she stared at Ben's crumpled, empty sheets. She knew, the moment she saw the house was quiet and dark, he had not gone to Mama.

If he had, every person from the boot boy to the earl himself would be up, searching for her and Robert.

Robert squeezed her fingers. "We'll find him," he murmured.

She followed him from Ben's room to the door to the tower, which stood open. The first few steps of the spiral stone staircase showed white in the moonlight, enticing the unwary, before they disappeared into the silent darkness.

"Will you wait here while I go up?" whispered Robert. She shook her head. He gave her one short nod, then ducked to go through the ancient door.

They climbed the narrow steps slowly, trying not to make a sound, lest it startle Ben. It was almost totally dark in here, with no windows to let in the moonlight. Jane held the rounded stone pillar the steps circled, and prayed they were as sturdy as they looked. She wanted to reach out ahead of her, to touch Robert's back and reassure herself he was still there, but she couldn't lest she cause him to miss his step and fall.

But oh! if she could! The desire to do so was so strong she could almost feel him...the thick wool of his coat, the flex of his muscles, strong and firm...

What was she thinking? As if he didn't already know her for a wanton! She clenched her fist and tensed her arm, as if that might keep it at her side, and continued up the stairs behind him.

"Careful," he whispered after they'd climbed for about five minutes. Her legs ached from the exertion, and she wanted to stop and stretch her back to ease the tension. She took one more step onto what must be a landing. It was wider than the steps and flatter, the stone more even, less worn.

She jumped when Robert took her arm. He apologized and drew her away from the top of the steps. "There's a door here," he murmured. "It opens to the roof." She felt his breath, warm against her ear and a shiver ran down her spine. "Ready?" he asked.

Jane nodded, then realized he couldn't see her. "Yes."

She heard a soft squeak as he turned the handle and pushed the door. A draught of cold air came in through the tiny crack. Jane shuddered. Then she tensed, terrified at the sound of Ben, crying out in anguish.

"No! Not want to! Let go!"

Desperate to help him, Jane tried to push through, but Robert blocked her way. "Easy," he whispered in the tone he would have used with a skittish horse.

"Ben's in trouble," she argued.

"He'll be in more trouble if we go racing out there halfcocked."

"But..."

"Janey, trust me." She stared at him. Although the sliver of light had helped her to get her bearings, Robert was still no more than a shadow against less densely packed shadows.

"It's a narrow ledge and a low parapet," he said. "If we charge out and startle him..."

She gasped. The thought that she and Robert might bring about the very tragedy they hoped to avert almost brought her to her knees.

"We'll go slowly," he whispered. "Don't alarm him."

Her chest hurt; her lungs refused to release her breath. She felt sick. *Please,* she prayed. *Please let him be all right.*

Slowly, silently, Robert pushed the door open. The draught increased, an icy blast of wind that forced its way past Jane and down the stairs. It tugged at her skirt and snatched her hair, and she had to put her hand on the wall to steady herself. The cold stone beneath her fingers steadied her, even as Ben cried out again.

"I not want it!"

The door was open wide enough for them to move through it now, and Jane followed Robert onto the ledge. About two feet wide, the walkway lay between the sloping lead roof of the tower on one side and a crenulated stone parapet on the other. The parapet, which was about three feet tall, was all that stood between the edge of the walkway and a one-hundred-and-fifty-foot drop to the gardens below. Jane glanced over the side and wished she hadn't. The ground, shades of silver and gray in the moonlight, seemed very far away. With her left hand, she clutched at the parapet, leaning awkwardly to do it.

The wind, which had been a gentle breeze in the park, was a roaring gale up here. It pushed at Jane and boxed her ears, then whipped her hair about her face. She narrowed her eyes against its force, gripped the parapet tighter, and followed Robert, her walk hunched and sideward, like an overgrown crab.

Ben's sobs led them more than three-quarters of the way around the roof before Robert stopped dead. Jane only just managed to avoid colliding with him. He pulled himself up, growing taller, and his broad shoulders widened as he gave a low snarl.

Jane leaned toward the lead roof and peered around Robert. What she saw stole her breath, her senses, her ability to think. Her mouth opened for a scream, but only a squeak sounded. Thank God, because anything louder might have been tragic.

Ben stood on the walkway in his nightshirt, shivering violently and pulling toward the relative safety of the lead roof. Lady Barwell stood beside him, the fingers of both hands gripped around his wrist, so tight Jane could see the white of her knuckles, and she pulled him toward the parapet. It was taking every ounce of Ben's strength to pull back.

"Jessica!" called Robert. His voice was mostly carried off on the bullying wind, but enough of it reached the countess that she whirled around, letting go of Ben's wrist and grabbing the parapet to save herself from falling.

Freed from her grasp, Ben took his chance and scooted past her, wailing Jane's name. Somehow, Robert sidestepped and let him pass on the narrow walkway, and Ben flung himself into Jane's arms. She wobbled a little before she steadied herself, then held him tightly, muttering soothing nonsense at him while she tried to listen to what was happening ahead of her. The wind at her ears, coupled with Ben's hysterical sobbing, made hearing difficult, and with Robert's back to her, she couldn't catch most of what he said, but Jessica faced Jane, and her words were much clearer.

"He was sleepwalking," she shouted. "I was trying to help him down off the roof."

Jane had seen how the countess had tried to do that. Gingerly, she peered over the parapet, then closed her eyes on the dizziness it caused. Nausea filled her, though whether it was because she was so high or because of the danger Ben had been in—was still in—Jane could not say. She took a deep breath.

"Come, Ben." She tried to keep the fear from her voice so he wouldn't grow any more alarmed than he already was. "Let's go inside."

"I scared," sobbed Ben.

"I know." Whispering nonsense to him, Jane led him along the walkway toward the door, moving awkwardly, partly because she tried to keep away from the edge and partly because Ben clung to her so tightly. Robert stayed put, hemming his stepmother in, preventing her coming after them. Jane looked over her shoulder and saw Lady Barwell, standing closer to him now, the look on her face venomous.

They were a few yards from the door when the earl came through it. He wore a nightshirt, his banyan open over it and leather slippers on his feet. His hair stuck up in clumps. Timmins stood behind him. Also in his nightwear, he did not follow the earl onto the roof but stood in the doorway, clinging to the frame as if his life depended upon it.

"What is happening?" bellowed the earl. In Jane's arms, Ben sobbed louder. Robert looked back over his shoulder and Lady Barwell took the chance to push past him, her attention focused on her husband. Jane watched in horror as Robert teetered at the parapet. The backs of his legs hit the wall and he arched backward, over the empty space between him and the ground below. He windmilled his arms and pushed his head forward in an attempt to straighten.

A thousand images crowded Jane's mind. All in a moment, she saw their first meeting on Bloomfold High Street, the carriage accident outside her home, the sight of him in Mama's chamber, the kiss at the inn in St. Albans, the moments in the summerhouse today.

I should have said I love him. It was her only coherent thought. Her heart stuttered; her breath caught. Time slowed to an agonizing crawl. She could no longer hear her own cries, nor anyone else's, nor even the buffeting gale. She was still conscious of Ben in her arms, but she could not feel him there. The entire world condensed to the man leaning backward over the parapet.

Moving in slow motion, Robert pulled his center of gravity toward the lead roof. His frantic fingers reached for something, anything to grab, and he caught Lady Barwell's arm.

Jane felt a moment of relief. He had hold of his stepmother. All the countess need do now was pull back toward the tower roof and the momentum would bring them both to safety.

Instead, whether by instinct or design Jane could not say, Lady Barwell pushed Robert again as she struggled, trying to free herself from his grip. Robert teetered again, but he did not let go of the countess. Her lips parted in a silent snarl, and she scratched at his fingers. Still, he held firm.

The earl pushed past Jane and Ben and moved toward his wife and son.

From the doorway, Timmins yelled.

Ben left Jane's arms and ran to the valet.

The countess pushed Robert again, and this time he went over the parapet, past the point of no return. Jane screamed. Both Ben and the earl yelled.

Robert clung to the stone wall with one hand, his other hand still gripping Lady Barwell's arm. She pulled back, desperately trying to get away from him, but she could not. His weight dragged her forward. She dug her heels into the walkway, but she could not fight him and she, too, toppled over the side.

The earl reached them as she tumbled over. He tried to grab at her but missed. He grasped at his son's arm instead, his face contorted in agony as he strained to pull him up.

Jane also grabbed at Robert's arm, her hands just below the earl's. Robert's face was a mask of determination and pain as he fought to stay alive. His other arm dangled, his fist gripped tightly around Lady Barwell's arm. She kicked the air and squirmed, howling like an Irish banshee.

"Stay still, Jessica!" Robert said, through gritted teeth. "I—can't—hold—you."

The shoulder seam on his coat ripped, and he jolted down a few inches. Jane tried to reach for something other than his sleeve, but he was out of her reach.

Lady Barwell kicked again, and slipped through Robert's grip. She dropped an inch and screamed before his fingers tightened on her. He shook with the effort of holding her.

"Get help!" yelled the earl. Jane prayed Timmins and Ben had gone to do that.

Jessica reached out with her free hand, grabbing at Robert's back. For an instant it seemed she succeeded, as his cravat bunched under his chin and his shirt tightened against his throat. He gagged and his eyes widened in the instinctive panic of breathlessness.

The back of his coat tore, dropping Lady Barwell farther. She came to a sudden, jarring stop. Then her weight pulled the torn jacket apart and the sleeve slid down Robert's arm. He lost his grip on her and she fell, still clutching what remained of his coat, her brief scream ending as she hit the ground.

Servants appeared, all in their nightwear. It took six of them to haul Robert back up, over the parapet, and onto the walkway where he sank to his knees, shivering and trying to catch his breath. Jane desperately wanted to go to him, to hold him as she had in the summerhouse, but she could not, not in front of his father and the rest of the household. Instead, she backed away and fled down the stairs to Ben's chamber.

Ben sat on his bed, sobbing, while Mama did her best to comfort him, her nightgown almost completely hidden under her thick robe, her hair in papers. He saw Jane and held out his arms. She walked into them, gave him a tight hug and let him cry until his distress subsided into hiccups and an occasional sob. Then Jane sat on one side of him, Mama on the other, and both rubbed their hands up and down his back in a reassuring caress.

Finally, Mama asked, "Would you like to tell me what happened?" Her voice was calm, as if she'd asked what Ben would like for breakfast, or if Jane thought it would rain.

Ben said, "Janey save me. I not want do what she say. Not go there 'gain."

As succinctly as she could, Jane told Mama all that had happened since Lady Barwell had confronted her in the hall. Every now and then, Ben interrupted with pronouncements of his own, such as, "She not nice," and, "She hurt me."

Mama was silent throughout the telling of the tale. Not by so much as the flicker of an eyelid did she give away her thoughts. When they were finished, she swallowed once, and asked, quietly, "Is she dead?"

Jane shrugged her shoulders. "I would think so."

There was a scratching at the door and a maid

entered. "Begging your pardon, ma'am, but his lordship sent me to make sure Master Ben is all right."

"Where is his lordship?" asked Mama.

"He and Master Robert are in the drawing room, ma'am."

"I shall dress and join them." She directed Jane to come with her and left Ben in the care of the maid, promising him she would not be gone long. Since the maid had also brought a pot of hot chocolate, Ben was not too distressed at Mama's leaving.

Fifteen minutes later, Jane followed her mother into the drawing room. Mama wore a simple black dress, the one she'd worn after Papa died. The material was thin in places and looked its age, but it was the only mourning outfit Mama possessed.

"Not," she told Jane on their way downstairs, "that I will truly mourn someone who tried to kill my son, but I have enough respect for the earl to do as I ought."

Jane had also changed. She'd had no choice. The dress she had been wearing was filthy and torn, and beyond repair, and like Mama, she knew she ought to wear something suitable for mourning. She'd changed into a somber brown round dress, the darkest outfit she owned.

The gentlemen stood as the ladies entered the drawing room. Two lamps had been lit, and a fire roared cheerfully in the hearth, painting everything an orange red that seemed out of step with the tragic night. Robert wore a fresh coat and shirt, though he had not replaced his cravat. The earl, too, had dressed. Both men wore black armbands.

"Come in," said the earl, and he gestured that they should take a seat before offering them tea, or something stronger, if they preferred. Mama opted for a glass of brandy, while Jane was thankful for the reviving cup of tea Robert brought to her.

"I do not rejoice in her death," the earl said, quietly contemplating his own drink, "but as Mr. Cowper had it in his hymn, the Lord does move in mysterious ways. The lady is spared a public trial ending in imprisonment, transportation, or even the noose. I am spared the ignominy of a divorce, and my family's name is not to be dragged through the mud."

"Jane said she tried to poison you," said Mama. Her eyes filled with sympathy for him.

The earl nodded. "William has been arrested. He's willing to tell all if it takes the rope from his neck." He raised a cynical eyebrow. "Apparently, Jessica paid someone to distill the flowers from the rhododendron bushes on the island. They are lethal in large enough doses, and they build up within the body." He sighed, suddenly looking old and sad. "She thought to make Barnaby the earl." He swirled the brandy in his rummer and took a sip. "Not that it would have done her any good. I made provision in my will for my youngest son should both Robert and I die before Barnaby reached his majority. Jessica would not have been his guardian, or the trustee of his estate."

"It was all for nothing?" Jane shook her head at the suffering the countess had caused. She glanced at Robert, then looked away when she saw he watched her, intently. Her cheeks burned.

"What happens now?" asked Mama.

"Her accomplices will be gathered up, although for Barnaby's sake I don't want the affair made public if I can possibly avoid it. He will grow up without his mother, as it is. He doesn't need to be gossip fodder, vilified before he is even old enough for school."

"You may, of course, rely upon our complete discretion," said Mama.

"Thank you." The earl smiled at her. "Dear lady, I have a boon to ask of you. I hesitate, since you have already taken great care of one of my sons, at considerable cost to yourself. In doing so, you've proven yourself trustworthy and honorable. So I now ask, would you consider supervising the care and instruction of my youngest son? I'm sure he and your granddaughter could be schooled together, and I will make the dower house available to you forthwith."

Mama smiled. Jane turned to Robert, her eyebrows raised in surprise. Robert's lips twitched and he inclined his head, indicating she should follow him. Quietly, without drawing the notice of their parents, who now discussed the earl's proposition, they left the room and went to the library. Here, the fire had not been lit, nor had the lamps, and the room was dark and cold.

Robert pulled back the drapes, revealing the navy-gray of predawn. It was enough to see by, although not to make details clear.

"How are you?" he asked as he pulled her into his arms and kissed her.

The thought flitted through Jane's mind that, had Lady Barwell succeeded, she might have lost him tonight. Which meant she would have lost herself, too, for she would never have recovered. Now, though, she wound her arms around his neck and pressed against him, reveling in his vibrant touch as she kissed him back. His tongue danced against hers, and his warmth enveloped her as the evidence of his desire for her pressed at her stomach, igniting fires that spread through her body and pooled low in her belly.

All too soon, he stopped. She missed him immediately.

"I've been wanting to do that for hours," he said, resting his forehead against hers.

Jane laughed. "At risk of sounding wanton, so have I."

He grinned, then became serious. "I thought I would die tonight. I couldn't see that you and Father would be strong enough to hold me for long, and Jessica was…" He took a deep breath and exhaled sharply. "I had just one thought." He smiled, uncertainly. "I didn't want to leave you. I wanted, needed, to survive, to tell you how much I love you. And I promised myself, at the first opportunity, I would do this." He lowered himself, rather stiffly, to one knee. Jane's heart beat faster than she could ever remember it beating before. She hardly dared breathe.

"Jane Winter, you are the most precious woman in the world to me. I love you with everything I am. Would you do me the honor of becoming my wife?"

Tears sprang to her eyes, even as her grin spread. She nodded, enthusiastically. "I love you, too," she said, and then she was in his arms again and they were kissing as if their very lives depended on it.

As the sky lightened and the sun warmed the land, he told her what his father had said as they sat in the drawing room, recovering from the night's events.

"Ben will be the next earl, and I'll be his guardian, along with your mother. But there is a problem. Apparently, the law allows the Crown to confiscate the property and assets of any peer deemed unfit to hold them."

"What?" Jane was horrified. "How can that be fair and just?"

"It isn't. But the Regent is an expensive man who needs all the wealth he can lay his hands on. You may be sure he will exercise his rights, if it enriches him."

She shook her head in disbelief and anger. "There must be something we can do to protect Ben."

Robert smiled. "Fortunately, there is. Father has already taken the necessary action by changing his will. Luckily, nothing of the estate is entailed, so when Ben inherits the title, I will inherit the wealth and the land. I will take care of Ben, and Barnaby, and see they want for nothing. Father believes the chances of Ben siring an heir are minimal, which means I, or my son, should I be blessed with one, will one day take his place. At which time, the title and the estate will be reunited."

Relief flooded through Jane and she pulled him closer. "You are a good man," she whispered. "My man."

"Always," he replied, and he kissed her.

A word about the author…

Caitlyn Callery lives in Sussex, southern England, near the Regency towns of Brighton and Tunbridge Wells. She is passionate about writing and suffers withdrawal symptoms when she takes a few days away from her work.

Before becoming a full-time writer, she worked in banking, as a waitress, in the motor repair industry, in a call centre, and for a charity. As part of this last job, she helped build a school in Kenya, and drove a vanload of wheelchairs from the UK to Morocco.

She also loves reading, knitting, walking by the sea, the theatre, and spending time with her family.

CaitlynCallery.com

Thank you for purchasing
this publication of The Wild Rose Press, Inc.

For questions or more information
contact us at
info@thewildrosepress.com.

The Wild Rose Press, Inc.

Milton Keynes UK
Ingram Content Group UK Ltd.
UKHW022052110624
443988UK00015B/640

9 781509 255207